# STAR CRUSADER

# HERO OF THE ALLIANCE

MICHAEL G. THOMAS

# PREFACE

*The* Star Crusader Fighter Combat Simulator *is the most advanced and realistic pilot training package ever created for the Alliance Navy. Flight control, battle strategies, and combat tactics are realistic and perfectly suited to the latest generation of military hardware. The simplified Star Crusader Public Platform is a prized recruitment tool, capable of isolating those perfectly suited to space combat. While retaining only some of the main systems functionality, it has a proven track record in training and identifying candidates for future fighter pilots.*

*The Star Crusader Simulation*

**The Battle of Retribution**

"Pull up! Pull up!"

The computer's voice was incredibly calm, yet equally assertive. Each word become louder, forcing Nate to act before it was too late. He pulled on the control column and narrowly missed hitting the stern of the Alliance cruiser, ANS Farragut. His stomach tightened as he expected to feel the impact, and then he was through.

*That was close!*

A bright flash to the left marked the death of an enemy fighter. Nate instinctively pulled hard left and spun his fighter around to avoid more fire from a second fighter. His wingman took the shot and cut the fighter apart in a single devastating volley.

"Good shooting, Hornet Five. Close up."

The fighters rejoined their formation and altered course to take them away from the nearby Biomech battleship. Streaks of projectiles fired almost continually from the powerful ship, making it deadly to approach. The enemy ship surged forward, with its engines on full-burn. Another volley struck from the other direction, and Nate put his fighter-bomber into a long roll. He spotted the battered hull of the Alliance ship as the crew of the Farragut fought desperately to get away.

"Stay in formation and move in behind the battleship."

Nate was not a pilot; he was not even in the Alliance military. He was a civilian cadet, seventeen years old, and in his final year. What set him apart from almost every one of his peers was his skill in the advanced Star Crusader videogame. He had fought his way up through the public contest and reached the final event. If he was successful, a prize waited for him beyond compare.

*I can do this. I know I can.*

Nate knew the warship's guns had locked onto him before the computer could even tell him. The angles made it easy for him to track, and by heading right at the target; it was almost impossible to miss. He had also managed to draw the gunners away from another Alliance escort, a small frigate that desperately tried to avoid the attention of the larger ships.

*And...now!*

He had performed this particular manoeuvre a hundred times before and knew the timing to the second. A quick course change threw the craft about and then ducked past a smaller vessel. It was a subtle shift in direction, but it instantly broke the ship's turret lock. It wasn't just Nate in the scenario; there were another five contestants, and each of them led a squadron of fighters. Though in direct competition, each was being scored on more than just individual kills. Contribution to the battle was equally as important.

As each of his unit twisted about in space, they dumped a series of countermeasures, to confuse the trackers as well as giving any missiles ghost targets to attack. These devices were barely larger than a tennis ball, but could trick sensors into thinking they were something as large and significant as a full size fighter. They spun about while panels opened and closed to distort the energy readings.

Behind Nate came the rest of the squadron, as one by one they unleashed a barrage of deadly Sea Skua anti-ship missiles. Each of the powerful missiles blasted great holes in the side of the ship, yet still it fought on. The final missile must have struck an ammunition or fuel storage unit because a large part of the ship disappeared behind a great explosion and vanished from view.

*Yeah!*

"Good work. Regroup at..."

Cheers rang out amongst the squadron, and Nate was convinced he could hear them in the public simulation hall. There were hundreds of cadets from the Alliance Academy, and every one of them would be shouting and cheering for one of their own from Kerberos to have made it through.

*Another seven minutes, and we'll have survived in this battle more than anybody before us.*

An indicator on his secondary display showed that the team competing from the planet Spascia had just been destroyed. It looked as though they had found themselves caught between a squadron of Biomech escort ships and were destroyed to a man.

*Bad luck, guys.*

He felt for them. A loss at this point was a guaranteed failure. Only one of them could go through. But by losing an entire squadron of Lightning fighters, they had also weakened his chances of making it through to the end of the battle. Nate had read about this fight, and though details changed with every re-enactment, one detail always remained true. The enemy would overwhelm the defenders until the marines could fight the final battle aboard the enemy Worldship.

It might have been a simulation, but Nate had a lot riding on this. Law might guarantee his place in the Academy, but the exchange programme was something else. Only six cadets from thousands of possible candidates would be chosen. He was competing against every school and academy in the Alliance, and there was nothing he wanted more. It was a chance to travel the stars and see new worlds, all while competing as a Star Crusader fighter pilot.

*We can do this...I can do this.*

Nate closed his eyes for just a moment, and when he reopened them, his senses were completely cut off from the rest of the world. He quickly sank back into the battle as though he'd never left it. The helmet and visor blocked all of his primary senses apart from touch, and for the public contest, the organiser had even constructed a mock-up of the fighter's cockpit. The controls and buttons were positioned where they should be for the antiquated fighter. The squadron of aged Thunderbolt heavy fighter-bombers moved on in a dispersed v shaped formation. There were seven, and all of them had seen hard use in the war. They were four-engine heavy fighter-bombers, and while the most powerful fighters in the Alliance arsenal, they were also the least manoeuvrable. Most squadrons had traded up to the newer Hammerheads or even the new experimental drone fighters. With the endgame in sight, all remaining war stocks had been released, and this threatened to be the last battle of the old design.

"I'm detecting turret lock. They've got us!"

He prepared to take evasive action as he listened to the cry from Hornet Ten. His gut instinct was to pull the stick, but they had been forced to bunch up due to the number of ships in their path. With wingmen so close, he could just as easily crash into them and kill them all. Nate instead looked left, then right, before flipping his spacecraft around. It was a tiny delay, but enough to confirm where he could move safely. His change in direction was just in time to avoid the point-defence turrets fitted along the dorsal spine of the battleship. Hornet Ten was too slow, and three turrets converged on the one craft, blasting it apart before his eyes. The wings, engines, and cockpit all vanished in a horrific mess of broken parts.

*Another one gone! We're getting crucified out here.*

Nate shook his head in irritation. No matter what decision he made, his wingmen were still being shot down, one by one. His fighter-bombers were tough craft, but there was little they could do against such overwhelming fire. Their thin armour plating could offer only a modest level of protection against fighter gunfire, and almost nothing against the powerful motorised

4

automatic cannons fitted to many of the enemy escorts. He shunted to the left just three metres, narrowly avoiding another burst of gunfire.

The faint voices of those in the tournament hall dissipated as the wreckage of Hornet Ten vanished before him. Nate watched in horror as the Biomech ship appeared out of the flames and smoke. At least a third of the ship was burning from within, and though crippled, it refused to die. The crew of any other vessel would already be aboard their lifeboats, but not this one. Entire sections rippled off as explosions rang out through her hull, and still the ship moved on.

*Not good. Not good!*

It may have been a simulation that had more in common with a videogame than something the military used, but the further they made it into the battle, the more real the entire thing felt to him. When a fighter was destroyed, he knew that meant one or two of his comrades were now dead, and that one fact alone kept the entire event a sombre one. Perhaps in the past the illusion would have been hard to maintain, but with such realism, it was easy to slip into another world, and another life. Only in the lulls of combat did he have a moment to realise none of this was the real battle, and he was in fact sitting in a pod, playing a highly realistic videogame.

"Scratch that order. Concentrate all fire on the battleship. Hit it hard."

The squadron of heavy fighters arced around their position and opened fire with guns and missiles. The battleship was now only four hundred metres from the stationary ANS Farragut, and both were blasting each other apart. At this range, they were able to hit each other, and they were quickly surrounded by hundreds of flashes, like great clouds of flies. A mixture of kinetic railguns, automatic cannons, and particle beams flashed back and forth, causing untold damage.

"Keep firing."

The fighters swept overhead, dropping another salvo of missiles. Their turret mounts traversed and added their own gunfire to the maelstrom below.

"Hornet Leader, what about the nukes?"

It was Hornet Three, and Nate was very tempted to give in and use the weapons. They were the most powerful carried by the Thunderbolt fighters, but each carried just one of the devastating torpedoes, and he knew he had to use them carefully.

"No, not the nukes. Save them for the prize."

For some it may have seemed a callous decision, but even a full volley of the torpedoes had no guarantee of success. They were slower and less agile than the missiles and easier to shoot down. Even if they hit the target, a battleship was a massive warship. Unless totally crippled, it would continue to fight.

*No, our job is to hit the cruisers with the atomics.*

For a second Nate thought they had been lucky, but then a single white flash erupted at the heart of the Farragut. The battle between the two capital ships had been decided, and Farragut was paying the price.

"Break formation and withdraw!"

He hit the engine override and pushed the engine to maximum, as the Alliance cruiser broke apart. He shook his head and changed one of his displays to show an external view. The Farragut was as tough as any cruiser in the fleet, but nothing could withstand the hundreds of warheads striking deep inside its hull as the Biomech Ravager battleship performed the coup de grace. The ships were poorly matched, and even with the firepower of an entire Thunderbolt squadron, they had failed to stop the Biomech ship. Nate's instinct told him he should have used the nukes, but deep down he knew it would have made little difference, if any.

*Could we have stopped that ship? How many lives are gone because of that decision?*

He knew that with each capital ship lost, their chances of holding back the enemy fleet would diminish. All of them had a job to do, and there might be one ship in the battle that would decide the outcome. His fighters could not stop them alone. All he could do was to help stave off heavy ordnance, engage fighters, and harass their smaller capital ships.

*I need to turn this around.*

The battleship gave no quarter, as it accelerated ahead and crashed bow first into the crippled vessel, finishing off any chance it might have of limping away. A small number of lifeboats tried to escape, with most caught in the blast. A final explosion shattered the stern, filling the void of space with spent ammunition and wreckage. The Biomech ship finally succumbed, and the remains of both vessels were quickly shrouded in flames and debris. It was a bitter victory for the allies, but at least Nate had the satisfaction of knowing the battleship had gone.

*That's nine of their ships gone in ten minutes, but how many have we lost? We cannot keep going like this. The Biomech main fleet isn't even all here yet.*

Nate knew how many hundreds had just died in the collision and the explosion that followed. The scene of carnage left him with a sick feeling deep down in his stomach, as he imagined what it would have been like in the real battle. All of the cadets discussed what the reality of space combat would be like compared to the Star Crusader simulator. Many of them, him included, had family members who fought in last space battles of the war. Right now Nate would rather not know. He'd read the history of this battle, and it was still known as one of the bloodiest events in human military history.

*Concentrate, Nate! Concentrate on what you can do, not on what you cannot. The battle is not over, not yet. Stay on course and attack!*

Another explosion off to the right marked the death of a troop transport. It was a violent end to another faceless ship, and with each loss Nate found their situation ever more precarious. The only saving grace he could see was that most of the passengers had escaped via lifeboats; four Mauler heavy landing craft were already there and escorting the lifeboats to the safety of a nearby Alliance Battlecruiser. The fleet continued to put pressure against the Biomechs, but the losses on both sides rose with each passing minute.

*We have to end this, and before we run out of ships.*

His squadron had done well, and so far counted three ships and four fighters to their credit. This was already quite a feat, yet for every kill they made, the enemy seemed to bring on two more fresh ships.

*It is like the Hydra from ancient myth. Each time you cut off a head, it sprouts two new ones. I need a new plan.*

The sound of multiple voices filled Nate's ears as the captains of different ships called in their positions. As each second passed, more and more ships arrived to give battle. One stood out far and above the rest, the mighty ANS Warlord, the biggest in the Alliance fleet, and flagship of the allied force.

"The vanguard is in position," said Admiral Anderson, the commander of the allied armada, "Commence the attack. All capital ships hit the Rift Engine. Everybody else clear the escorts."

Nate had been waiting for this, and after minutes of combat, he began to think something had gone wrong. His squadron had launched along with the rest of the vanguard. Their job had been to contain and slow the enemy long enough for the primary fleet to arrive. With the Admiral in position, battlecruisers, battleships, and cruisers would bolster their fleet. There were even assault ships teeming with marines, each readying their warriors for the multiple boarding actions that would be necessary to end the battle. The voice of the Admiral returned, and Nate completely forgot for that moment that this was actually a recording from the battle, and not the man himself speaking to those engaged in battle.

"All of our battles and campaigns have brought us here to the Black Rift, and to face out greatest enemy. This is it, the moment the future of every race in the known galaxy will be decided. Not one kilometre back. We fight and win, or we die here today. Engage the enemy and collapse the Rift!"

Nate had heard the same words before when watching documentaries and archival footage. The battle was so much more than just a great event. It was also the scene for nearly every kind of space combat ever witnessed. Battleships slugged it out in one on one duels, fighters swirled about, and dropships deposited companies of marines into enemy ships. This time the battle was different, because this time Nate had a personal stake in the battle. Never before had so much ridden on a single event for him. If they lost this battle, it was over, and everything until now would have been wasted. He spotted the timer running just above his eye. There were three more minutes to go if he wanted to beat the score set by the Terra Nova Academy of

Science, and give him a chance to compete for the lowest ranked space. Their team had finished in first place less than a day earlier and already had three candidates through. That was unless Nate could beat them, and he had every intention on replacing their third winner.

*One of those places is mine!*

He took a deep breath, and then checked the navigation orb just below the forward view. Though the contest was to decide his own particular fate, he was also well aware the simulation could not be a success without working together. On his own, he could do little to turn the tide of battle. This was no minor skirmish. It was the final battle of the Biomech War, and both sides had marshalled every resource to win it. The rest of Hornet Squadron was necessary for his own safety, as well as to provide the firepower to create any realistic change in the fight. Ultimately, only the heavy capital ships could win this fight, and if his squadron did their part, it was all possible.

*We won this battle in 2463 AD, and I can do it again. I just need to keep my head, and make sure the capital ships can do their job.*

Even as Nate considered the ultimate goal, it reminded him that there was one major threat to the Alliance ships, the dreaded Biomantas. These massive cruiser class ships were fast, tough, and built specifically to engage and destroy ships of their class and larger. The mission scenario was relatively vague, but the briefing had been very clear about the danger posed by these powerful cruisers. His squadron had been specifically tasked with keeping them occupied, and the only reason why the fighters still carried their torpedoes.

"This is it Hornet Squadron. Stay close and follow me."

Nate pointed the nose of his heavy fighter at the swirling maelstrom directly ahead, a terrifying tear in space-time known as the Black Rift. It was a wormhole that connected directly to the home world of the invincible Biomechs. The ancient race had been dormant for so long that most had thought them little more than a myth. Now their armadas of ships and millions of warriors were running amok, burning cities, and overrunning world after world. A prophecy had told how this was the beginning of the end, but Nate refused to believe that. He focussed his attention on the groups of ships coming through the tear in space-time and made his plans.

*We can win this. I know we can.*

For the first time in living memory, it was open, and the Biomechs were surging through to bring an end to the devastating Biomech War that the alliance of races was losing, and losing badly. If they won, the Biomechanical monsters would take the worlds of the Helions, and then spread out to conquer every one of their neighbours. It would be the beginning of the end for all life in the known galaxy. The dawn of a new Dark Age, and there was no way Nate would let that happen.

*This is it.*

Every ship near the Black Rift lay smashed and burning, and still the enemy came through. The Biomechs advanced so callously through the Rift that they smashed their way through friend and foe alike, no matter the risks to their own craft. There was only so much space at the Black Rift, and anything that got in their way was paying the ultimate price.

He activated his primary weapons and then flipped off the safety on his guns. Compared to the enemy, his fighter seemed puny, but he had a job to do, and like his wingmen, he was not going to stop until they were victorious.

"Watch for hostiles. The next wave will come through any moment now. Get ready."

There had been twelve of them at the start of the battle, but the first wave of Biomech fighters had taken their toll. At their flanks moved two more squadrons of the lighter twin-engine Lightning interceptors.

Another burst of bright blue lightning crackled through the Rift, and from the centre of the whirlpool emerged the nose of a single massive ship. The vessel was as big as a mountain and moved through slowly, while dozens of smaller capital ships hung close to its flanks.

"I've got contacts. Looks like a Rift Engine and escorts," said Nate.

Reports had already arrived of the massive ship, but this was the first time in the battle that one had appeared. According to the brief, the Rift Engine was a construction designed to stabilise the Rift back to the enemy's homeworld. Once its work was complete, there would be no way to hold back the limitless resources of the enemy. Only half of the vessel emerged, with the remainder on the other side of space, deep inside the enemy's territory.

"Hornet Squadron, this is Hornet Leader. We have our targets. Let's clear a path for the heavies."

The fighter-bombers were optimised to attack small to medium ships, but with such numbers, they had just enough firepower to deal with one or two of the larger ships. While the Lightning fighters took on the enemy fighters, they would do their part to help the capital ships do theirs. A quick movement of his retina selected a pair of the mighty Biomanta cruiser class warships. Though short in length, their wingspan gave them the appearance of the large cartilaginous fishes known as Manta Rays on Earth. The Biomechanical hulls made them almost impossible to scan, and they moved as quickly as frigates.

"Break and engage, I repeat. Break and engage."

The large formation of fighter-bombers split apart into two smaller groups, just as more flashes appeared around them. Scores more Alliance ships arrived nearby, as the last group of warships arrived from throughout the sector. Nate spotted dozens of heavy cruisers, destroyers, and even a mixture of alien ships. There were newer designs such as the Crusader and Liberty ships, as well as much older pre-Uprising ships that had been hastily pressed into service. It was a mighty armada, but as he looked back at the Black Rift, he wondered if it could ever be enough.

*This is gonna be a close run thing.*

The communication indicator flickered, and the voice of Tiger Leader came through loud and clear. The squadron was positioned less than three kilometres to their flank, yet in such confusion it was almost impossible for Nate to find them.

"Hornet Leader, we have bogies launching from the carrier. I repeat; we have bogies at the Black Rift and launching from the carriers. We are moving to attack. Watch your back."

Nate licked his upper lip as he listened. Tiger Squadron was led by one of his fellow cadets, but right now he had little interest in trying to surpass him. None of them would be going through at this rate. He could worry about the specifics later. He had a ship to kill. Nate connected to the rest of his squadron and selected the new targets.

*There they are.*

His gut told him to turn from the Rift, increase power, and maintain a safe distance while the Lightning fighters dealt with the enemy. Normally, that would have made sense. His fighters were slower, less nimble, and larger targets for the enemy to hit. None of that mattered today, though, as all that did was time. Every second they delayed battle was more time for the Biomechs to bring in reinforcements. Either they fought now, or they lost the battle and with it, the war.

"Hornet Squadron. Activate your atomics and engage the enemy. Nuke 'em!"

Nate blipped the burners on his heavy fighter and began accelerating towards the Black Rift. The swirling patterns were mesmerising, and as the shapes shifted about, yet more enemy craft came through. The largest were the Cephalon command ships and the equally massive Ravager battleships. Around them swarmed large numbers of Biomanta cruisers, vessels that had proven their worth in a dozen battles already.

*Here we go.*

He led the formation of four Thunderbolts, while the other three moved off to attack their own targets. The nearest Biomanta must have spotted the fighters because its myriad of defensive turrets had opened fire. The capital ship was covered in turrets, each more than capable of tearing a fighter apart. Standard Naval doctrine was to keep out of range of defence turrets, especially due to their high-tracking speeds. Nate selected more than a dozen waypoints for his fighters and then moved in close to the nearest command ship. The fighter-bombers were forced to keep making adjustments to avoid hitting the myriad of gantries and pylons jutting out from the ship's vast superstructure.

"Stay close. Activate your atomics."

The command ship concentrated most of its fire on an approaching Alliance Conqueror class battlecruiser, and instead the nearest Biomech cruiser opened fire on them. At this speed they were hard to hit, and hundreds of rounds overshot and struck the command ship instead. By the time they'd covered half the length of the ship's hull, Nate sent the command.

"Now!"

As one the formation of four fighter-bombers lurched out from the shelter offered by the command ship and bore down on the cruiser. Multiple shots penetrated the left wing of Nate's spacecraft, but he ignored it and targeted the underside of the Biomanta.

"Fire!"

Each of the four craft launched the remainder of their missiles while simultaneously holding down the triggers on their secondary guns. All of this was for show, though, and the real prize was the single tungsten reinforced torpedo sitting under the belly of each of them. It was the most powerful weapon that could be carried by a single fighter, and now four of them were heading towards the Biomantas.

"Split and create openings."

The four fighter-bombers broke formation, each approaching the cruiser from a slightly different heading. Most of their missiles were either destroyed by turret fire, or struck the thick plating of the cruiser's armour. Nate wasn't concerned, though. All he wanted to know was that they had opened up breaches in the hull. They were so close now he could see the tall markings written in garish colours along the ship. All of his secondary guns, including the multiple turrets, now opened fired, each one opening up tiny gaps in the thick Biomechanical plating.

"And...withdraw!"

The countdown clock on his cockpit had reached the marker, and as the torpedoes hit, he realised he'd made it past the marker. There were Biomech fighters all around him, and the fighter-bombers' turrets tracked and fired almost continually. It was a brutal firefight as shells struck both sides.

Biomech fighters exploded; Alliance fighters were cut to pieces.

"Bank right."

A quick roll to the right, and once again Nate managed to avoid a pair of radar tracking missiles. That was the point at which the salvo of torpedoes from Hornet Squadron finally reached their target. White flashes marked the destruction of the first few torpedoes, but two made it through the defensive fire and slammed into the already weakened armour before detonating. One by one, they sent the energy of their low-yield tactical warheads deep inside the vessel, literally burning the ship from the inside out.

"Yes!"

He was so excited that he didn't see the pair of tiny Biomech fighters coming right at him. Both put a hail of armour piercing slugs into his cockpit with such a ferocity that they chewed through armour, fuel lines, and electronics with ease.

"No...not now!"

Two of his supporting fighters tried to move away, but one rolled too quickly and clipped the other. The wreckage of the two spun past him, and he was forced to go above them, right into the path of a second Biomanta cruiser. The ship had been hit by the second squadron of fighter-bombers and was already shattered.

"I've got fighters. Coming in on..."

It was the sound of Tiger Squadron. Before Nate even worked out where they were, the last few were destroyed. The whole Biomech fleet was now in position and the cold void of space full of ships, each desperately trying to attack another while keeping themselves safe. A constant twinkling, like that of stars at night, marked the death of one fighter after another. It was a bloodbath.

"Break and follow Hornet..."

A short burst of gunfire struck the nose of the fighter-bomber and knocked out the guns, as well as the communications and radar system. One engine ripped apart, and Nate quickly diverted power to the other engines. More shots came in, and he was forced to break from his current position and move in close towards the nearest capital ship. He used every trick he knew, pushing the Thunderbolt to its limits, desperate to shake off his foes. Although crippled, the turrets across the surface of the ship continued to fire at him. Nate managed to get close enough that the enemy fighters were unable to get a clear shot. They gave pursuit and just as they reached him, a massive flash erupted from the heart of the second cruiser. Nate's fighter, as well as the group of Biomech fighters were instantly was torn apart in the inferno.

His visor went dark, and for the briefest of moments, he thought he'd actually died. It was a painful, worrying experience that faded as quickly as it had arrived.

*What?*

Without even directly intervening, the visor lifted up, and he was greeted by the increasing brightness of the simulation hall. He blinked twice in an attempt to get rid of the blurriness. Hundreds of people were cheering, yet all he could see were bright shapes. His eyes had become so accustomed to the interior of the fighter that he found it hard to focus for a few seconds. Willing hands lifted him from the seat, and somebody nearby removed his helmet.

"Great work, cadet."

It was a man's voice, slightly gruff and completely unfamiliar. He shook his head and found the view already clearing up. There were people nearby, but he was on a stage with the Principal of the Academy right next to him. Directly opposite were five other cadets, each in the uniform and colours of the own institution. The man looked away from him and signalled for Nate to join the other five. He took a step and nearly stumbled. A waiting hand helped him, and soon he was standing alongside the most beautiful cadet he'd ever seen. Her long straight, blond hair ran down past her shoulders, and her eyes were wide open, as though something had surprised her.

"Hi. I'm Nathaniel Lewis."

She shook her head and sighed.

"Yes, we know. All of us do."

Nate was hardly surprised; this was the usual response he'd found with girls in the Academy. His attention turned to the Principal who now moved in front of the group.

"Ladies and Gentlemen. May I present the six winners of the Interstellar Tournament! They will now go on to represent the Academy schools of the Alliance in the goodwill tour of our neighbours."

Nate couldn't believe it. By luck or judgement, he'd managed to beat hundreds, perhaps even thousands, to join this group of elite cadets. They would now travel far from home, visiting alien races and competing in friendly contests, all in the name of promoting the Alliance. As the audience clapped, the man moved along the line, calling out their names. Each barely registered with him until he reached the girl right next to him. He turned and looked at her as the Principal spoke.

"Cadet Cassandra Hurley, of Terra Nova!"

She must have noticed him watching her and glanced sideways, giving him the faintest of smiles. It wasn't much, but it finished off the day as perhaps the best Nate had ever had. He looked out to the crowd and imagined what adventures were to come.

*This is going to be...epic.*

# CHAPTER ONE

*Our armed forces are the guardians of the peace and freedom that our citizens enjoy. It is the duty of the Alliance Navy to protect our interests throughout the galaxy, from keeping shipping lanes clear through to transporting Alliance ground forces directly into action. The hardworking crews of the Alliance Navy Auxiliary support the warships of the fleet. While the Navy secures the shipping lanes, ground combat remains the role the Alliance Marine Corps. The Corps takes recruits from throughout the Alliance, from the hardy people of Earth to the monstrous synthetic warriors known as Jötnar. This elite force is supported by the planet bound reserve Marine Corps units, classified as part of the Colonial Guard forces. There is no greater role a citizen can play than to offer up their life and liberty to defend the ideals of the Alliance.*

*Naval Cadet's Handbook*

**October, 2472 A.D.**
**Starbase 'Mognathus 7', 3rd Quadrant, Byotai Empire**
**Six months later**

Nate and his friends had never seen death until the bloodbath on the Mognathus Starbase. Future historians would know the events as the Mognathus Mutiny, but for them, it started like any other day at the Academy. While they sat at their desks and continued their assessment, a momentous event was gathering pace around them. It was to be the day the social cohesion of the Byotai finally cracked, and after years of growing resentment, they turned on their leadership caste and began a bloody purge that seemed to never end.

What started at Mognathus would spread from planet to planet until the entire Empire and its immediate neighbours were engulfed in turmoil. All it took for this terrible revolution to begin was a single symbolic act. There was no general call to arms over the public network, no great blast of sound or music. In later years, this single act would become the focus of propaganda on all sides. But few could argue that it was that day, in October 2472 when the Byoti state crumbled, and it began with a mutiny in the heart of the sprawling Imperial shipyard of Mognathus.

The firing on the Imperial patrol ship, Plethodon, marked the infamous event. The vessel was small, little bigger than an interplanetary shuttle, and crewed by thirteen Byotai sailors. Plethodon was designed to conduct searches, check cargos, and ward off the occasional pirate or corsair attack in the immediate vicinity of the shipyard. It was not a ship of the line, and this far from the frontier; it was fair to assume there was little chance of any action. The small ship orbited the space station just as it did every day. According to the training manual, it should use a different route each day. The Byotai were no different to any other race in this regard, and routine quickly settled into something easy to follow. Without any indication something was happening. This far into Byotai space the crew were relaxed, and never suspected what was about to occur. When the guns opened fire, she never had a chance.

Waiting just inside the two massive docking arms of the station was the large black shape of the Sword of Mognathus, a Byotai heavy cruiser and would ever be remembered as the ship that started the mutiny. Like all ships in the Empire, this one was designed to look like a living creature. The long hull was broken up into bulbous segments, and massive masts extended out with micro-fine wings attached, giving the impression of a dragonfly or other equally massive insect. The motorised armour plates moved aside to reveal the barrels of large calibre guns. One by one the guns fired, and the heavy energy blasts struck Plethodon's flank and punched massive holes in her hull. The vessel depressurised before her crew had any idea what had happened.

It was a bloody opening to what could have been a peaceful revolution, but that was not to be. Trouble had been building quietly for centuries, the majority of the reptilian species being kept in thrall by their patrician class. Only those from the few privileged families could expect high office, or promotion to the command of starships in the fleet.

None of this mattered to Nate, though. As he sat there, his mind wandering to the events of the last few exciting days, the shots were being fired. The mutineers aboard Sword of Mognathus were all experienced warriors, and they quickly turned the powerful weapons against other ships currently docked in the shipyard. The mutiny had begun, but the violence was far from over.

As ships were being torn apart, there was nothing but calm and serenity inside the vast space station. With nothing there to transport the sound vibrations, the noise of battle vanished into the void. Only those actually watching would ever have an inclination as to what was happening, even as the powerplant of Plethodon went critical and the ship exploded. The only sign of trouble was the bright flash outside the classroom that not one of the cadets noticed.

Until that fateful day, Nate and his friends had lived the carefree life known only to young cadets this far from home. Each had been selected from their classmates to represent the Alliance Academy in the tournament. It was to be a friendly contest with their peers in the Byotai Empire, one of many projects to cement the new bonds with the Empire. They'd been selected from the thousands of cadets in the Alliance's military schools due to their unique aptitude in a single area, that of the popular simulated arena known as Star Crusader. It was a commercial spinoff from the military simulation software and had quickly become the single most competitive sport in both Empires. Of all things the two peoples shared, few would ever have expected a computerised simulation would rise to the top.

Now Nate and his five comrades were here and aboard the Byotai starbase known as Mognathus 7 to complete in a specially sanctioned military version of the simulation. Unlike the commercial edition, this would involve the use of real physics and damage, as well as fully realised modelling of both weapons and spacecraft. Mognathus 7 was one of the major Imperial shipyards and home of the elite fleet training academy for the reptilian race known as the Byotai, a strong and reliable ally of the Alliance. This was the place where all officers underwent their initial training, and Nate and his five comrades were the first human cadets to ever set foot on the starbase; six young cadets far from home and aboard the alien space station deep inside Byotai space.

They sat at their desks, alongside the eighteen Byotai cadets who gave them nothing but irritated looks. There were hundreds of Byotai cadets at the starbase, but it was almost impossible to tell their age from just their looks. Once they reached maturity, they appeared little different to each other; their skin shed and changed their apparent look day by day. Little did any of them know that on that day in October, what started with classes on engineering and computer science, would end with death on a massive scale.

The light flashed again, and this time Nate just happened to look up. As his eyes moved up, the room flashed with the light, and he found himself looking directly at the Byotai instructor, Captain Vidsara.

*What was that?*

Their eyes met for a moment, and he instantly knew he should be looking back down at his assessment. The Captain was a war veteran and had seen service when Nate was just a young boy. Like all of the Byotai, his leathery skin and bony face was the first indication that he was not human. His cold-blooded species was one of the many discovered by the Alliance, and ruled a vast domain of more than fifty colonies, spread over nine distinct quadrants. They were one of the largest empires that had been discovered, and also one of the most secretive.

Nate moved his eyes to the windows, yet he could feel the gaze of the instructor burning through him as he waited for the students to finish their assessment. The alien opened his mouth, and a brief moment later the translator fitted to Nate's ear converted the sentences into something he could understand.

"Cadet Lewis, return to your work."

The mention of his family name immediately caught Nate's attention.

He'd been born Nathanial Edward Lewis, but to his friends, and even his rivals, he was simply called Nate. He looked back down at the diagram of an engine intake system on his portable Secpad and sighed. The design was complex and broken apart into more than fifty pieces. Unlike the Byotai cadets, Nate and his friends were there simply as exchange students for a single semester. They were not even military cadets, not yet. First they would return home and continue their studies in other subjects before graduating; then, and only then, would their aptitudes be fully assessed and options given to them. Nate already knew what he wanted, and he'd settle for nothing less than a starship.

*Maybe I should have spent more time revising, and less time at the observation window. You won't command a battleship if you can't even remember how to put an engine back together.*

It was all just wishful thinking. Like any new cadet, his mind constantly moved to the thought of starships and of the great battles of the past. From the first day they'd learnt about the great ship duels of the Uprising and, of course, the one event every single military officer seemed to bring up in his presence, the death of Admiral Lewis, his uncle.

He turned his mind from the task and to the day before. It was the cadets' first visit to the simulation centre where the Star Crusader system had been up and running. He'd racked up thousands of hours on the public system available on the Cortex, but this was something very different. The Byotai had been given access to the military version, and had taken the thing to heart. The engineering teams at the station had even created a dedicated area for the teams to compete, as well as space for the senior officers to observe. They had been given control of simulated Byotai fighters. To the surprise of their instructors, the human cadets were more than capable of surpassing the scores set by the previous students.

Nate smiled to himself, recalling the last round of the simulated battle, where the six of them had defeated last year's Byotai graduates in a free-for-all dogfight, all as part of the warm-up for the main event. It was his first battle with the safeguards removed, and he found exposure to real world physics exhilarating.

*That was a good game, a very good game. Now, if only we can do the same in the contest.*

Nate didn't particularly enjoy the studies, and much of it reminded him of the military school he'd been sent to back home. With his family gone, his guardians sent him, like so many other youngsters, to join the Alliance sponsored Academy programme. Though run by the military, it was not a direct path into military service, but intended to the lay the foundation of a general advanced education, one that would be suitable for enrolment in both public and private sector service.

Unlike the majority, he'd shown an aptitude in one specific area, one that the Academy placed great value, in space combat. Only a handful had passed the tests to join the exchange, and that meant travel to strange and exotic worlds as he trained with the new allies of the Alliance. It was all a far cry from his early years back on Kerberos, growing up in the household of a long-established military family. Now it was only him, and Nate was determined to succeed.

*What's going on?*

Something odd caught his attention, and he looked to his left where the entire side of the room was filled with large, slightly curved windows. Outside, the inky blackness of space, interspersed with the gantries and docking arms, reminded him this was no mere starbase, but a military outpost. This was a Byotai station and with a strong military presence. There were not just Byotai warships in the shipyard; there was also a small Alliance fleet, flying the flag for politicians back home.

Nate had spent the last ten minutes trying to piece the system back together, and as he moved his finger on the device, he noticed the instructor moving to the window. He appeared nervous and was speaking into the communication's unit implanted in his forearm.

*What is going on out there?*

He recalled the public information films he'd been shown back at school. Even though he was only seven or eight years old, the videostreams had bordered on something close to a horror show. Back then the information film was on what to do if you were attacked by the dreaded Biomechs and their ground troops. He had never seen this enemy, but the information film had stuck with him after all this time.

*Look for your exits, and plan your escape.*

The words came back to him as if he'd been watching it five minutes ago. Nate remembered the imagery showing black shapes that were supposed to be the ships of the enemy. As they moved over a city, the children were seen running to shelters or to secure parts of their homes. It was frightening, made all the more terrifying by the news reports of the constant defeats against the dreaded enemy. Nate looked to his left, but there were only the windows, so he turned to the right of the instructor where the main doorway in now seemed so far away.

"What is it?" Cassandra Hurley asked.

Nate glanced over to her, noticing that as usual she seemed more interested in what the others in the group had to say. He pointed to the window.

"Something's going on out there."

He felt a pain in his shoulder and turned around to find Rex Hampel pulling back his arm. Though the same age as Nate, he was much bigger built, with a pale complexion and vivid blonde hair. He lifted his eyebrows in an attempt to intimidate Nate into reacting.

"Yeah?"

Nate shook his head but then spotted another door off to the far corner, partially blocked by four metal cases. It was a smaller doorway, one of the older bulkhead doors that linked many of the compartments together. Rex looked away and pointed at the windows just as another flashed lit up the room. This time, the yellows and reds of explosions were all too obvious. Some of the cadets rose from their seats and moved to the windows.

Each of the Byotai cadets stayed close to DuFarl, the alien group's star pupil and highest scoring pilot in the simulation contests. He looked over to the human cadets and muttered something in his own tongue. His words

23

were so fast that the translator circuits failed to understand. Nate looked back to the others.

"I think we should..."

"Should what?" Rex snapped back.

Nate rubbed at his forehead, knowing too well that he was once again going to be ignored.

"We should get out of here."

Rex walked over to the window and began laughing. Nate was still sitting down when he heard the sound of shouting coming from off in the station and behind the main door. The instructor moved away to examine, and Nate jumped up from his seat.

"What the hell?" Rex said.

He looked back to the group but at no particular individual.

"There's a fight going on out there."

He turned back and watched as more lights flashed back and forth, like a massive firework display for their eyes only. The lights and colours betrayed the different types of weapons, and from their experience in the simulated combat, they knew exactly what they were. In the last round they fought a battle between two groups of matched Byotai fighters and a single cruiser. It was their first real exposure to the weapons used by the alien race, and now Nate was seeing them with his own eyes, right outside the station.

"Who is it?" Billy asked.

Rex looked back and watched the display of weaponry with morbid fascination. The energy weapons were impossible to see without some medium to reflect the light. Luckily for him, there was enough small debris and dust to do just that.

"Kinetic rounds, phased plasma...and what is that? Proximity missiles?"

He stumbled backwards as a volley of phased plasma struck a ship moving slowly away from the station. One flash after another marked the impacts, yet still the ruined vessel continued to move away. Rex shook his head in astonishment.

"Those are Byotai weapons."

Rex then looked back to the others, but while the humans seemed shocked by what was happening, the majority of the Byotai cadets appeared almost disinterested.

"Something weird is going on out there."

While Rex and the others seemed more interested in the battle, Nate was much more focused in what he could see inside the classroom.

*They know something. What the hell is going on here?*

"Then we need to move...fast!" Nate said.

He was already on his feet and at the secondary door. The boxes were light, but as he moved them, he found his path blocked by a security panel and coded access unit. He placed his finger on the black pad and pushed the button, only for the hexagonal inner section to flash red.

"Nate, move it!" Rex yelled.

With a rough shove, he pushed Nate to one side and began to strike the panel, all the while the sounds of violence continued to increase in volume. An alien voice called out loudly, and Nate turned left. The instructor waiting with them. His mouth was open, and he was taking in more air than normal. His eyes were bloodshot, but Nate already knew the signs.

*He's worried.*

"Let me open the door," said the electronic voice in Nate's ear.

Nate grabbed Rex by the arm and pulled him away.

"I said, get out of the way!"

Rex stumbled, and the instructor moved in, pressing buttons in a bizarre sequence. The mechanism clicked, but the door remained shut.

"Now we're in trouble," moaned Cassandra.

All of the human cadets were there now. The instructor pushed the door, and it hissed open. Rex stepped in first, activating the lamp on his portable Secpad to check the way. As always, his right-hand man Jack was there to watch his back. Wherever Rex was, Jack was always somewhere nearby.

"It's an access shaft."

He stopped and looked back. The main door clicked but refused to open. Voices called out in the Byotai language, and even though neither Nate nor his friends understood the words, they could easily tell from the tone they were not there to help.

*The instructor, he's locked us in.*

Nate began to talk to the old warrior, but then he spotted DuFarl and two of his friends heading to the main door. They were calling out to whomever was on the other side.

"No, DuFarl. Don't do it!"

The Byotai youth looked back at Nate and lifted his arm to point. He said several words that were clearly insulting, and then moved his hand to the pad next to the main door. A pair of the students leapt on a third, one of the older Byotai; Nate recalled him being from one of the patrician families that had fallen on hard times. He hadn't wanted to be in the military, but without money, his family had little choice.

"Go, run. You have no time," said the instructor.

Nate looked at the face of the wizened old instructor. He'd never talked about his past life, but his exploits in the last war were on public record, and Cassandra had made a great show of presenting her findings to the entire group. He was descended from one of the old patrician families and had fought as a marine in the same great space battle as his uncle.

"Come with us."

The Byotai pushed Nate so hard that he stumbled into the complaining Cassandra. She tripped but righted herself before hitting the smooth wall. Nate took three steps and heard the door groan. It pulled back towards the frame to seal down shut. The computerised voice of his translator spoke again in his ear.

"If you want to live, hurry! This is a revolution."

The group of six were now inside with Rex and Jack at the front, and the rest staggered behind. The shouting turned into gunfire, and Nate glanced back. The old instructor was still there, blocking the doorway, and with two holes in his stomach. He looked to Nate and muttered one word before pushing himself against the door and sealing them inside.

26

"Hide!"

The door seemed to close ever so slowly, giving Nate the perfect view of the approaching villains. He stood there speechless as he watched the group of heavily armed Byotai moving into the room. The instructor lifted something from his flank and then came another bang. This time it was closer, and the shouting increased. The Byotai scattered and then returned fire. Their shots were erratic and panicked, while the instructor took careful aim, firing two shots at a time.

*He's fighting them.*

These were not uniformed Byotai marines of the kind frequently seen patrolling the station. They looked like regular Byotai, dressed in civilian clothes and carrying military weapons. Nate swallowed, and it felt as though something the size of a golf ball had become lodged down in his throat. Even worse, he could see the Byotai cadets seemed to be running about helping them. DuFarl called out and waved his arm at the door just as it locked shut, and they were trapped in utter darkness, temporarily making them safe from the intruders. The gunfire continued, and every few seconds a round would strike the blast door or the nearby bulkhead walls.

"Keep moving," he said.

They inched their way along, stepping carefully over the cables and pipes that ran along the floor of this section. It was perfectly big enough to walk through, but with so little light there were more than enough obstructions to cause a fall. After what seemed an age, they reached an intersection with passageways leading off in four directions. In the middle was a hexagonal space, big enough for all of them to stand in. At the centre of the space was a raised plinth, with a ladder hanging down to stand just a metre from the floor.

"What now?" Cassandra asked.

She lifted up her Secpad and aimed the light to the ceiling. The shaft continued upwards before vanishing into the blackness.

"Keep moving," said Rex.

Nate looked to Cassandra and activated his light on his Secpad unit.

He'd never been this close to her, and her long hair dropped down over his shoulder.

"I...uh...we need to get out of here. Get help."

Rex moved into view.

"Yeah, brilliant idea, Nate. You saw the Byotai out there. Something is going on and they are after us, and anybody that helps us. Who on this station will help us now?"

"The marines," Nate said, trying to sound confident, "There is a single squad here as part of the exchange."

He nodded to himself.

"If we can get to them, they will help us."

Rex sighed. "Nate. Nate, you fool."

Rex stepped away, still shaking his head. Jack tried to persuade the others to follow him in the same direction they'd already been walking. Nate stopped to think. Rex went to grab him, but he twisted away from his grasp.

"If there's fighting on this station, you can guarantee they will be the first to go." said Rex.

Billy pushed up between them. He was of a similar height to Nate, and his rough, ginger hair looked almost like a mop. Even in this low light he looked something of a mess.

"It doesn't matter," said Billy, "Either we hide, or we run."

Rex held up his Secpad and showed them the connection lockout notices.

"They've cut off our access to the Cortex. So how do we find our way out?"

Cassandra checked hers and shook it, trying to get the thing to connect.

"I sent out our distress code when we got inside. I don't know if it got out, though."

She sighed and rubbed her head, desperately trying to come up with a plan. The door they had so recently entered through made a clunking sound. Billy groaned nervously, and Cassandra put her hand over his mouth. She then looked to Nate. As she opened her mouth to speak, a series of high-pitched cracks silenced the entire group. More rang out, and then a small serious of thuds.

"Explosions," said Nate.

He looked to Cassandra again.

"It's not just us. This is an attack or a revolt or something. We have to get to our people before they find us."

Cassandra kept her eyes looking firmly at Nate's, even as they stepped around the hexagonal space, examining the four options before them. The only possibility each was avoiding was the chance of turning back the way they'd come.

"I've seen you exploring the station, Nate. Can you get us to the marines? Do you even know where they are?"

He gulped in air as he ran over the shape of the station. It was vast, and he'd only explored the small numbers of areas the cadets had access to. Even so, he knew where the marines were staying.

"Yeah, I can do that. They have their quarters in the trade sector. It's on the lower ring near the customs centre. We need to warn them."

He held up his device and showed them a bright blue schematic of the place. Cassandra pulled the unit from him and ran her eyes over the plans.

"I don't understand. How is yours working?"

He grinned, not that any of them could see in the low light.

"I cut the link the minute trouble started in the class. I've still got the mapping information in memory."

Cassandra grabbed him and held him firmly. He could tell it was relief and nothing more. But even inside this dark passageway, perhaps seconds from danger, he felt happy.

"Okay, gadget boy," said Rex, "What now?"

Nate licked his lower lip.

"Follow me. I know the route."

He moved to the front, with Cassandra and Billy right beside him. Rex watched the rear of the group, constantly looking for signs of their pursuers. To all of their surprise, Nate began climbing the ladder. Billy followed without saying a word. He was almost at the top before the others started to climb.

"Nate, you'd better not be wrong about this," grumbled Rex.

He reached the top and hit the release button. This time it was a mechanical unit, and the hatch opened, releasing cool air into the chamber, as well as casting a pale blue light back down onto their faces.

"Yeah, Rex, right now I'm worried about what you'll do to me."

He reached up and pulled himself off the ladder and into another hexagonal space. It took only a few seconds to check it was empty before he looked back and helped the others up. They all climbed through until Rex made it and landed down alongside Nate. He looked almost thankful to be there, but at seeing Nate and Cassandra side by side he scowled.

"Okay, hero, now what?"

Cassandra moved between the two of them.

"Let him work, Rex. He's got us this far."

Rex stepped back and began checking the metal racking fitted to the walls. There were all kinds of plastic storage cases, and he took whatever he thought might be useful.

"What are you doing?" Billy asked.

Rex opened another and took out a roll of metallic tape.

"I'm taking everything that might be of use. Why? What about you?"

Billy moved back to Nate and Cassandra.

"That guy is such an ass."

Nate kept his eyes focused on his Secpad while the blue light in the small room gave him a cool, sinister hue of colour. He ran his finger along the screen and tracked their position. Finally, he stopped and looked to the others.

"Okay. We're not too far away."

He signalled for them to come closer, but only Rex showed any interest. The rest were too busy looking out for their pursuers. Jack bent down and looked down the hatch and into the area they'd just left. Cassandra squinted as she double-checked the Secpad.

"Are you serious, Nate? That's where we need to get to?"

Nate nodded.

"It's not what I want, but this is the place. The customs level is where the marines are, and it leads to the docking clamps and the ships. It's the only way we can get to our own troops."

"Or get off the station," added Billy.

Even Cassandra seemed unimpressed with the plan.

"Wait a minute. You want to cross the plaza and move to the service deck. And then what, climb six levels to the customs level?"

Rex looked at the device for just a second.

"Or we run for it, get to the express elevators, and ride them all the way there?"

Nate shook his head while Rex moved off to the nearest hatch. He accessed the panel and ever so carefully opened the door. It was small, just big enough for a single person, and sealed around the frame with a smooth round material, much like rubber. The door opened inwards, and he peered around the corner, making no sound of any kind. Jack concentrated on the Secpad, even though the other three seemed more interested in seeing what was outside.

"No, we move along this route here."

He touched the unit.

"By using the service shafts and avoiding the public spaces. Until we know whom to trust, we have to be careful. We can climb the ladders up one level..."

Cassandra tapped the Secpad on the image.

"And then use the service elevators."

"Exactly," said Nate, "It won't take much longer, and we can avoid any..."

Rex was at the door and starting to move through it.

"Rex get back," said Nate.

Rex paused and then opened his mouth to complain. He must have seen something outside and immediately dropped down to his knees. Jack signalled for them all to be quiet. Nate stayed completely still, moving only one finger to disable the portable device in his hands. Though the gap was small, all of them could see the panicked groups of people rushing about. Most were Byotai, but there were also a number of the more slender-shaped Helions, and even a pair of Khreenk traders. All ran from the direction of the shouting.

*That's what I was afraid of,* Nate thought.

He moved closer to the door but made sure he stayed in the shadows of the poorly lit area. He moved alongside Rex, who was breathing quickly and speechless for a change. From here the panic inside the station was obvious, and Nate watched in stunned silence.

Cassandra knelt down along him and whispered in his ear, "You were right, Nate."

He felt a glimmer of pride, but more important, he was just glad they'd not rushed out into the path of what was clearly a dangerous situation. The six of them kept still while the sound of angry shouting increased. Nate felt the urge to run, to move in any direction, but with no idea what was happening, the safest thing for now seemed to be to keep still. Then came the screams of terror. Nate almost stumbled when he spotted a group of Byoti, all armed with firearms or brandishing improvised cudgels. They ran into the open plaza and called out to the few Byotai still there. Two Navy crew ran past directly in front of the group. A fusillade of shots rang out, and both slumped to the floor dead.

Cassandra lurched backwards and knocked a batch of metal pipes from the shelf. One struck the metallic floor with a clattering sound, but Nate and Billy caught the rest and held onto them, each terrified of making more noise.

"Great, now we're done," complained Rex.

When Nate looked back through the narrow crack in the door, he found the armed group had gone. He might have felt relief but was much more nervous not knowing where they were, and suspected they were coming for him. A shadow moved closer, and then a foot appeared near the doorway. Nate gripped the metal pipe and pleaded to himself for the individual to move on.

Then came the sounds of shouting again, and the figure moved away. Rex leaned forward and reached for the door to move it shut, but slipped and ended up pushing it further open. The wider gap gave them a good view of the plaza. Out in the middle were two bodies, and next to them a single older Byotai. He was dressed in light coloured clothing, his head bare and chest encased in a half breastplate. He faced off against the rowdy group, with his hand resting on his flank, above where his pistol was fitted. Just behind him, and low on the ground, was a single Byotai. She moaned from at least one leg wound and tried to crawl away from the violence.

"He's a Byotai officer. Look at the uniform," whispered Cassandra.

"Yeah," Matilda agreed, "And how does that help us? All it tells me is that this little insurrection is against authority."

The technical wizard of the group had been silent until now. Though quiet, she was the only one of the group with any real understanding of the Byotai languages and culture. She nodded as she watched the argument.

"He's a junior captain. He's telling them to turn away. And they are telling him to drop his weapon, or..."

Matilda paused, and Rex grabbed her shoulder.

"Or what?"

Matilda shrugged but didn't seem particularly fazed by Rex.

"Or die like the others."

Cassandra squirmed and moved away from the doorway.

"No. No, it's not fair. We didn't do anything. We're not..."

Nate lifted his finger to his mouth, and Cassandra quickly quietened down. A noise far off to the left caught the ear of the mob, and the angriest of the group pointed off into the distance. Two left to investigate and quickly vanished, leaving the other four to face off against the officer, who'd now drawn his pistol and was aiming it at the face of the loudest killer.

Billy whispered as quietly as he could, "This is going to go badly. We need..."

Nate's attention was off to the right where two other Byotai were

33

hiding. They looked about the same age as him, and one of them spotted him. Their eyes met, and Nate felt a shudder in his chest.

*Idiot, what if they say something?*

The officer lifted one hand and called out to the group. They then spread out with three taking aim with looted firearms, and the fourth brandishing cudgels. They were now in a semi-circle and still moving apart. Soon they would have both of them surrounded.

"What's he doing? What do they want?" Jack asked.

Rex looked to Nate, and then the others.

"We need to do something. They're going to kill the two of them, and then we'll be next."

Nate looked down at the narrow metal pipe that he'd caught. It was just over a metre long, and must have weight a minimum of two kilograms, perhaps more. When he looked back up, Rex was grinning.

"Yeah, I like your thinking, Nate."

He reached up, took one of the pipes from the shelf, and moved to the partially open doorway. Jack did the same, and Nate, fearing what would happen if only a few of them tried to help, did the same. He looked to the rest. Billy was already trying to come and help, but Nate blocked his path.

"Stay together. If we screw up, somebody has to pass on what happened."

By the time he stepped back, the other two were ready. Nate squeezed between them and looked out to the left and right, double-checking the other two were still away from the plaza. Apart from the bodies, the place was totally deserted. The four thugs had their right sides to the doorway and were angled slightly away, making being spotted unlikely.

"Okay, let's do this," he said.

The three inched out from cover and into the open. Nate felt immediately vulnerable and glanced off to his left, expecting more of the angry mob to arrive. The sound of shouting and gunfire had subsided, though, and now just the argument with the group continued. They moved past the bulkhead pillars, keeping them in the line of sight and making sure they were undetected. They made it halfway when Nate spotted the entrance to the service shaft. He pointed at it, but Rex was already moving along and getting ready to attack. They were now only ten metres away from the argument, and there was no more cover as each waited behind his pillar.

*A metal bar against guns...Are we idiots?*

"Surrender!"

It was the sound inside Nate's translator. He spun around and found himself looking directly at the face of an older looking Byotai female. She wore some armour, and a metal plate ran from her forehead and down her elongated nose. The plating followed the bony contours of her skull, giving her an even angrier look than her body language suggested. At her sides were five more Byotai, and two carried rifles.

"What now?" Rex asked.

Nate licked his lip. His heart said to go for it, to start swinging the bars and fight, just like the stories he'd read about. But his brain told him that would be stupidity.

"If we fight, we die."

He then looked to Rex and Jack.

"Drop the pipes."

Nate was already releasing the metal in his hand when there was a loud banging sound of metal on metal. At first he thought it was one of the pipes, but then more continued, and he immediately knew what it was. He'd been on the station long enough to be able to tell the difference.

*More boots. Now it's over.*

His throat turned dry, and he twisted his head around to look at the newcomers. There were four of them, and they were big. All were armoured from head to toe in protective plating, and in their hands oversized carbine weapons. The armour was faded grey, with black markings running horizontally like tiger stripes. Their heads were encased, and their collars hidden behind raised gorgets.

"Fire!"

# CHAPTER TWO

**Starbase 'Mognathus 7', 3rd Quadrant, Byotai Empire**

Nate closed his eyes involuntarily and tensed his body, waiting for the pain to strike at any moment. He'd never been shot before, but he'd take his share of punches and kicks throughout school. Guns erupted all around him, and the gunfire was so intense he could actually feel the heat through his cadet tunic. The sound inside the starbase was louder than he could ever have expected, and his hearing became muffled after just a few shots. Logic dictated that the first projectiles would hit his torso, but to his surprise his shoulder was touched first, and he instantly winced.

"Come with me."

The voice was loud, artificially enhanced, and boomed almost as loudly as the gunfire. He opened his eyes, expecting to find that he was on the ground, bleeding out and facing the mob. Instead, he was being pulled to the side of the plaza by an armoured arm. The soldier was a heavily armoured marine, and his chest plating bore the insignia of the Alliance Marine Corps. Nate instantly recognised it as being PDS Alpha armour, the latest issue that had now been in continuous use for more than a decade.

*Marines?*

A shot flashed overhead, and a chunk of masonry ripped apart and crashed to the ground nearby. The marine pushed him away just as a pile of masonry came down, narrowly missing his head.

"Rex!" Jack yelled.

Nate looked around for his comrades, but the group was scattered at different parts of the plaza. He saw Jack huddled behind a pillar with two marines nearby. The Byotai mob had gone, but they'd left two of their dead behind.

*Cassandra, Billy, where are they?*

The Byotai officer was leaning behind a bulkhead. Blood dripped from a graze to his head, but he was still upright and fighting. He took aim and fired twice before uttering an odd alien howl. One or two of the mob must have been hidden off into the distance because more guns fired.

"Covering fire!" said one of the marines.

His voice was muffled inside the suit, but with him shouting the sound was just about audible. The small group of elite warriors opened up with a crescendo of fire, far in excess of anything the mob could muster. Shapes rushed out in the open, and somebody fell. Nate couldn't tell who, but he immediately recognised a cadet uniform. He took a step, but the marine lifted his hand.

"Stay back, son. We've got this."

This time the marine was speaking to those outside of his squad, and the external speakers fitted to his armour amplified his voice into something loud, clear, and menacing. The way he moved and spoke gave the impression he was some kind of metal monster or demon. Inside his armour the marine was substantially heavier than Nate, and as his feet crunched on the broken masonry, it made a heavy thudding sound. The marine was calm and aimed carefully before blasting away at the hidden position. Nate, ever interested in the weapons and equipment around him, found this close-up look at a real live firearm to be fascinating. He instantly recognised it as a standard issue carbine, one he'd seen before in their lessons on Alliance technology.

*L52 Mark II carbine, triple-barrelled coil-gun with hardened slug rounds. They're marines, all right.*

From his position safely hidden hind a bulkhead, he had a much better view. He looked to the open and saw Rex with another marine. There was blood on Rex's arm, but there was no obvious wound. Nate wanted to move, but as the marines continued shooting, he found he was rooted to the spot and incapable of going anywhere. He watched as the two pulled Jack who was crying out from an injury, and leaving a trail of dark red blood on the floor.

"No...this can't be."

The marine looked back and deactivated his frontal visor. The plating moved away, and he found himself looking into the eyes of a man in his early twenties. His face was heavily tanned, and there were black tattoos running down his cheeks.

"Sergeant Perkins, from Relentless."

He took in a breath, and only then did Nate notice that he'd already taken two hits to his armour. One was high, just under the chin and had gouged a pit at the size of an eyeball in the gorget plate. The second was at the shoulder, and had left a series of indentations and marks. The marine seemed to find moving his one arm painful.

"Nathaniel Lewis, of the..."

The man smiled.

"Son, I know who you are."

He leaned in closer while keeping a careful eye out for their attackers.

"Nate, where are the others? We were told there were six students here. Your trackers are accurate only to a hundred metres. I need to get you all out of here, and fast."

Nate considered his question, but only for a second. He'd never met the marine before, and there was always a chance the man was as much a problem as the Byotai mob. More shouting from back inside the station quickly changed his mind. He nodded to the now almost completely closed doorway.

"Back there, three more."

The man nodded and reactivated his visor. Nate could see him speaking over his internal communications system as it closed down tightly, sealing him inside his fully enclosed suit of armour. The sound of his voice vanished the second the visor hissed shut. As he watched, a pair of marines rushed to the door, and then slid it open. As they did so, Cassandra and Billy leapt out, swinging the metal tubes. One struck a marine in the arm, but the next marine quickly stopped the second attack.

"It's okay. They're with us!" Nate shouted.

It didn't matter, though, both were quickly disarmed, and then Matilda was pulled from the darkness and brought back into the plaza. When Cassandra spotted the wounded Jack, she immediately forgot about the marines and rushed to him, bending down to check his wound.

"You have to help him."

The marine next to Nate gave a hand signal, and two of the marines moved back towards the service area already identified by Jack. A third went alongside Cassandra, checked Jack, and placed a small packet on his wound. He yelled in pain and reached out for somebody to help him. Sergeant Perkins rushed in front of the cadets and aimed his carbine once again, three shots in quick succession, each one precise. As he stopped, his left hand slipped down to his flank, and a small flap flipped open. He grabbed a metallic container and threw it over to Cassandra.

"You've been medically trained?"

Cassandra nodded quickly.

"Good. Come with us. As soon as we're out of sight, you can help him with the field dressing. Push it hard, and let the tool do the work."

The marine looked down at the writhing cadet. The man's helmet was still sealed up, and if he was trying to be conciliatory, it was wasted on the cadets.

"Son. It will seal the wound for a few hours, but it's gonna hurt like hell. Hang in there."

"Sarge! New contacts!" yelled one of the other marines.

Sergeant Perkins leaned to the right around the bulkhead post so that he could get a better look off into the distance. He then lifted his carbine and took aim. The sound of more Byotai was getting louder and louder. There were multiple entrances at the opposite end, and shadows were already dancing about from the bright lights cast further back in the passageways.

"I see them, multiple contacts, one fifty metres out and closing."

He glanced back towards Nate.

"It's time to get out of here. I don't know what's going on, but the

40

station is out of control. If we wait any longer, we might end up permanent residents. Our ships are ready for evac."

He gave a hand signal to his comrades and then called out over his external speakers.

"Let's move out. Bring the wounded officers with us."

With that, the marines moved to follow the first group. They didn't bother using cover and rushed as quickly as they could, the first two covering them. The Byotai officer moved in the same direction, and when he reached Sergeant Perkins, the two spoke in the Byotai language. With the marine's face hidden behind armour, Nate could only hear the synthesised voice.

*What the hell is happening on this station?*

An arm grabbed him, and he moved through the large doorway and into the service corridor. This was well lit, but far less salubrious than the plaza. Sergeant Perkins went to the front as they kept moving further into the station, and the Byotai officer went with him.

"Is this better?" Cassandra asked.

Nate hadn't even noticed she was there, right beside him. Rather than answer, he looked back, fearing that his friend might have been left behind. He needn't have worried; one of the marines was carrying him over his shoulder. Back in the passageway, and nearly thirty metres, away a head appeared. The rearguard marines opened fired, sending sparks flashing. Nate looked back at Cassandra and then ducked, narrowly missing hitting his head on an overhanging beam.

"They are Alliance. I don't know who else we can trust, right now."

Sergeant Perkins must have heard them and pointed off into the distance.

"We're using the back route to avoid the mob. Ten more minutes and we'll be at the customs level. There's another squad waiting there for us."

Nate nodded, and they continued through the maze of corridors and shafts. They moved far back in the starbase, into areas that didn't even show on his Secpad. As good as the marine's word, they emerged from the final shaft into the long and especially wide customs deck. This was designed much

41

like a smaller plaza, with a customs booth and security gate leading to the docking gantries. Large panes of smoked glass had functioned as security partitions in the past, but now all of them lay smashed or cracked in a hundred places.

"What happened here?"

Cassandra's voice was quieter than normal, but Nate could pick up the nerves and the fear from the way she spoke. None of them were soldiers, and the most violent thing any of them had committed over the last three months was in computer fighter simulations. That was it. They waited at the entry point, a large, triangular doorway and the last piece of cover before moving into the open area. Sergeant Perkins lifted his hand in the classic stop motion.

"This is it."

He looked back at the mixed group and seemed pleased to find Jack was moving more freely now. His eyes moved from each of them until stopping in front of Nate.

"Stay here. I need to check this out."

Without checking to see if they were listening, he activated his visor, and it hissed back into position, hiding his face entirely from view. The Sergeant then walked out into the open and onto the smashed glass. The broken pieces crunched under his feet as he moved ten metres ahead, and then stopped. He was there for almost ten seconds before looking back.

"We're clear. Let's go!"

They came out from cover and made for the Sergeant. Once there, they passed him and ran straight into a terrible scene of carnage. There were at least ten bodies scattered about, and Nate found a young Byotai of perhaps ten or eleven years old. He bent down to see if he was alive, but one of the marines grabbed him.

"It's too late for him. Protect yourselves and those you know. We don't have the time to do more. Not now."

The other cadets moved along silently, taking in the bloody scene and dealing with it in their own way. Not one of them showed fear, but there was a clear difference in body language between the marines and the cadets. Two more marines were the only people still present on the customs deck, and both took aim at the group of marines and cadets.

"Corporal, where's your squad?" Sergeant Perkins asked.

All of the marines had opened their visors, and the two that had stayed behind were dripping in sweat. As Nate moved closer, he observed the dozens of marks on their armour, and then the four more bodies on the ground behind their position. Three were Byotai and one was human.

"Sergeant, glad you got back."

Perkins glanced back at his unit and then to the marine.

"I've got the six cadets and no casualties. You?"

With the last word the tone in his voice changed. Rex moved up alongside Nate and then pushed closer to the Sergeant. He began to speak, but the Sergeant lifted his hand for him to be quiet while he listened to his exhausted Corporal.

"One dead, three wounded. I sent them back with the Ambassador and her staff."

Sergeant Perkins' expression instantly changed.

"What? The Mauler has left the starbase?"

The marine nodded quickly.

"Yes, Sergeant. We were getting pushed hard trying to hold this position. Thought it better to save some than keep them here."

"Yeah," agreed the second marine, "and risk losing them all."

The Corporal looked a little sheepish and nodded to the exposed doorway behind them.

"The Mauler will be back in three minutes."

More noise came from the opposite end of the open space and off behind the many shattered glass dividers. Shapes moved, and a single gunshot rang out. It was poorly aimed and struck the wall several metres from Billy's head.

"Marines, form a defensive perimeter," Sergeant Perkins ordered.

He looked over to the cadets.

"Get back behind the desks and wait for the Mauler. Three minutes and

43

we leave. Be ready to run. You'll get one chance for this. Screw around and you can stay behind."

Nate and Billy ducked down behind a large metal counter. The rest were a short distance away behind a series of large locker units. Long corridors ran the length of the starbase viewing point. Normally, the one side would be completely transparent so that visitors could see out into the open space of the shipyards and docking arms. Long metal safety shutters were now in position, and small flashing red lights served as a constant reminder of the dangerous situation all of them were in.

In the middle of the safety barrier was a single doorway, and four large articulated bars sealed it. Above the doorway was writing in the odd glyphs of the Byotai. Luckily, all the cadets had been taught the basic warning signs before they even arrived.

*It's the shuttle evacuation dock.*

"What now?" Billy asked.

He watched Nate looking at the doorway and then placed his hand on his injured flank. He immediately groaned and released his hand. Nate lifted his head a fraction above the desk. From there he had a reasonably good view of the customs area. What remained of the smoked glass dividers gave the space a weird, maze type look. That was when he spotted the mob. He ducked back down and looked to his friend.

"We do what the marine asked us to do. Stay down and wait for the shuttle."

Billy said something else, perhaps another question, but his voice was drowned out as the shooting started. This time it was very different, and rather than wild, sporadic fire was careful shooting from Byotai in concealed positions. The six cadets ducked down as glass, masonry, and metal splintered, shattering all around them. A shot hit a marine in the chest, and he staggered backwards, tipping over and crashing through a smoked glass tabletop. Nate watched him fall and started to crawl along the floor to reach him. By the time he was there, Rex had joined him. Three more rounds struck nearby, and then a fourth took a chunk of metal from the ankle of the marine's armour.

"We have to move him," said Nate.

"Yeah, come on."

They grabbed the marine's arms and dragged him. The wounded warrior groaned, and it seemed to take an age as they moved him metre by metre until back to their original position. Once there the marine deactivated his visor and revealed the pale face of a young woman, perhaps twenty or twenty-one years old.

"Get back! This thing will burn your face off," she said through clenched teeth.

Rex moved away, but Nate stayed where he was and leaned over the fallen woman. She tried to push him away, but he avoided her hands and moved towards her sternum.

"I can see it; you've got something embedded in the armour. Let me help."

He looked around for a tool, but all he could see was the debris from the fight. There was a dead Byotai nearby with a bar still grasped firmly in its hand, presumably something they'd elected to use as a cudgel in the battle. The marine tried to grab at the white hot projectile as it continued to hiss away, every second getting closer to melting through the thermal layer of the armour and to her flesh.

"I know I've taken a hit, jackass!"

She tried to pull at it one more time and only succeeded in scorching the fingers of her armoured hand. Several more rounds struck overhead, quickly followed by the meaty staccato sound of multiple L52 carbines opening up.

"Okay, cadet. Help me get it off."

Nate slid along the floor and grabbed at the bar. The Byotai must have had a death grip on the thing, and he was forced to put his left foot on its arm to release the piece. Now that it was in his hands, he could see it was actually a small crowbar, probably one of the many tools taken by the mob.

"Keep them back!" Sergeant Perkins shouted.

The marine was calm, and his comrades took careful aim, making sure their rounds struck true, without causing excessive casualties. Significantly, more fire came back, but this time the mob was cautious. Rather than rushing headlong, they fanned out, using every piece of cover and trying to outflank the defenders.

"I've got armoured Byotai marines coming in. Change to maximum power settings. Do not let them get through!"

Nate was back at the fallen marine, and Rex moved up with a bent piece of metal he'd found from somewhere else.

"Well, what now?"

Nate looked at the projectile. The white light was so bright it actually hurt his eyes just to look at the thing. As he leaned in closer, the heat became almost unbearable. Only the advanced multiple layers of the PDS Alpha armour were keeping the marine alive.

"No idea, just dig and pull."

Nate pushed his tool up against the super-heated projectile and then pushed down to one side. The metal on metal groaned, but still the object remained jammed in tightly.

"Come on, you, too."

Rex shielded his face from the heat and then jammed his piece of metal against the side of the round. The two pushed and twisted until after one herculean effort, the thing popped out and struck the floor. Pale white smoke rose from the penetrated section on the marine's armour, but she was already starting to relax. She reached towards Nate and grabbed his shoulder, pulling herself back up to her feet.

"My weapon?"

Rex looked to his left, found the carbine, and grabbed it. Against him, the triple-barrelled gun looked massive. He handed it over, and the marine checked its status and then clipped on a new power pack.

"Thanks, guys, I owe you."

She activated her visor, and it clamped shut in a fraction of a second. The woman was as though she'd been jolted by a surge of electricity, and knowing the burning projectile was gone invigorated her into action.

"Now stay down. It's my turn."

A small number of shots clattered to the right. The marine rose to her feet, took aim, and fired. This time the weapon was changed to the high power setting. It was something unique to the coilgun, a type of electromagnetic railgun that launched magnetised projectiles from each of the triple barrels. By firing all three together, and with an extended burst of energy, it was capable of unleashing devastating firepower at short to medium ranges.

"Nate!"

It was Cassandra's voice. Both Nate and Rex looked back to the direction of the sound. Cassandra had moved slowly along the floor until reaching a knocked over cabinet, and now little more than ten metres from the sealed airlock system.

"What?"

He was forced to repeat himself because of the gun battle raging all around them. With every second the Byotai seemed to be gaining ground, but then he saw what Cassandra was so preoccupied with.

"The door, there's something behind it."

Even as she said the words, the metal bars began to move. At first it was a short distance, and then all of them pulled outwards, and the door split at the middle. There was enough space for three people to enter side-by-side, but with the steam still venting out there was no way to see what lay on the other side.

"Everybody, move to the door, now!" Sergeant Perkins called out.

The marines moved back, taking it in turns to withdraw while the others emptied their clips in a last, desperate volley. They had switched back to the standard rapid-fire mode, and the guns made a buzzing sound, unleashing magnetised slugs at an incredible rate. The marines couldn't keep this up for long, but they didn't have to. The return fire from the Byotai reduced for a moment, and it was just enough to cover the ground for Nate and the others. The doors finished opening, and in walked a great hulking machine. It moved out from the doorway and kept going until it cleared enough space for everybody to get past. It then stopped, braced itself, and lifted both arms to take aim.

"Go!"

The machine spoke in a low, mechanical tone that sounded almost as though it was entirely synthesised. Nate had no idea if it was a human inside or a pre-recorded message triggered as a command. Rex and Cassandra were through the doorway and to the other side of the mist.

"Nate, come on!" Cassandra cried out.

The clatter of small arms fire, and the arrival of two thermal projectiles embedded in the wall, quickly pushed Nate along. He glanced at the large fighting machine as he ran past, and then he was through. That was the point at which the machine opened fire. Unlike the marines, this great behemoth didn't bother to find cover. It seemed to want to be a target.

*A Vanguard!*

He would have liked nothing more than to stay back and examine the thing in more detail, but there was no chance of that. The last he saw it was standing at the entrance, its arms raised and blasting away with its weapons. Like the other marines, this much larger model was equipped with a pair of the same weapons on each arm. It was twice the size of a man, and made a whirring sound as it articulated joints and motors moved. The sound of projectiles striking its armour was almost as loud as the gunfire. Most bounced off the curved surfaces, but some managed to breach the layered material, and Jack heard its occupant howl in rage via the external speakers.

"This way, Nate," said Billy.

He rounded the corner in the tunnel, and there were his friends, moving as fast as they could and mixed in with the marines.

"Billy, that was a Vanguard. Incredible!"

His friend gave him an exasperated look.

"Really? That's what you're thinking about, right now?"

Nate said no more, and they continued to move down the straight passage, each jumping through a narrower airlock, barely big enough for the mighty Vanguard marine to have used. He caught up with them and jumped over the lip to crash inside the Mauler. The doorway gave the impression it was small, but in reality, it was just one of the airlock entrances that led inside. Once there, Nate could see the interior was big enough to carry anything up to a hundred armoured marines. Apart from those escaping the station, it was completely empty.

"What is this thing?" Jack asked.

Rex looked at him and laughed, enjoying the chance to get rid of the nerves and fears he'd clearly experienced on the station.

"It's a Mauler, like the Sergeant said."

Four marines jumped inside, one after the other and then moved back, making sure there was plenty of space around the hatch. Then another two marines joined them, almost crashing into the others due to their speed. One looked back and deactivated their visor. It was the female marine that Rex and Nate had helped.

"Two left plus the Vanguard. Who's piloting that thing?"

The last two marines came in and slid each side of the doorway, their weapons at the ready. Behind them came the bloodied, but still alive shape of the Byotai officer. He crashed down alongside them and dropped to the floor, panting with exhaustion. A marine deactivated his visor. It was Sergeant Perkins.

"Everybody in?"

The female marine shook her head.

"Just the Vanguard, Sergeant."

The marine gave her a grim smile.

"Okay, then, Private, seal up the door. It's time to get out of here."

Her face changed, and from where Nate was standing, he could see she was not happy with the order. Even so, she reached out and hit the seal lever. The doors clamped down tightly, and a high-pitched whine announced the completion of the air seal.

"Sergeant, the Vanguard?"

Sergeant Perkins tapped his helmet.

"SWD tech. Remote controlled sentry drone. It will buy us the time we need."

A private nodded in appreciation. "Yeah, I like it."

The Sergeant lifted his arm and pointed to the many brackets attached to the floor of the craft. One by one the marines stepped over them and then hit a button to the side. Clamps lifted up from the floor, and a harness moved in around the body.

"Cadets, get on the clamp brackets."

All but Rex moved to the designated spots.

"You, too, son, unless you want your head attached to the bulkhead."

He nodded to the metal frames above them, none of which looked particularly comfortable to crash into. At that moment, the Mauler unclipped itself from the station and shuddered as the final links were detached.

"We'll be away from the gravitomagnetic field in a few seconds."

Rex needed no further persuasion and moved to the spot just in time. As the clamps moved around his body, the artificial gravity produced by the station quickly dropped off until they were in the zero-gravity environment of space.

"Okay, people. Hold on, this is gonna get a little dicey."

The Mauler performed a one hundred and eighty degree spin and then activated its main engines. Though bulky, the craft was as nimble as a heavy fighter in a zero-gravity environment. They continued to accelerate away from the docking arms and towards the protection of the waiting ship. The marines had access to the open channel feeds from the Alliance ships, and even the external feeds from the Mauler; the cadets had nothing.

"What's happening?" Cassandra asked.

Sergeant Perkins pointed to the front of the craft.

"We've got three ships in the area. We'll land, and then get the hell out of Dodge."

"And the Vanguard?" asked Nate.

The marine did his best to look conciliatory.

"Son, the Vanguard is just tech. That one is expendable, but we only have a few control packs. They are not cheap."

* * *

DuFarl had never seen a battle before today, and with every second that passed, he was beginning to realise he loved it. The fear, the tension, and the blood all combined to send his heart racing. He'd wanted to do this for so long, and now the uprising had begun, he couldn't wait to do his part. All of that would have to wait, however, until the orbital starbase was secured. If they failed, the rebels would spend the next decade in a prison cell, instead of bringing in the great change they all desired.

Part of the wall collapsed, sending heaps of rubble on top of two wounded deck workers. Neither were armoured or protected in any way, save for their work tunics. Before the dust even cleared, the guns from the Alliance Vanguard Marine opened up again. These were not the high-velocity metal slugs from the Alliance's usual firearms, but the large, 12.7mm intelligent rounds. Each was hardwired to detect nearby targets, and exploded as it moved over the heads of those hiding. Nowhere was safe from the devastation the war machine wreaked. Those rounds that failed to find a target simply embedded in the walls, but just as many struck further back and penetrated into the attached rooms.

Smoke and dust mixed together in such quantities that many of the Byotai fighters were forced back to avoid choking to death. Yellow flames flickered off into the distance as one of the side store rooms caught fire. Two Byotai civilians rushed out and fell to the ground, both screaming in pain from the flames spreading through their clothing. A third grabbed a box extinguisher and doused them in a cloud of deoxygenated air.

"Steady!" said one of them.

The voice was calm, in the clipped accent of a patrician. DuFarl looked up but could see little more than a large group of civilians as they moved through the rubble of the customs level. Glass and metal lay smashed in every direction, and more than a dozen rebels were dead.

51

"Help..."

DuFarl dropped down as another volley flashed by overhead. Bullets struck metal, glass, and flesh with equal measure. Some cried out, others screamed from the pain. One fully armoured Byotai marine ran past and took two hits to the torso. He went down hard and crashed into the floor.

*They'll pay for this.*

DuFarl stayed as low as he could and grabbed the marine's arm. He was heavy under all that plating, but another of DuFarl's comrades from his class helped to pull the marine away from the open space. As he looked down at the injured marine's face, he coughed violently, spurting warm blood over DuFarl's neck and chest. He pulled back in surprise, but when he looked back the marine was clearly dead.

"He's gone," said another.

The leader of the ad hoc unit of Byotai leaned over and pulled a snub-nosed pistol from the dying Byotai's flank.

"Take his weapon and help the others."

DuFarl took the weapon, checked the safety slider, and activated the unit. It buzzed gently as it powered up. Some of his classmates were there, intermingled with the odd mixture of civilians and mutineers. The majority were clearly not full-time warriors, but one in particular wore the breastplate and body armour of an Imperial Navy Marine. He was no bigger than the others, but the way he moved and commanded respect made him the obvious leader of their rabble.

"Those with rifles, keep the enemy busy."

"How do we kill it?" asked one of the older Byotai.

The marine struck him in the chest.

"I didn't say kill it, did I? Now, take aim and shoot it. Do not stop until I've dealt with it."

He then signalled to DuFarl and the others. It was a motley group; with the only thing they shared being their race. Some of the civilians wore no armour; others had stripped everything from breastplates and helms down to leg armour from the dead. All carried a strange mixture of pistols, cudgels, and blades. It was not particularly impressive, but as every minute went by, their numbers increased.

"The rest of you, stay with me and keep low. The humans cannot leave Byotai space, not under any circumstances!"

He looked back in the direction of the Vanguard. It was still firing, but now it was only shooting at targets that were visible. The guns unleashed long burst of flame as the barrels started to overheat from the firepower being sent against them.

"We have to outflank it, now!"

A small blast struck the wall, and a civilian was hit first in the arm and then the stomach. He staggered backwards and collapsed against another before both crashed to the ground.

"Covering fire, now, damn you!"

The fire from the other Byotai was sporadic at best, and DuFarl might have laughed at some of their ineptitude, if it were not his own life on the line. He crawled along the ground with a small group until they were on the left-hand side of the machine. From here he could see its legs under the nearest desk. The senior marine looked back at the group that were scared but still confident of victory.

"Youth! Where are the Alliance cadets?"

DuFarl snarled at the insult. He was old enough to be a regular soldier, or even to serve on a warship.

"They are all in that passageway, escaping."

"Very well. It is time to end this. With me!"

DuFarl picked up the helm from a dead Byotai marine and pulled it onto his head. He checked the pistol one last time and then ran around the corner towards the Alliance machine. Its arms moved from left to right as it tracked targets and opened fire. The left arm must have spotted them because it twisted about and fired. Three Byotai fell, and then something happened. The arm squealed, then nothing but a puff of steam or smoke blew out from the barrels.

"Now!" yelled the senior marine.

Nineteen Byotai surged from their cover out on the flank. Another six moved up to join them but scattered as shells struck nearby. The rest were now on their feet, and turning back would simply mean a bullet to the back, so on they went. Seven more approached head on, running straight at the Vanguard marine with little care for their lives. DuFarl shouted as he ran at the thing, his excitement and adrenalin overruling anything his brain might have been trying to tell him. Two more Byotai were cut down until they were able to physically throw themselves at the marine.

"Bring it down!" yelled a Byotai marine.

It might have been tall and heavy, but nothing that size could withstand the force of so many at once. Several of the attackers screamed in pain as the motorised limbs crushed metal and bone with ease, and still it fought on. Finally, it lost its balance and crashed onto its side. One after the other they surrounded the thing, pinning its arms down. Others hacked, stabbed, and blasted at the motors, joints, and less armoured parts. DuFarl took aim with his pistol and then stopped.

*What's that?*

The young Byotai bent down and placed his head closer to the metal body. It was quivering, like a mortally wounded beast facing its last few seconds of life. He strained his hearing, half expecting, almost wanting to hear the sound of a pleading human. Instead the sound was a beeping, and it was increasing in tempo. He lifted up to his feet and looked at the shattered machine.

"What's that noise?"

Another pair of civilians, not feeling confident in attacking their fallen foe, scrambled past. Both leapt at the thing and hacked away at the metal armour with their cudgels. The shooting had stopped, but the sound of violence, and the crying out of the wounded seemed equally painful. DuFarl looked down at the machine and saw a red light under the arm and embedded in the torso. It was flashing quickly and then so fast that it almost became continuous.

*No...it can't be!*

DuFarl looked and found the leader of the Byotai marines. He opened his mouth to shout, but there were no sounds. Instead, the Alliance marine detonated with such ferocity that it hurled those around, including him through the air. DuFarl was unconscious before he hit the bulkhead, and never even felt the heat from the blast as it burned through his clothing and flesh.

# CHAPTER THREE

**Alliance Mauler 'ANS Mongoose'**
**3rd Quadrant, Byotai Empire**

The Mauler was perhaps the ugliest craft in the Marine Corps inventory, but there was a reason for its continued use. The four massive engines could lift a company of marines from a planet's surface, and then carry them up into orbit to join a warship. The armour was thick enough to allow direct frontal attacks against defended installations, and best of all, it was easy to maintain and keep running. The Mauler was something of an antique, a relic of the time when armour and engine power was valued over weaponry. Now its ability to sustain punishment was being put to the test like never before.

Base defence systems were only partially active, but already they were blazing away with guns designed to engage capital ships. Slow to turn, and with long reload times, they were poorly suited to hitting something as manoeuvrable as the Mauler. Even so, one triple burst of kinetic projectiles came close, only missing its hull by little more than a metre. The second volley would have hit, had the pilot not tipped the craft to starboard and then blipped two of its four engines. The sudden change in angle and power management spun the vessel out of the path of the starbase's gunnery systems. It was only a temporary measure, but against such inexperienced gunners it bought them a few more seconds.

"That was...interesting," said Lieutenant Higgins.

He was a young pilot, no more than in his late thirties, and larger built than most. Blood dripped from a minor cut to his head, and his Naval fatigues were only partially zipped up. Like all of the officers, he'd been caught by surprise and had chosen to do his job instead of wasting time with trivialities such as dress code.

"Get your helmet on. This is gonna get rough."

Both men opened the access hatches above them and pulled down the special Naval issue PDS helmets. Although designed as part of the slimline Naval uniform, neither had found the time to use them in the rush to rescue those on the starbase. The units would provide critical head protection in a fight, but more important they contained independent life support systems that could seal in an emergency, and provide oxygen for up to three minutes. It was enough time to fix a single problem, little more.

"Hold on, Sergeant."

With another tug on the control column, he rolled the Mauler along its axis and dove down to slip between the multiple shattered parts of the docking arm. The larger parts were bigger than the Mauler, but there were still hundreds of smaller sections, some of which glanced off the craft's hull. One hit engine number one and tore off a section of plating half a metre wide. Alarms sounded, and Lieutenant Higgins punched the override button, quickly silencing them.

"Not much further."

To his left the co-pilot position had been replaced with a gunnery pod. Instead of another seat there was a semi-enclosed control pod, with multiple displays and controls fitted inside. The unit was slaved to the four turrets positioned along the front of the vessel, like two pairs of horns. In front of the pilot two displays showed a forward view much like a glass cockpit would, but without leaving the crew vulnerable. They were large and gave better visibility that would normally be expected on something like a Lightning space fighter.

Sitting inside the elaborate contraption was the gruff Sergeant Popwell. He was one of the marines that fought his way back from the station after rescuing the Ambassador and her family. Now he'd returned to take control of the Mauler's primary turret.

"Yeah, not bad, Lieutenant, you might make a pilot after all."

He banged his left hand on his display, right on top of a flashing red shape.

"We've got more problems, though. I've got three Byotai fighters coming right at us from behind. They don't want us to leave."

"I'm on it," said the Lieutenant.

The young man pressed a sequence of buttons, and the Mauler deactivated its drive engine. Almost immediately after that the manoeuvring engines spun it around a hundred and eighty degrees so that they were flying backwards.

"Eleven seconds, Sergeant. Make them count."

The Mauler continued onwards, and the pilot's displays altered to show the rear view so that he could see where they were heading. His current course put them behind the broken docking arm, but in eleven seconds they would need to pull up, or risk utter destruction in a high-speed collision.

"Got 'em!"

Sergeant Popwell might not have been a Naval crewman, but his gunnery was second to none. With the Mauler spun around, they had placed their heaviest armour facing the fighters, and now he unleashed the firepower of the four antique turrets. Each was fitted with a pair of Uprising era L48 rifles modified for spacecraft use. They unleashed 12.7mm hardened slugs that easily punched through the frontal armour of the fighters. Every five rounds was a special proximity high explosive charge, and after the second burst, they began to have an effect. The first fighter spun off to avoid the shooting, but it was too little too late. The armour piercing rounds opened up holes in the armour that the high-explosive rounds could exploit.

"Three seconds."

There was just enough time for another burst, and then Lieutenant Higgins rotated the engines and hit maximum boost. They pushed up from the debris, leaving one of the pursuing fighters to crash nose first into the twisted metal.

"Now we will take our chances in the open." he said under his breath.

Gunfire filled the emptiness of space around the Byotai starbase as the

Mauler moved faster and faster from it. What had once been a safe harbour in the heart of the Empire was no more. The captured Byotai ships ran amok, striking without mercy the small number of foreign ships still moored there. Most had already given up without a fight, including a number of massive transport barges, and even a single luxury liner from Spascia that had stopped for repairs. The occasional flashes of light from inside the liner showed that a major gunfight was spreading through her many decks. The majority had been taken so completely by surprise, they had no chance to put up even a token resistance.

There were scores of vessels connected to the multiple docking arms. Each of these extended out like long tendrils, the largest moving out to more than a kilometre. They were capable of taking even the largest bulk haulers and the most powerful Naval warships.

The largest of the docking arms lay broken in three places. The massive structure was twisted and bent, and one particularly large section had ripped from the starbase and now drifted dangerously close to the other moored ships. This scene of structural carnage was a subtle reminder as to where two Alliance ships had broken free. Hundreds of small holes peppered the ruined gantries and docking arms, marking the impact of heavy guns. The escape had not been peaceful, and scores of small fires now burned in this part of the starbase.

"They got Adamant," said the Sergeant through gritted teeth.

Lieutenant Higgins nodded but kept his eyes fixed firmly ahead.

"She won't be forgotten, Sergeant, I promise you."

They passed the single largest conflagration and into the open space around the base. The shattered hulk of the Alliance Navy Auxiliary replenishment ship, ANA Adamant was now all that remained. The bulk of her hull remained attached to the broken docking arm, though both were now crippled beyond hope of repair. She had been boarded, and some of her crew executed in the opening minutes of the mutiny. She lay burning from a series of explosions that had ripped through her powerplant and stores in matter of minutes. These were not from fighting, but due to the courageous last actions

59

of her captain, who upon seeing the hopelessness of their situation had given the order to scuttle the ship. The officers of all three Alliance ships present at the starbase had refused demands from the mutineers to relinquish their vessels, with terrible and violent repercussions.

"Nearly there," said Lieutenant Higgins.

A bright yellow flash obscured their view, and for a moment both thought their escape was over. The Mauler could certainly take a beating, but there was nothing they could ever do against a full volley from a ship-of-the-line. The Byotai high-energy weapons could destroy a frigate with a single well-placed volley. All it would take was a hit to the engines, and they would drift in space with no hope of making it back one piece.

"Yeah, that's what I'm talking about," said Sergeant Popwell.

In front of them were two vast starships, although massive compared to the Mauler, but miniscule to the vastness of the starbase. They were the only two ships to have successfully broken free of their mooring clamps, leaving large chunks of metal drifting in a trail behind them. Because this was space, there was nowhere for the broken metal to go, so it drifted on whatever course it had started out on. The larger of the two was the Armoured Assault Ship ANS Relentless, and the first to escape. She was a recently reactivated training ship and beginning to show her age. Instead of the heavy particle projectors fitted to modern warships, she was armed with railguns, the latest technology two generations earlier.

"Gorgon made it, too," said Sergeant Popwell.

"Yeah, but look at her hull."

They were already passing the ship and could see the armour and weapons in all their glory. ANS Gorgon was a Liberty class destroyer, one of the standard Alliance middle-size modular warships, and a powerful escort vessel. There were great scars along her port hull, and flashes continued to erupt along one section, leaving a trail of debris behind her.

"Better than being stuck behind...like Adamant."

The mention of the ship lowered his spirits, and he moved his attention fully to Gorgon. This particular vessel had been fitted out for fleet defence, and as such her three mission bays were configured for defence against projectiles, rockets, and missiles. The three modules were attached like panniers, suspended under the heavily armoured skeletal structure. Each module came equipped with a pair of quadruple 20mm coilgun mounts, on top of the two mounts fitted fore and aft. The ship even carried a set of torpedo tubes under her nose to fire anti-ship ordnance when required. Back in the Biomech War, the Liberty class had proven flexible, if sometimes a little under-armed. Lieutenant Higgins looked to his gunner and smiled before activating the internal comms system to speak to his passengers.

"We'll be on board Relentless in less than thirty seconds. Get..."

"Watch out!" Sergeant Popwell suddenly shouted.

The Lieutenant instinctively pulled on the controls, but that moment of examining the damaged ship had turned his attention away from the danger. A single Byotai heavy raider arced around the destroyer, heading for their starboard flank.

"Open fire!"

Sergeant Popwell was already in action. Inside his control unit he spun around the two starboard turrets and put out a storm of projectiles. His shooting was off, and though he was quick, the pilot of the heavy raider had already anticipated his shooting. Using the manoeuvrability of the craft, he rolled it and put a burst through the side.

"Alert, hull breach," announced the computer in a monotone voice.

Lieutenant Higgins shuddered as multiple rounds punched through the plating and struck around the cockpit. One embedded in the control system for the guns, and half the controls went dead. The depressurized compartment whistled and howled as the internal defence systems pumped coagulant sealant gel into the gaps. In less than five seconds, the craft was repressurised, but the damage had been done.

"Lieutenant!"

Sergeant Popwell hit the release level and drifted out from his harness. Globules of blood drifted about inside the cockpit, some striking metal, or even the two men. The Mauler continued drifting towards the assault ship, but with one engine damaged, and fuel pumping from the hull, it was beginning to move dangerously out of control. Lieutenant Higgins tapped the side of his helmet, and the visor opened. He groaned but was still conscious.

"Sergeant."

The older man grabbed the pilot's arm and tugged on him.

"I can't land this thing on my own."

Lieutenant Higgins did his best to smile, but his face was already turning paler by the second. Sergeant Popwell had already grabbed the field dressing pack from the mount on the ceiling, pulled off the lid, and pushed it against the wound on the Lieutenant's chest. It was a fully automated medical pack, and both sealed the wound and pumped in a series of painkillers.

"Sergeant, enter the auto-land command, and..."

The young officer's eyes flickered, and then he was gone. Sergeant Popwell couldn't tell if he was unconscious or dead. All he knew was that they were still tumbling towards the warship. A quick glance at the screen confirmed they were spinning, so he grabbed the manual override wheel and twisted it. The last remaining thrusters activated, and they began to twist back around. Coming right at them was another of the heavy raiders, and in that moment, he knew they were all dead. He could have stayed there and watched, but even though he knew it was too late, he still kicked away at the wall and reached over for the gunnery controls, forgetting they had already been knocked out. His hand grabbed the controls, and he depressed the triggers. Nothing happened, not even the whine of the ammunition feeds.

*No, it can't be happening, not like...*

The fighter exploded in a bright yellow flash that tore the craft apart with incredible ferocity. All fighters contained substantial supplies of explosive fuel and ordnance, and it appeared the entire lot had been ignited. The centre of the explosion turned black, and then through the flames appeared the shape of a winged fighter, its forward guns blazing away as it continued to shoot at the ruined Byotai fighter. With a flash of power, it made a last minute course change and activated its main engines to fly overhead, leaving the small fragments of the Byotai fighter to clatter against the reinforced forward armour of the Mauler.

*Thank you!*

Sergeant Popwell had no idea who was piloting the Lightning fighter, but whoever it was, they had just saved him and everybody on board. The problems for them were still far from over, and he pulled himself back to the controls and continued moving them until they were aligned with the assault ship. He had no idea where the main drive engines were controlled from, but the manoeuvring column seemed reasonably straightforward and instantly overrode the standard control system. With the warship now in view, another series of icons appeared, and at least one he recognised.

"Landing system and glide path," he said quietly.

"Alert...Proximity alert," said the computer.

He looked around at the myriad of controls, sweat pouring out and sticking to his face, doing little to cool him down in the stressful situation. He'd been in plenty of combat scenarios before, but had never been expected to know more about the Mauler than how to use its weapons.

"Where the hell is it?"

Though mainly computerised, there were still plenty of physical buttons, levers, and overrides to allow a crewmember to control the vessel, even after a major system failure. He almost panicked but then found the button display. He leaned forward and almost punched the flashing shapes.

"Auto-landing sequence activated, following approach vector. Landing confirmed. Locator beacon and glide path approved."

Though the gun battle around the ships continued, the Mauler remained on the landing programme, oblivious as to what was happening all around. Sergeant Popwell didn't react until they were through the outer doors and passing through the multi-stage airlock system and to the landing deck. He looked to his young officer and placed his hand on the man's shoulder.

"Sir, Sir! We made it. I don't know how, but we made it."

The man's red-shot eyes opened, and he nodded to the Sergeant, incapable of saying or moving any further.

**Alliance Armoured Assault Ship 'ANS Relentless'**

Nate had never been inside a Mauler before, and certainly not in a combat environment. The excitement he should have felt was abated by the so recent memories of the destruction aboard the starbase. Until today, the only death he'd ever seen was pre-recorded on a videostream, or in one of the many combat simulations he and his friends played. There was nothing more terrifying than landing under fire. The knowledge that a single well-placed shot would see the craft depressurise and all of the occupants killed in a slow, cruel fashion. He began to close his eyes but saw Cassandra staring right at him. They were clamped into position, so they simply looked towards each other and waited for it all to end.

The landing inside the vast warship was every part as rough as the flight from the starbase. Seconds after they hit the metal flooring, the mag clamps were released. Nate's first reaction was to breathe a sigh of relief at having made it. It had taken seven terrifying minutes to travel from the starbase to the ship, and every second was an opportunity to be blasted out of space. With no access to external video feeds, and no windows of any kind, there was simply no way for him to know what was going on.

The doors opened, and cool, dry air flooded the Mauler. He was second out and assumed the vessel would be packed with crew, pilots, and marines. He could not have been more wrong. The landing bay was in reality a massive series of hangars, and inside them a bizarre collection of craft, but Nate counted no more than five deck crew in the entire place. He was expecting at least five times that number.

"Sergeant, where is everybody?"

The marine tried to smile but ended up giving little more than a grimace.

"This is it. We've got only a skeleton crew, and a quarter of those were on the starbase. What you see is what we have, nothing more."

Cassandra choked as he said the last words.

"On the starbase? Did you get them out of there?"

Sergeant Perkins nodded proudly.

"Yeah, most of them. We took losses, though."

The ground beneath their feet shuddered and then again.

"What's that?" Jack asked.

The Sergeant called over to one of his marines and spoke to them for several seconds. As he finished, two of them peeled off and moved into the distance. He then turned back to the cadets.

"What did you say?"

Jack pointed back at the inner hangar doors. "The sound."

Sergeant Perkins grinned.

"Oh, yeah, well, that's the sound of the Byotai trying to keep us here."

He looked at each of them in turn, scanning their faces and assessing them in seconds. At the same time, a small group of pilots climbed into their craft on the deck, and motorised tractor units moved them into position. Nate was astounded to see deck crew removing cables from the power clamps of Lightning fighters. He'd seen the snub-nosed fighters before at shows and demonstrations, but he'd never expected to see them being armed for combat.

"Billy, look, Avengers."

Both looked on in awe at the shape of the deadly X57 Avenger III drones. They were covered in thin sheets, but their shapes were still unmistakable to those familiar with the designs. They were roughly the same size as the Lightning fighters, but that was all they had in common. The Lightning fighters were a throwback to the fighters of the last two wars, but the Avengers were the latest iteration of the venerable drone programme. These designs had only come into service over the last two decades and were already revolutionising space combat. Apart from the obvious advantages of remote control or autonomous operation, the fighters were able to take full advantage of the extra space to fit more armour and weapons. The end result was a medium-sized, eight-engine fighter much more heavily armoured than its size would suggest.

"Avengers. On a ship like this?"

One of the deck crew overhead Billy and stopped what he was doing for a brief moment. The man was filthy, but not from dirt or neglect. His overalls bore the telltale signs of oil, grease, and other fluids commonly used on the spacecraft. The man's face told a whole other story, and Nate saw he was tense and worried, the lines on his face appeared to widen every second, making him look older and older.

"What exactly is that supposed to mean?"

Billy looked to the grubby mechanic and shrugged, evidently not realising he'd just insulted the old warship, and therefore by association, its crew. He started to answer, without thinking about the impact of what he was saying.

"Well, Relentless isn't exactly..."

Nate struck him gently in the chest. It was far from subtle, but at least it stopped him speaking for a moment. Billy looked back at his friend who answered him with a withering stare.

"I think what he meant to say was that Relentless is fitted for manned fighters only. We're both surprised to see drones on board. Aren't they normally restricted for use aboard ships like the Crusaders and Liberty destroyers?"

The man's lip lifted a little at the corner, and he chuckled. It was a good save, and he had more than enough work to do.

"Yeah, okay kid. Something like that."

A small team moved around to the front of the Mauler and helped remove the injured pilot from the cockpit. The cadets watched as the bloodied body was taken away. A battered looking sergeant followed along with them, a man that didn't even give them a cursory look as walked on by. Nate moved his attention back to his friends.

"We were real lucky back there."

Rex laughed, but there were still nerves that he couldn't hide.

"Luck was nothing to do with it."

Cassandra looked directly at him and nodded politely.

"If it wasn't for Nate, we'd still be on that station, and their prisoners."

Jack groaned as he lifted his arm, so Rex grabbed the limb and pushed it back down.

"If it hurts to do that, then stop."

Nate noticed Billy was much more interested in the spacecraft that filled the interior of the ship. He looked at the array of equipment, but no matter how hard he tried, he could not drag his eyes away from the small number of aged Lightning fighters.

"Lightning IIA fighters," he said under his breath.

"Yeah," Billy agreed, "You can see they're the modified versions. Look at the wing mounts. They can carry heavy weaponry."

Both looked on as though they were on a school visit to a military museum. The fighters sat there, waiting on battered sleds, like relics from a long lost past. The Lightning was a simple winged design, with a pair of large engines attached to its flanks. The tail section consisted of a pair of boom extensions, each bearing an elegant looking rudder. Hardpoints under the wings were fitted for external ordnance, and a pair of guns sat atop the nose and directly in front of the bubble canopy. It might not have been fancy, but it had served first the Confederacy, and now the Alliance with great success. This revised version carried improved avionics, heavier frontal armour, and the ability to carry more powerful weapons on its revised wing mounts.

"Cadets," said Sergeant Perkins.

Nate and Billy looked around to the man, and he stepped closer to them all. Rex lifted himself up taller, clearly making himself look the biggest and most important member of the six cadets. Sergeant Perkins looked at each of them in turn before Rex spoke.

"What do we do now?"

Sergeant Perkins lifted an eyebrow just before he answered.

"You're safe for now, but the fight is only just beginning. If we want to get out of here in one piece, we're gonna have to fight our way out."

Rex took a step towards the marine, separating himself from the rest of the group.

"Uh...what are you saying exactly? You know we're exchange students. We're just cadets."

The marine looked less than impressed with his interruption. Instead of answering Rex, he looked past him and at the other five.

"I'm saying that this mutiny is Empire wide. I've just heard the same is happening to all Byotai territories, and we're taking losses. We have orders to withdraw immediately. That means each of you will have to do your part, no different to the rest of the crew. Understood? There are no passengers on Relentless."

Nate nodded and looked to his friends. All of them were there, including Jack with his new bandages applied en route to the ship.

"We understand, Sergeant. Whatever we can do."

Rex placed his hand on Nate's shoulder in a dismissive gesture.

"Speak for yourself, hero cadet. What exactly do you expect us to do, Sergeant?"

He ignored Rex and looked at the rest of them.

"Now, which one of you is Admiral Lewis' nephew?"

Cassandra looked at Nate instinctively even though she said nothing. Rex laughed and then pointed at him.

"Nate's the guy you want. His uncle's the war hero."

Normally, Nate would have struck out at him for that, but there was something about the ship that made him feel sombre and more serious minded. What few crew remained were busy preparing craft and weapons for a potential fight.

"I'm Nathaniel Lewis, Sergeant. Why do you ask?"

The marine moved in and examined him, like he expected to find something special about the young cadet.

"No idea, son, it comes from the Captain."

He turned to the other cadets.

"You will follow Private Valentine here. I want the rest of the squad to get to the armoury, reload, and get to your stations. This ain't over yet, and if any Byotai come knocking, we are gonna be ready."

"Sergeant!"

The marines scattered, leaving just Private Valentine with the cadets, and Sergeant Perkins waiting alongside Nate. Rex looked over to the female marine and nodded his head with amusement.

"Yeah...now that's more like it."

The marine shook her head.

"Park it, cadet, and come with me."

The marine walked off to the right, with three of the cadets behind her. Cassandra and Billy held back near Nate. Sergeant Perkins was speaking briefly to one of the mechanics on the deck and noticed the three were still there.

"Go with the Private. She'll find you somewhere to stay."

Billy shook his head.

"With respect, we're staying together."

Cassandra nodded quickly in firm agreement.

"We're not Alliance military, Sergeant. You can't..."

The man laughed and rubbed the back of his hand across his cheek.

"Cute."

He considered their words but not for long.

"With me."

They moved off through the hangar deck, constantly changing direction to avoid running into a motorized weapon trolley, or clamped spacecraft that seemed to fill the vastness of the hangar. In the background was the constant din of the war klaxon, a tone that reminded everybody of the seriousness of the situation. Finally, they reached a modestly sized elevator unit. There were no guards present, and the doors were already open and waiting for them. Sergeant Perkins moved inside and signalled for the three to join him. Once in, he entered the code sequence, and the door quickly hissed shut.

"You see, cadets, Relentless wasn't always a relic. Back in the day, she was state-of-the-art. She was finished thirty-five years ago, and right after the start of the Zealot Uprising. You've heard of it?"

Billy and Nate nodded politely, but Cassandra was less than amused at the history lesson.

"Yes, Sergeant, we're well aware of the Uprising. It wasn't that long ago."

The marine cleared his throat.

"Maybe not, but I wasn't alive when this vessel was first put into action. She was built as an armoured assault ship. That meant she would be used to lead assault teams and other ships directly against starbases, stations, and even capital ships. That's why her armour was made so thick."

Nate glanced over to Cassandra, and she seemed just as intrigued in what the man had to say as he did.

"Now she might only be a training ship, but she's still got what it takes. You won't find a tougher assault ship in Orion Command, and I can tell you that."

Billy started to speak, but Nate stamped gently on his foot, quickly distracting him. The two shared a glance, and Nate shook his head just as the doors opened. As the metal panels parted, they revealed another passageway filled with far more crew than at the hangar. At the far end was a wide-open bulkhead section that was packed with officers.

"Where are we?" Billy asked.

Nate looked on in awe as they moved from the express elevator and onto the open bulkhead.

"This is the CIC."

"The Combat Information Centre," Billy said in astonishment.

Just as they reached the entry point, Sergeant Perkins turned to the three of them.

"Don't touch a thing, or speak to anybody unless spoken to. Understood?"

The klaxon continued to sound, and as they passed the guards and entered the CIC, they were granted a glimpse of the command crew. There were at least eight officers, all clustered around a single vertical tactical display that glowed with light. Small holographic schematics of ships and the station provided a perfect three-dimensional model of their predicament.

70

"Brace for impact!" said a loud voice through the speaker system.

Nate immediately looked for something to grab and spotted one of the many emergency grab handles fitted through the ship. They were far more than normal, and as he looked up, he noticed them repeated in the most bizarre of places.

*She's an old ship. When she launched, there was no artificial gravity.*

Nate had never been on a ship before that lacked the gravity generators now so common. He looked around the CIC and examined the faces of the older men and women in command. They were all serious people, and though he knew they were in danger, not one of them showed any sign of nerves or fear.

*This is what I want.*

"Captain, we have five frigate class warships on an intercept course," said the XO.

The second-in-command was an older man, his face pockmarked with a hundred indentations. He sported stubble, and a rough white beard that had been recently trimmed.

"Wait. Make that six. Sword of Mognathus has changed course and is returning to the starbase. She is launching fighters. Gorgon is taking fire."

He looked away from the vertical display and to his Captain, a tall, bald woman with a face as hard as granite.

"My passengers? Are they all aboard yet?"

Sergeant Perkins approached and spoke quickly.

"Captain Galanos, all of the cadets and the Ambassador accounted for. We located the nephew of the Admiral. They didn't get to him."

The Captain glanced at him, then back to her XO. She seemed to relax a little, but was far from happy. That was the moment she noticed Nate and the others. Her brow tightened as she looked at him, and then her attention returned to the Sergeant.

"Good work. The garrison commander threatened his execution, and that of the Ambassador if we didn't hand over our ships. You've saved them, and our crews."

She looked briefly back at Nate.

"I will not compromise, young man. In the Alliance Navy there is no negotiation with hostage takers. You understand?"

Nate swallowed, his throat feeling dry and uncomfortable.

"Yes, Sir."

That was all she said, although he was convinced there was more. She opened her mouth, but a series of bright red lights on the vertical display quickly distracted her. The number was so great her head glowed red from the effect. He watched as a swarm of them moved in around the model of the warship, like insects moving in on a carcass or piece of rotting meat. He looked over to his friends.

"This is going to be bad."

The klaxon roared for what must have been the tenth time since they'd come aboard. Nate suddenly felt that they had moved from one metal coffin and into another, one from which there was absolutely zero chance for escape.

"Brace! Incoming missiles," said the XO.

The ship let out a great groan, and steam blasted down into the passageway outside as two coolant pipes burst. A crewman yelled in pain, and a repair team quickly moved in to repair the damage. The interior lighting flickered and returned as quickly as the trouble had begun. The Captain seemed completely nonplussed about what was happening, and her crew continued with their duties, even as the ship was continually pounded.

"What about the trade delegation from Carthago? They cannot be left behind. We have our orders."

The XO pointed to a group of three civilian craft near the station. As he moved his hand, the three green shapes flashed and bright green circles appeared around them.

"We have a squad bringing them out now. All civilians are accounted for, but it's cutting it fine. They won't make it past the Byotai guns without help."

The Captain clearly wanted to get out of the area of control provided by the starbase, but until all were aboard, her hands were tied. She made the decision before Nate even had time to assess what was going on.

"Bring us about and take us directly to the station. Launch fighters and send them to escort the transports."

She leaned forward and tapped the shape of the other Alliance ship.

"Captain Granger. What's your status?"

"Captain. We've got fires on three decks, but the ship is in one piece. Weapons are primed and gun ports are open."

"Good. Follow my tracking and come aboard to protect my port flank."

As the Captain spoke, she created a diagram showing the position of the two Alliance warships, the approaching light transports, and the fighter cover.

"We will provide a flak corridor for the transports. Use whatever stores you have available and fill the skies. We need to buy time for the transports. When we're clear, activate your engines, and meet us at the rendezvous."

"Affirmative."

The Captain considered her options as the mighty ship groaned under the new pressures of her manoeuvring engines. The Sword of Mognathus was now heading directly at Relentless in a desperate attempt to cut her off from rescuing the transports. It was too late, though, and Relentless was already positioned in such a way that her air-defence turrets could provide a protective screen for the transports.

"The Byotai heavy cruiser is targeting the shuttles," said the XO, "They can't withstand a concerted attack."

"Very well," replied the Captain, "Focus our primary weapons on the station and open fire."

The XO appeared stunned.

"The starbase? But there are civilians on board."

Captain Galanos' expression could not have been angrier at that moment.

"That station turned on every one of us. It is a nest of vipers, and the only thing standing between our people and safety. Now...target their noncritical section, and open fire on the station."

"Aye, Captain."

Both capital ships continued to unleash a hail of projectiles all around them in a devastating flak cloud. But when they turned their guns on the starbase, the battle transformed. Arcs of energy and long trails of armour piercing slugs moved back and forth, like a group of wooden ships battling it out on the high seas. The turrets of the Alliance ships raked the station, setting off hundreds of explosions and starting fires throughout.

"Wait for it," said the Captain.

The officers on Relentless clearly had no idea what was happening, but as Nate watched, it all became clear.

"You're forcing them to make a choice."

The Captain smiled for the first time since Nate and his friends had entered the CIC.

"Indeed. What is more important to them? The starbase, or those people heading for our ships?"

With perfect timing, the massed guns of the Byotai warships changed direction and continued their attack against Relentless. The ship shuddered as she had before, but it was enough to give the Captain a moment to savour the moment.

"More like it."

She turned to her XO.

"Status of our fighters?"

The man looked pained to answer her question.

"All our pilots are in action. Three lost, two are still fighting, but they've sustained damage. They cannot stay out there much longer. We're just not equipped for prolong combat."

Captain Galanos sighed.

"Very well. As soon as the transports are aboard, get the fighters inside. We cannot wait much longer."

# CHAPTER FOUR

**Alliance Armoured Assault Ship 'ANS Relentless'**
**3rd Quadrant, Byotai Empire**

The vibration from the massive impact sent Nate and Billy crashing against one of the vertical display units. Billy managed to right himself, but due to the awkward angle, Nate slid right past and struck his cheek on the side. Cassandra fell backwards, almost into the waiting arms of a grey-haired junior officer. Another bent down to help Nate and extended a firm hand.

"Use the grab rails. Until this is over, you need to keep hold of something."

He held onto the rail with his left hand, and with his right he checked his face. He could feel the warm, damp fluid, and as he checked his palm, he found fresh blood. Another hand grabbed him and then pushed a field dressing pack to his head. The pain was relentless for a few seconds as the device bonded the wound, as well as cleaning it. When the Naval officer removed the unit, he found Billy and Cassandra staring right at him.

"Yeah," said Billy, "That will scar up nicely."

The older officer moved away, but not before pointing towards the nearest rail.

"Use it this time."

Nate looked sheepish.

"You both okay?"

They were completely speechless, and all Nate got from either of them was a nervous smile. He looked over to the vertical tactical display. He was even closer now, and the detail provided gave him the perfect view of the unfolding battle. It was awfully similar to the overviews given when playing the Star Crusader simulation as a tactical commander.

"Look, they want to keep us here."

Billy, ever the optimist, pointed at the large number of ships.

"Most of them aren't moving. Maybe it's not as serious as we thought."

Cassandra laughed at him. "Billy, you're such an idiot sometimes. Of course it's serious. You saw what happened back on the starbase."

Captain Galanos reached for one of the nearest grab rails as another volley struck the dorsal plates of ANS Relentless. Sword of Mognathus completed her final turn, repositioned her armour plates, and brought her primary weapons to bear. Unlike the other races, the Byotai were famed for their use of movable armour. As they moved aside, the barrels of the massive phased plasma cannons extended outwards. At the same time, she continued to fire with her broadside batteries. Due to the massive energy requirements, containment generators and launch tubes, the primary weapons could only be fitted inside the bow. As the ship swung around, it lined up on the Alliance ship and took aim with her powerful guns. These were much more damaging than the railguns fitted on older Alliance ships, and in their own way more dangerous than the particle beam weapons on more recent ships. One at a time the guns fired, hurling projectiles capable of vaporising fighters and escorts in a single shot.

The initial strikes were marked by a series of white and green flashes along ANS Relentless' hull. Each shot unleashed incredible levels of energy, but they still struggled to penetrate the inner compartments of the warship. The great vessel shuddered continually as she absorbed a barrage that would have already crippled a conventionally armoured cruiser, but against the massed layers of frontal armour they were fighting it was completely different. It was more than just thick layers of plate. It was actually more than fifty layers of ablative armour, each carefully spaced apart from the next using a secret honeycomb style mixture. Captain Galanos tapped several sections on the schematic of the enemy vessel.

"Alter heading by fifteen degrees and transfer all our forward guns to the Byotai heavy cruiser's left flank. Target her propulsion and communication system here, here, and here."

The two capital ships continued towards each other on what appeared to be a collision course from those further away. With ANS Relentless now moving on a slightly angled heading, she'd freed up more defence turrets, as well as allowing the two to pass by each other in just a few more seconds of travel. Each opened fire, sending even more projectiles into the void. Sections of metal tore off both, and one of the large wing structures ripped away from the Byotai ship and drifted off into the blackness.

"Keep firing!"

The ships passed by with less than five hundred metres between their hulls. With the forward guns now unable to fire on her, the Byotai ship reverted to using her myriad of small and medium sized guns to rake the hull of Relentless. Though less able to fight back, the heavily armoured ship was supported by the Alliance destroyer ANS Gorgon, whose own guns fired continually. The smaller ship travelled less than a kilometre away and on the port flank of the assault ship.

A pair of Lighting fighters moved between them, taking care to avoid the defensive fire from the turrets. There were also now more than a dozen much smaller ships, and the majority did their best to get in the way of the escaping Alliance ships, and three even opened fire with the few weapons they carried. One fired three missiles at ANS Gorgon before sustaining a massive broadside from the destroyer's low-slung turrets. It exploded and then vanished, leaving little but small chunks of debris drifting about in space.

"Captain," said the XO, "The cruiser is performing a lateral rotation. It will be completed shortly, and I suspect they are attempting to move into position to strike our rear quarter."

Captain Galanos looked unperturbed at the news.

"Yes, that makes sense. Maintain course, and bring us around in a reverse heading. Bring our bow to bear, but follow on our present trajectory."

Nate watched in awe as the officers performed the textbook operation with calm and precision. As the vessel spun about on its axis, he looked to

Cassandra and Billy.

"See what she's doing?"

Billy shook his head, but Cassandra clearly had a much better idea as to what was going on. She pointed at the imagery of the assault ship and shook her head.

"Impressive, very impressive. The Captain is swinging around in one-eighty rotation to keep our bow facing them."

Billy tightened his brow, and then his eyes widened, as he understood.

"So, like sliding with the fighters?"

Nate seemed amused at his answer.

"No, Billy, not like, more like exactly the same."

The ships were once again facing each other, but this time they were moving in the same direction. As before, the Byotai heavy cruiser unleashed a volley from its forward phased plasma batteries. These high-energy pulses moved little faster than conventional space-based artillery, but embedded in the outer plating and then exploded, ripping off great chunks of plating from the ship with every impact. Each shot used superheated plasma encased inside a shell that was magnetically shielded. When the shell struck an object, it would explode with incredible energy.

"Hit them, hit them hard!" said the Captain, "I want to see holes in her hull. Relentless might be an old lady, but she's got it where it counts."

Two more phased plasma shells struck below a bow-mounted gun port and tore off an entire compartment, sending twisted metal off in a cloud of debris. None of the defensive weapons on board could do anything to stop them, so Captain Galanos ignored them, and proceeded to hit the heavy cruiser with a bewildering array of gunfire. The damage was light, but continuous, and designed more to harass than to destroy. The XO spun around, an almost excited look upon his serious brow.

"Captain, our fighters have cleared a path on vector six-three. The transports are coming in right behind them. It's going to be close, very close."

"Good work. Get them aboard fast."

One of the larger screens changed its view to show the transports and their fighter squadron moving to the port side of the ship. The fighters peeled away at the last moment, giving the transports space to land. The landing deck outer airlock doors were wide open as the transports flew in at high-speed. Gunfire raked the hull just as a group of six Byotai fighters strove into view. Nate held his breath and watched in awe at the sight of the incredible landing. The speed of the approach was much higher than normal, and the manoeuvring thrusters glowed bright with energy as they slowed the transports down. Even the engines were not enough, and they were forced to rely upon the triple layer of crash nets installed for such an occasion.

"No," said Captain Galanos, her expression changing from relief to concern in an instant.

"Drive those fighters back!"

It was too late, and the fighters broke through the light defensive screen and put hundreds of rounds into the outer landing deck. Many struck the deck, some even hitting the transports. The Alliance fighters spun around and engaged them at close-range, but it wasn't enough.

"Captain, look!"

The XO pointed at the vertical tactical display where ANS Gorgon had drifted further away to provide a more accurate curtain of defensive flank. Captain Galanos observed the group of small ships making their way to towards the flank of the Alliance ships. Her jaw hung open as she watched the first burning tug. The vessel was not Byotai, but it was most definitely heading towards them, and it was flanked by another three similar craft, each heading right at the ships.

"Target the tugs. Destroy them!"

They were half the size of a standard frigate, and though unarmed, surprisingly tough. The defensive turrets on ANS Relentless tore chunk after chunk from them, but that wasn't enough to stop the hulls from hurtling towards the huge open sections along the hull, and even as the assault ship rolled to avoid them, they altered course to match the position.

"Close the landing doors, now!"

The doors were massive sections of reinforced plate, capable of blocking the path of something up to the size of a Mauler. There were two open on the port flank to give the transports and fighters access to the outer landing deck. Though partitioned from the main deck, it was still a major vulnerability that if exploited, could cripple the ship in seconds. Nate watched the models of the ships, as well as the space-time distortion lines that normally showed when close to large astronomical bodies. The Alliance ships in particular created an odd distortion around the powerplant sections of the hulls.

*It can't be, surely not.*

Nate looked again and counted the lines for the third time. Each time the carrier exerted more power, the field changed. It wasn't much, and the fighter crews were already trained to avoid getting too close during their manoeuvres. He looked back at the tugs and immediately spotted where they were heading. Nate knew immediately what was going to happen, but he couldn't believe for a moment the rest of the crew were oblivious to the danger. Even the ship's computer appeared to have utterly failed in identifying this new threat.

"Captain," he called out.

The Captain looked back, saw it was the cadet, and turned back to look to her XO. At the same time, the guns on both capital ships continued to fire at the tugs. Nate spoke again, but a junior officer stepped in to block his path and called over to Sergeant Perkins.

"Escort them from the CIC, Sergeant. This is a combat environment. It's not a place for...cadets."

"But, Sir, the tugs are not coming for..."

The Sergeant moved in quickly and reached for Nate, but he ducked to the side and managed to avoid his grasp. Again the man tried to grab him, so he twisted away, and then moved around the tactical display with the man hot on his heels. He reached the unit and pointed at the incoming ships just as the Sergeant grabbed him.

"It's too late. Look!"

Captain Galanos saw what he was pointing at, and though annoyed at his interruption, she knew instantly that he was right. The Captain took another step to the right and moved her hand around the shape. Vector lines showed the affect of the powerplants and artificial gravity units on all the major vessels.

"Of course, they are using the residual pull from our gravitometric wake to swing around us faster than expected. It will improve their rotation speed by up to...fifteen percent."

She moved nearer to the unit and used her hands to change their projected course. Instead of hitting the carrier, they actually moved around. Normally, their engines would not be quite powerful enough, but by staying close to the gravitometric generators, they could use the distortion to boost their manoeuvrability enough to do it.

"They will swing in against Gorgon from the opposite side. Very clever, I should have seen that."

She tapped the icon for the ship and called out anxiously to the Captain of the destroyer. The delay in answering seemed like an age, and as she waited, the crew continued directing all of their weapons at the ships. Finally, the image of the veteran Captain appeared on one of the main displays.

"Captain Granger. Take evasive action now. The tugs are swinging around my dorsal section and coming for your flank. I repeat, they are not intending on ramming my ship. It's yours they are going for."

"Understood, Captain."

She shook her head in irritation.

"By removing our escort, we will be left defenceless and alone in Byotai territory. They can see how well armoured Relentless is, so they are hitting the weaker link in our defence."

The XO offered no argument or discussion, just the matter of fact tone so rarely seen in the civilian world. The wire diagram of the destroyer started to move, but it all looked too slow and ponderous to have any beneficial effect on the Alliance warships. Nate felt the marine's arm on his hand, and he began to slide away from the CIC. The XO saw what was happening and shook his head.

"He spotted this. Maybe he'll see something else. Right now, we cannot leave a thing to chance. Leave him be."

"Sir," said the marine.

His tone was stern, but like all of the marines, he was quick to react. The man then turned around and went back to his position near the entrance to the packed room. Nate looked at the displays and found the largest showing a view of the space battle outside. Even though the ship continued to shudder as projectiles hit it, it still felt far removed from the battle raging outside. Cassandra leaned in and whispered to Nate. The air from her breath tickled his ear and made him shudder, to both their surprise.

"Good work, Nate. You just got yourself noticed."

Nate looked at her for a moment, but try as he might, he could not tell if she meant noticed by her or the crew.

"They are awfully close," said the XO.

Captain Galanos watched the Liberty class destroyer perform a bizarre twist for such a big ship, simultaneously putting a volley into the tugs. Three missed by a matter of metres, but four managed to make a final adjustment and struck her aft, just a short distance from the engines. At first there was no clear sign of damage, and then came a series of small flashes as those controlling the tug detonated her engines. The final blast was followed by a large section of the destroyer breaking off, taking one of the primary thrusters with it.

"No...that...is not good," said the Captain.

She then looked to Nate.

"You were correct, cadet. Never be intimidated by those around you, even me. I was wrong, and you were not."

Nate wasn't sure what to say, so just nodded quickly. The Captain had little interest in continuing the conversation in any case, and moved along the CIC to speak with the other officers. Cassandra and Billy joined Nate and looked carefully at the imagery. Billy looked pale as he watched multiple sections rip off the destroyer. Then a colour image of the Captain appeared on the large viewscreen.

"Captain Galanos. I've sustained major engine damage. We can follow, but not at full speed. I recommend you withdraw from battle now. We can cover your exit."

A heavy volley of phased plasma shells struck the assault ship, and this time one of them managed to penetrate deep inside the bow. Multiple alarms blasted, warning those inside of the danger. Then a series of bright shapes popped up on the far left side of the tactical display. The XO was already examining them, and when he looked to the Captain, it was clear they faced a bigger problem.

"Two Byotai cruisers, plus escorts. They'll be here in less than ten minutes."

More alarms activated at the engineering display, and the XO shook his head nervously. As every second went by, so did more warnings of failed systems, breached hull sections, and damage to the outer armour.

"Captain, we can't take much more of this."

Captain Galanos lifted her hand to her chin as she considered her options, limited as they were. They could stay and fight alongside the damaged destroyer, or they could flee and leave them to their fate. ANS Relentless was a tough durable ship, and she knew they could fight three or even four ships on their own, even with a limited air group on board. They still had the station and its own squadrons of fighters to deal with, and now there were more ships coming in.

"How long until we can activate the main engines?"

The XO checked with the navigator who was already plotting a revised route.

"Sir, engines are spooled up ready, and the course is plotted in to avoid the minefield. As soon as the fighters are aboard, we can activate the engines."

The Captain looked dubious at his suggestion. Relentless was a big ship, and the gaps in the minefield were difficult enough to navigate even without the chance of them exploding upon impact.

"That is a very small window, less than a kilometre between the mines.

Can we make it through without sustaining major damage?"

The man nodded quickly.

"Yes, Sir. The mines are proximity high explosive charges. We will be moving too fast for the debris to be a serious issue."

Captain Galanos shook her head.

"I don't like this, not at all. I want to stay and fight, but the lives of our crew and of our passengers outweighs the desire to hurt the enemy."

She lowered her eyes momentarily before looking back at him, her eyes hard and focussed with purpose.

"Send the signal to our fighters. It's time to leave."

Both watched in silence as the Byotai warship shifted course and focussed its attention on the damaged destroyer, rather than hitting the more durable shape of ANS Relentless. Though much more heavily armed than the carrier, she was far less able to take a beating. One round after another hit her flank until an extra mission module exploded and breached the ship's spine, leaving the vessel dead in space.

"No!" Captain Galanos exclaimed, "Not Gorgon."

The XO tagged the remaining fighters and contacted them directly.

"Get back now. It's time to leave. I repeat; all Alliance fighters withdraw to Relentless immediately. We leave in one minute. Get on board, or stay behind."

Both watched the screen as the spacecraft moved towards the final remaining open hangar door. They made it to within three hundred metres before the wing of fighters bearing black painted markings appeared. They carried the symbols of the Mognathus training squadron and were heavily armed. Apart from their integral gunnery systems, half of them also carried a number of missiles and heavy anti-ship torpedoes in large launch pods. Nate pointed at the first fighter.

"That's DuFarl's squadron. The Black Hunters."

Captain Galanos turned her attention to the young cadet.

"DuFarl?"

"Yes, Sir. He is the senior Byotai cadet, a graduate of the last intake and their ace. He is in charge of the base's Star Crusader competition team."

Captain Galanos shook her head. The XO continued issuing orders as the ship prepared to activate its main drive engines. For a fraction of a second, he glanced at the tactical display.

"Fighter ace? These kids might ace the simulation, but real combat is not the same thing. Our pilots will shoot them out of the sky. That much I promise you."

Captain Galanos sighed.

"We were misled, all of us were. These Byotai cadets are not just simulation veterans; they all have actual combat experience. This has been planned for a long time. Look at them. There is no way they are just simulator pilots."

As if to clarify her point, the fighters performed a tight spinning manoeuvre, and then split up, four heading for the damaged destroyer and two more chasing after the Alliance fighters. Every twist, roll, and slide performed by the Alliance pilots matched by the Byotai, leading to a violent free-for-all between them. The Captain looked to her officer.

"These are not just cadets!"

One of the Lightning fighters lost an engine and spun off into space, pursued by the lead fighter. It spun about as though out of control, but then managed to loose off two bursts, one of which caught a pursuing fighter. Sparks flashed along the fighter's hull before one detonated and tore apart the cockpit. Billy's face flashed yellow, and Nate looked at him as he watched the bright explosion.

"DuFarl is a combat pilot. Can you believe that?"

Billy moved his focus from the battle to his friend and shrugged.

"Yes, well, I suppose so. You saw what he was like in the simulation. He took it seriously, even the training bout."

Cassandra gave him a hard look, but he didn't notice. The battle was unfolding just like the simulated battles they'd fought so many times before in the Star Crusader simulation. Nate spoke quietly to them both, doing his best not to be heard by the senior officers.

"We've seen DuFarl in action already. And he's flying that fighter no differently to the simulated drones."

Cassandra nodded.

"He's not a cadet, is he?"

Captain Galanos rubbed her forehead gently, waiting for the last remaining fighters to make it back. All eyes were on them as the craft weaved in and out of fire from both enemy fighters and the Byotai capital ships.

Captain Galanos called out to her crew, urging them to work harder and harder, "Protect those fighters. They must make it back in one piece."

Smoke poured from one of the engines of the nearest craft, a rudder section had been blasted clean off. Two missiles moved close by, and it vanished from view for a fraction of a second. There was silence in the CIC, until it appeared with its remaining engine roaring at full burn. The two were just a few seconds from the closing doors.

"Start the countdown. We leave in thirty seconds."

The XO looked flabbergasted.

"Captain. We cannot leave Gorgon and our ejected pilots behind. They'll..."

The Captain looked to her XO and shook her head.

"No, we cannot stay. There is nothing more for us to do. All of them have bought us time with their very lives. If we stay, we dishonour them all."

She nodded at the nearest display.

"Set the clock to twenty-five seconds."

Another officer called out from the other side of the CIC. Some of the lights had failed, leaving an entire section in almost total darkness, lit by nothing more than the displays strewn around the room.

"One fighter aboard."

Captain Galanos swallowed uncomfortably.

"One? What about the second?"

They all knew the answer, but she had to hear it for herself.

The XO said what they were thinking, "That's it, Captain. Only one made it home."

There was a palpable sense of loss inside the carrier. The vessel was only lightly equipped for the diplomatic visit, with little more than a skeleton crew and a handful of fighter pilots. Now all of those were gone, save the one pilot that had made it back.

"Outer door shut, retracting inner decks. We are launch ready," said the XO.

Captain Galanos turned her attention to the crippled destroyer. The vessel was clearly dead in space, yet while explosions ripped through her hull, she still fought on. The squadron of Byotai fighters spun about to avoid gunfire from the destroyer, and that brief moment gave the carrier one last moment to activate its engines. Captain Galanos reached out for one of the convenient grab handles, knowing the initial burst of power would be equal to more than thirty thousand kilonewtons, and then increasing by the second. The inertial dampeners linked to the gravity system would be able to compensate, but all those aboard would still feel the effect.

"Captain Galanos, he's coming back," said Nate.

All eyes turned to the formation of Byotai fighters. He was correct, and a single craft had turned back to point right at their flank.

"Ten seconds!" yelled the XO.

It took a moment for the ship's sensor to track the target, and no sooner was it on the tactical display, when it broke up. Instead of an object, there were now eight, and each displayed the same mass an energy signature.

"Anti-ship torpedoes," said the tactical officer, "They are tracking and on course. Our weapons are off-line and retracted."

The man looked to the others, but there was little point in saying anything more. The engine sequence was active, the defences lowered, and the course laid in. Either they would blast away from the carnage of the starbase, or they would remain alongside the wreckage of ANS Gorgon. Nate looked to his friends. Billy looked on nervously, but Cassandra knew as well as Nate did, this was going to be close. One of the displays flashed white as something exploded on or inside the destroyer. Nate felt nauseous, knowing how many people would have been on board the Alliance vessel.

"Five seconds. Engines activating."

"Brace!" said an unseen officer.

The sound of his voice called repeatedly though Nate's ears, but he couldn't tell if it was intentional or his mind playing tricks. The ship shuddered violently, and he looked up at the countdown. Each second moved away so slowly it almost felt he was watching minutes ticking by. As the unit reached two seconds, the CIC lights deactivated, and a great hammering thud filled the space, the sound of exploding systems mixed with screams and shouting. The last thing Nate saw as the lights cut off was the look of sheer terror on Cassandra's face.

# CHAPTER FIVE

**Alliance Armoured Assault Ship 'ANS Relentless'**

**Day** 3

The beeping sound must have been playing for more than five minutes. Nate knew it was playing even though he was asleep. The sound was continuous, with an odd pulsing that was designed to get your attention. At some point it stopped, and for some bizarre reason that was when he opened his eyes. The place was dark, and he could hear the sound of snoring a short distance away. For a short while he might have forgotten where he was, but then the continuous, gently but irritating drone returned.

*What was that sound?*

He lowered his legs down from the top bunk and looked down. His head was swimming but not from pain or discomfort. The odd feeling was simply due to lack of sleep and that constant sound that was starting to drive him insane. Since the escape from the Mognathus 7 eighteen hours earlier, he'd managed just three hours of sleep, and every minute had been spent thinking about what he'd seen since the violent start of the mutiny.

"Billy. You awake?"

There was no sound so he turned his attention to the rest of the bunkroom. It was bigger than he might have expected, three large bunks on each side and doubled up to provide berths for up to twelve. A single massive bulkhead divided the room, with a single gap at the centre to allow movement through, while the rough arch shape ran along both the floor and ceiling. Opposite him were the sleeping forms of Matilda and Cassandra. The lights were dim but provided enough illumination for him to see that both were fast asleep. Nate stretched out with his legs and then spotted Jack off to the right. He saw Jack watching him, and then he vanished from view.

*Typical Jack, Rex's lackey.*

He lowered himself down to the floor, shivering as his bare feet touched the cold metal. Jack was one of those people that you never truly knew. While Rex was a classic case of an extrovert and used to public attention, Jack was the opposite. The cadet followed Rex around like a lost puppy, and was always there with moral and physical support in case of any problems. Nate had seen Jack drag other cadets away when involved in an argument with his friend. The two were like brothers and never apart.

"So, you're finally awake," said Rex.

He moved through the bulkhead gap, his feet moving slowly and deliberately. Jack followed right behind him and slightly to his left. Near them was a wall-mounted display, something old that possibly dated back to the original commissioning of the ship. Small green lettering filtered the display, but it was too small and too far away for Nate to be able to read the thing. He took a step to move closer, but Rex lifted his hands and blocked him.

"I've already read it."

"So?"

Nate again tried again, but Jack moved alongside Rex and completely blocked his path.

"I'll tell you how this is going to work, Nate. And it starts with you listening for a change."

Rex's voice was getting louder, and Cassandra had now woken and lowered her feet over the side of her bunk to touch the cold floor. She was still hazy and looked confused by the voices in the room. Like the others, she wore the loose underclothing given to them by the crew of Relentless that looked much like civilian pyjamas. They were far from flattering and consisted of a dark blue undershirt and trousers bearing the Alliance Navy insignia. She began speaking, but a voice interrupted and drowned out the others.

"Engines are on, and the alert system is inactive."

She lifted her head and looked first to Nate, and then to Rex.

"What's happening? Is there a problem?"

Rex pointed to Nate.

"That's what I'm trying to explain to your little boyfriend."

Cassandra looked to her right and to Nate. He watched her until she shook her head and groaned. She might have been annoyed, but Nate was convinced he could see a little embarrassment on her face. Cassandra pouted, and her voice became even more clipped and proper than normal.

"Boyfriend? Are you kidding me?"

Nate had heard many insults over the last few weeks, but this one comment seemed to hurt the most. He didn't know Cassandra as well as he'd wanted to, but he thought they were at the very least friends. She might come from a privileged family on Terra Nova, but that hadn't been much of an issue so far. This was out of the blue and knocked his confidence right when he wanted to stand up firm in front of Rex and Jack. It was made much worse by the mocking tone she appeared to use as she almost spat out the words.

*Thanks for that.*

Nate had hardly made any kind of move towards Cassandra; in fact of all in the group, he was the one that had gone out of his way not to. Jack's mouth was open, and at first Nate thought he was panting. In reality it was that he was silently laughing, enjoying Nate's discomfort.

*Even better, Rex must love this.*

Cassandra appeared oblivious to it all and pulled out her second generation Secpad bracelet. It was something all members of the Alliance military were now equipped with. They were given them when shown to their new quarters. It was small enough to fit inside a pocket, but most people these days just kept them on their wrists. It was much more than a unit to communicate with. It was a mobile device that gave access to the public Cortex, as well as the way to manage and control all manner of technologies.

"Okay, let's have a look then, shall we?"

Cassandra's voice had taken on the tone of the Terra Novan elite, an accent she often tried to hide with more common rolling vowels and dropping certain letters. Her long, frail looking blonde hair dropped down over her brow. With a flourish, she shook it back and continued to page through the latest reports.

Rex looked to Jack, and though he tried to hide it, Nate could see he was snarling. Cassandra tapped the bracelet, and the entire unit pulsed white. She then dragged her right index finger along her arm. A page appeared, hovering directly over her flesh. The result was much like the antiquated Secpad they'd been given as children, but it was in reality being projected by the device on her wrist.

"That's odd," said Cassandra.

"What is it?" Nate asked.

Rex shook his head and moved closer. Jack waited near the bulkhead.

"It's the Captain. She wants to see everybody in..."

Rex then glanced to Jack who mouthed something back to him.

"Yeah...in ten minutes."

Matilda was now upright on her bunk and busily scrolling through masses of data on her own unit. Cassandra looked up to her and indicated towards the others.

"Have you..."

"Yes. I know," interrupted Matilda.

Cassandra shook her head in irritation. Matilda might be the most intelligent of the group by far, but she was also the one with the least sense of etiquette or social awareness. While Cassandra was always mindful of the way she sounded or looked, Matilda often completely forgot what she was doing. Nate had seen her arrive to simulations and training sessions half-dressed, without make-up, and often with her hair in a frightful state.

"So what are you doing?"

Matilda still kept her eyes glued to the holographic detail until she finally stopped and looked down to them all.

"We are approaching the Arnos Cluster. It's home to an abandoned Byotai research station."

Rex laughed.

"What? Why the hell would we be heading towards a Byotai station

93

after everything we've just been through?"

Matilda sighed.

"Because we are seven weeks away from the border and running out of provisions. I saw the display in the CIC, and the Arnos Cluster was flagged as the destination."

Rex continued to laugh at her.

"Seven weeks, what the hell? You know there is a Spacebridge six days travel from Mognathu, don't you? We can just use it to travel directly to the Helios Prime nexus. And from there we can go wherever we want."

Now it was Nate's turn to enjoy watching his nemesis suffer at the intellect of Matilda. He would have liked to say it himself, but Nate and Rex were always at each other's throat. It was nice to see somebody else there for a change.

"The Spacebridge between the Byotai Trinity and the Helios Nexus? You are of course correct, oh, genius."

Rex's eyebrows lifted at the insult.

"If we travelled to the Spacebridge, we would have to ask the Byotai military for permission to use it. They would then activate the unit, and we would be away and safe in Alliance territory."

She then looked to Nate. He was happily smiling as she spoke.

"Clearly we won't be doing that. Not unless we want to be blasted to atoms by the Imperial fleet. Do you think they will grant passage to a renegade ship deep inside their own territory?"

Nate leaned over his friend who still lay on his back on his bunk. He was fast asleep, and every twenty seconds or so would let out a long, rumbling snore. He leaned in close and called out loudly.

"Billy!"

The cadet opened his eyes and stared at him.

"What?"

Nate turned away and grabbed his overalls. They were Naval crew issue and nothing particularly fancy. Grey seemed to be the order of the day on the ship, with the only sign of colour being the utility strap around the waist.

Fitted to the wide band were a number of narrow pouches, all of which were empty.

"The Captain wants to see everybody. It's important."

He looked back. Rex and Jack had left, leaving the four of them inside the room.

"Good work," grumbled Cassandra, "We need to stick together. Unless you want to get us all volunteered for cleaning duty."

Nate didn't seem overly impressed with her wishes, and he wanted more than anything to show her that he was no longer the follower, the one that always did as Rex and the others told him.

"Maybe, but somebody needed to say it. If we're to get home alive, we're going to need to use our brains for a change."

Matilda laughed, but it was not a laugh like the others might utter. The young cadet's voice almost howled before she returned to her normal conservative state.

"Nice fake laugh," said Billy.

The teenager's voice was slow and slightly slurred, made worse by the yawn midway through the sentence.

Cassandra rolled her eyes as she listened to them both.

"Whatever...Nate."

Cassandra then walked to the doorway and opened the blast door. Nate looked despondent as she left, only now realising what a fool the two had made of themselves. In his attempt to build himself up, he'd made it simpler to knock him back down. Cassandra was a stickler for details, and she had probably already worked out what each of them would be doing for the next week. Then she looked back at them.

"Well? Are you coming?"

Nate in turn looked to his scruffily attired friend.

"Come on, Billy, we need to go."

Nate wasn't sure, but he was pretty certain he saw a glint of a smile on Cassandra's face. That or she was merely laughing at the two of them.

* * *

The landing deck might have been exactly the same as when Nate and the others had arrived, but in just three days it had incurred a surprising amount of change. Many of the stores from the rest of the ship had been brought down, and the place was now filled with the weapons and equipment of war. It was a radical transformation, yet the interior was sparsely filled with spacecraft. Nate and his friends moved past the groups of people and to the front, where a metal gantry was lifted up nearly three metres tall. At the top was the Captain.

"Is this it?" Rex said.

Nate hadn't noticed his fellow cadet, but with there being so few people about, it was impossible to avoid him. He lifted his hand to get his attention, but Rex intentionally looked away and to his friend Jack.

"Such an ass," said Billy.

He nodded in agreement and started to speak, realising Cassandra and Matilda had vanished. He looked off to his right. They were speaking with a marine. The hum of conversation vanished as the Captain called out loudly to those in the hangar.

"Your attention, please. We have an urgent situation to discuss."

Nate listened but turned his attention to those waiting in front of the gantry. At least half were military, made clear by their clothing and bearing. The rest were a mixture of traders, scientists, and diplomatic staff from their mission. He saw the Ambassador, a short stocky woman with a fearsome expression on her face. Her two guards, as always, surrounded her. They were plainclothes marines, both expressionless as they looked out at the group. One noticed Nate watching, and as their eyes met, he gave him a low nod.

*What?* Nate thought.

Another officer, one he didn't recognise, was helped up the first few steps and then leaned forward on the metal barrier. He wore the stripped down Naval version of the PDS armour, but without a helmet or attached webbing and firearms. Unlike the similar gear worn by the marines, this was

96

designed to provide a sealed environment and protection from blast and flash damage. The resulting armour was little thicker than the clothing worn by the civilians, but instantly marked him out as an Alliance officer. Ambassador Delorax approached the gantry, but she did not climb it and waited at the bottom, with one foot on the lowest rung.

"The mutiny at Mognathus has spread far and wide. The last contact we received from Alliance Command was mixed, but clear. Something has happened inside the Byotai Empire, and they are turning on any allies of the ruling caste. Military and civilians alike have been murdered, and there is no way of knowing how far this goes."

She looked to the Captain and nodded politely.

"On behalf of all civilians on Relentless, and for my family and staff, I thank you and your crew."

She then turned her gaze out to the small crowd.

"I call on you to do whatever the Captain asks of us. We all have a part to play, and if we are to survive this treachery, we must work together."

With those last words, she stepped away, leaving the deck in silence. There was no talking, just the gentle click of her shoes as she moved from view. Captain Galanos lifted her arms slightly higher to encompass them all.

"My last orders were to recover all Alliance personnel, military and civilian, and to fall back to our emergency rendezvous with the fleet, and that is exactly what we will do."

A few in the audience spoke quietly, and she waited for complete silence before continuing, "We escaped the munity at Mognathus, but our ordeal has only just begun. Relentless is a tough lady, but she still suffered as badly in the fight. Even worse, the losses sustained by my crew. If we are to survive this, we will have to work together. I no longer have the manpower to operate her effectively."

The Captain paused, letting her words sink in. The implication was clear, and as Nate listened, he almost felt excited at the prospect of being able to help in some way.

*Anything is better than waiting and wondering what's happening.*

"In three days we will rendezvous with the fleet, but, and this is a big but. We have no idea what ships made it out in one piece, or even if the enemy knows this location. We need the ship in the best condition we can make her, and we must be combat effective."

She glanced at one of her crew, took a breath, and continued, "We came to Mognathus with more than a hundred crew. Now we are down to just twenty-seven plus our thirteen marine guards. I am short of crew in almost all areas, especially medical and engineering. When we arrive we have to be ready, and that means each of us will have to do our part."

She then nodded to the wounded officer.

"Please listen to the assessment by our senior pilot, Lieutenant Higgins. He is the sole survivor of the battle of Mognathus, and responsible for allowing us this one chance to get home alive."

The man nodded and stepped slightly to the right. He moved awkwardly, and that, combined with the short description by the Captain, left the hangar deck in a somewhat sombre mood. A few clapped, but they soon stopped when realising how few they were.

"The escape from Mognathus was costly, incredibly costly."

He fidgeted as he spoke, and even grimaced as his right elbow brushed against the railing.

"As well as the loss of personnel, we lost a large quantity of fuel, and over half our ammunition was expended getting out of there. For this ship to be combat effective, we need manual gunners, fighter pilots, and support crews. The only defence the ship has is behind its guns and fighters, and right now we cannot operate either of them."

He pointed behind the assembled group.

"Everything we have left is on the deck. The rest has been stripped for parts. Every member of this ship's crew is here, right now."

That revelation sent a shockwave through the group. A normal ship's complement was in the hundreds, and a carrier would expect to double that with a full-strength air wing. Even with all the civilians, they could barely muster seventy souls. Two of the civilians started to talk, and then a third joined in, his voice nervous and worried. The Lieutenant increased the volume of his powerful voice, and it boomed out into the open hangar.

"All my pilots are dead or missing in action. Only Major Williams and I made it back here. The Major is an outstanding pilot, with a history of combat flying going back to the Biomech War. He was our best hope at defending the ship. I have to inform you that he died of his wounds less than an hour ago. That leaves me as the only qualified pilot."

He lifted his right arm so that all could see the bandage still wrapped around his wounds.

"And I am far from able to fly anything, right now."

That sent a hush throughout the hangar. None of them had been spared the sight of the dead, but there was something much more disconcerting when aboard a carrier, with no pilots remaining. The ship was sturdy, and that much was obvious, but it was just as clear that for a carrier to punch its weight, it would need fighters.

"We've got just one Mauler still functioning, six Avenger combat drones, and four Lightning manned fighters."

He then shook his head and sighed.

"And no pilots. Apart from me, we lack any formal combat pilots on this ship."

As he waited in silence, Captain Galanos continued. As she started to speak, Nate noticed the marks on her face. At first he thought it had been little more than a trick of the light, but the more he looked, it was obvious she'd been badly hurt. There were deep lines running down her face and disappearing inside her uniform. A Naval officer stepped in front of him and held up one of the older model, hand operated Secpads.

"Any formal engineering or medical experience?"

Nate almost stepped back at the question. His engineering knowledge was limited to what had been covered in school, nothing more. While his medical knowledge was even less impressive. Off to his right two civilians were being escorted away by one of the marines.

"Do we have anybody with experience of combat flying here?"

The man sounded subdued as he asked the question. There were no immediate responses, and rather than wait longer, he gave a signal to those off at the sides of the ship.

"My officers will come to you shortly, to assess your capabilities and match you with a role on my ship. I need everything from gunners and engineers, to cooks and cleaners."

From one side of the hangar came a small group of Naval personnel. They fanned out in front of the small crowd. No sooner had they arrived than the first protests began. Nate looked to Billy and leaned in close.

"We have experience. We could help."

Billy lifted his eyebrows in stunned surprise.

"Pilots? Are you kidding?"

Nate grinned.

"Or would you rather be a cook or cleaner?"

Nate then lifted his hand up high and called out.

"We're pilots."

The noise in the hangar quickly faded, and a small group of the civilians moved away, creating a rough channel to the temporary podium. Lieutenant Higgins looked out to Nate and scowled.

"You're a cadet, son. I need combat pilots. Men and women with experience piloting fighters."

He looked away from Nate, who took the opportunity to move closer to the gantry.

"The six of us came to Mognathu to compete against the Byotai pilots. We're all high-tier pilots in the Star Crusader simulation."

A couple of the civilians laughed, and one of the marines called out to silence them. Nate looked back to his friends, but only Rex had stepped forward.

"Yeah, he's right. We're..."

Another marine stepped in front of Nate and looked him up from head to toe. It was Sergeant Popwell, the gunner of the ship's last remaining Mauler.

"You're the cadets we rescued from the station, aren't you?"

He might have been trying to sound friendly, but along the way his voice twisted slightly, and turned the question into something more closely resembling an order. Nate felt his throat tightening up, but Rex appeared unaffected.

"Yeah, we're the six cadets from the exchange programme."

The Sergeant looked back at the podium while more marines spread out to speak with others in the hangar. The noise has become louder again, and as more people talked, the more difficult it became to speak. The Sergeant said a few words via his helmet communication system, nodded, and then looked back at Rex and Nate.

"We'll see. Get your friends and come with me."

The Sergeant moved off towards the podium. Nate and Rex followed close behind. By the time they reached the base of the frame, the Captain was gone. In her place were a handful of more junior officers.

"Where are the others?" Nate asked.

He looked around and finally spotted Cassandra and Matilda heading in their direction. Neither looked very happy, and behind them came a young Naval ensign.

"Where's the other two?" Sergeant Popwell asked.

Nate shrugged.

"I don't..."

Rex pointed off to the left.

"There, to the side of the fighter."

While they were looking about, none of them noticed Lieutenant Higgins had moved next to them. He hunched over a cleaning rod he was currently using as a walking aid. Nate was stunned at the marks on his body. The field dressing and medical kits on the ship had done a good job, and there were no open wounds. Yet his flesh was puffy, and there were deep lacerations and cuts on his hands and face. As he moved, he winced, but that didn't stop him from taking a commanding position in front of the four cadets.

"So! You think you have combat flight experience, do you?"

Cassandra arrived and immediately answered, drowning out the others with her matter-of-fact tone."

"We are experienced with the simulation, but not actual combat, obviously. The six of us were chosen from by lot from all high scoring cadets in the Academy."

The officer seemed less than impressed as she continued, explaining their many successes until finally he lifted his hand to stop her.

"That's enough. You might have simply said no."

Matilda was now there, and she opened her mouth to argue. Lieutenant Higgins put his finger to his mouth and shook his head. The cadet continued to speak, so the Lieutenant cleared his throat, drowning out her voice.

"This is a military ship, and you are now under military discipline. So silence!"

Matilda closed her mouth, and the sound from the others in the background quietened for a moment. It was rare for anybody to be able to keep her quiet, and Nate was quickly drawn to the memories of so many times where she'd gone on and on for hours at a time.

"Cadets. Experience in the Star Crusader public simulation is one thing, but combat is quite another."

Nate lifted his hand in an attempt to placate the man.

"Sir. We are not saying we're combat pilots. But we also do not use the public simulation. For the last three months, we've been competing on the military closed servers, with all safeties removed."

The officer straightened up a little and listened. Matilda nodded quickly as he continued to explain.

"We are all certified to control trainer drones in Alliance space."

Lieutenant Higgins grinned.

"Trainers, huh?"

He rubbed at his chin with the back of his hand.

"I'll tell you what. Meet me in the training suite. You can show me what you've got. Impress me, and you might get to help defend this ship and all

102

that reside in her."

"And if we fail?" Cassandra asked.

Rex muttered at her question, but all six listened patiently for the officer's answer. The man indicated in the direction of a group of civilians busy moving away from the hangar deck.

"If you fail, you will go back into the pool. We still need cleaners and medical assistants."

For the first time since leaving the starbase, Nate felt a moment of excitement. The escape was far from over, but even the slimmest chance of piloting an actual military drone was more than he could ever have expected. He looked to his friends and found little more than worry and nerves.

"We can do this, don't you think?"

Cassandra and Jack were silent. Matilda lowered her head to consider the problem. That left Billy who appeared completely stunned by the suggestion. Nate grabbed him by the shoulder and shook him.

"Well?"

Billy tried to speak, but his nerves got the better of him. Another hand came down and rested on Nate. He looked back around to look into the eyes of the Lieutenant. His face appeared to have softened, at least for a short moment.

"Nerves have taken him. Now imagine defending this carrier against a concerted assault. The lives of everybody depend on your skills and training. Can you do it?"

Rex stepped alongside Nate and nodded slowly at the officer.

"Yes, Lieutenant. We can do it."

"Very well. Wait here. You have a few minutes. Then you will come with me, and we will find out what you're made of."

They were left alone. Nate looked to Rex and found him looking right back at him. His expression was as hard and unfriendly as it always seemed to be.

"Okay, Nate. Don't screw this one up. I'll lead, and you'll follow. Just like always."

He walked off, saying no more, other than to whistle for Jack to follow. Nate shook his head and turned his attention to the other three.

"You know what they are asking us to do, don't you?" Cassandra asked.

Nate couldn't help but beam in happiness at them.

"Of course. We're getting the chance to be fighter pilots."

# CHAPTER SIX

**Fighter Control Suite**
**Alliance Armoured Assault Ship 'ANS Relentless'**
**Day 3**

The hangar deck was already in the process of being dispersed as Nate and his friends left. They may not have been in combat, but the sense of urgency was clear and obvious. Cassandra and Billy were at his side, Matilda trailed behind, her chin up and busily looking about. Rex and Jack were at the front, and barely a metre behind the Lieutenant. Billy seemed out of breath as he looked across to his friends. It wasn't through lack of fitness, but something else.

*He's worried. He's right to be,* Nate thought.

"Looks like Rex wants to run this one," complained Billy.

Cassandra nodded in agreement. The three had only met when brought together at the Academy finals, but already they were proving close friends. Cassandra might have been something of a know-it-all, but both Nate and Billy knew her skills were significant. Nate tried to make light of it with a low laugh.

"When doesn't he want to run things?"

Rex glanced back at them, but he either hadn't heard what they were saying about him, or he'd chosen to keep it to himself. The three said no more, and he turned back to speak with Jack. Nate relaxed, but only a little. Billy spoke quietly so that only he could make out the words.

"We can do this, right? We can do what the Lieutenant asked?"

Nate shrugged.

"Maybe. We've flown enough simulated missions before. This should be little different."

As they passed the empty corridors and ramps, nearing their destination, it became clear how empty Relentless actually was.

"She's like a ghost ship," said Nate.

His voice was quiet, but not enough that the others couldn't hear. Lieutenant Higgins heard him speak and nodded, as they kept moving.

"You're not wrong about that. We have enough crew to travel a modest distance in friendly territories. When it hits the fan, we'll have some problems. The defence for the carrier is always its fighters, and if that fails, you need engineers, medics, repair teams, and marines to defend against borders."

He threw his head back and raised his eyebrows.

"And that is something we have damned little of."

They moved on in silence until Nate spotted the imagery of different fighters that somebody had scrawled on the wall. It was fine work, and he couldn't help but lean in for a closer look.

"They date back to the last war."

There was a sense of reverence as he ran his left hand along the cool metal. The images were quite small, and many showed ships of various alien designs. One even looked similar to the diagrams he'd seen of the dreaded Biomanta capital ships. Cassandra spent only a few seconds looking at them. She was much more interested in the people and the events than the images themselves.

"What happened?"

Lieutenant Higgins didn't stop, but his composure altered just a little. They passed a single marine who, like so many of his comrades, had picked up an injury during the fighting to escape the starbase.

"Relentless was not a glamorous ship."

He pointed to the walls of the passageway.

"You see; back in the war there was a major lack of carriers for use in the convoys. They were needed for the war fleets, and anything capable of carrying large numbers of fighters was transferred to the front-line squadrons. Carriers like Relentless were at the bottom of that list."

106

"Why?"

Matilda had scrutinised the images and answered Cassandra's question while the Lieutenant considered his next words.

"Relentless is not like the other carriers."

"That is true," Lieutenant Higgins agreed, "Do you know why?"

Matilda nodded.

"She's an armoured carrier. Where fleet carrier have bigger hangars, she has armour plating."

"Indeed," They moved on a little further while the officer continued with his explanation, "Back in the day, the extra armour was critical, but with the advanced weaponry of the Biomechs, we needed warships to go toe-to-toe with them. As an old carrier with limited hangar space, she was relegated to convoy duty where her extra protection would be more useful when fighting raiders."

He looked back at Matilda.

"She had an unremarkable war until running the blockade of Spascia."

Again he touched the metal walls with his fingers.

"She stood alone while sixteen transports broke the line and delivered infantry and supplies to the defenders of Spascia. The last stand of Relentless went on for nearly two hours, and by the end of it she was adrift, with no fighters, and all but nineteen crew still alive."

He chuckled.

"The Biomechs thought she was a dead hulk and abandoned her to engage the rest of the newly arrived fleet. Since then, she's been repaired, refitted, and put back into service. She's a tough old girl."

They said no more as they made the final journey inside the ship. The trip to the Control Suite had not been long, but for Nate it seemed like an age. For the first few passageways he'd felt rather self-important. Other civilians were being shown to their new posts or handed jobs to carry out, but not Nate. While this continued, he was being taken to the heart of the ship's defences, the Drone Control Suite. He hadn't seen it yet, but from what he understood, it was designed to operate as both a training hall and command suite for drone fighters. A female voice caught Nate's attention, and he looked to the right as they passed by a pair of female crew.

"Sir," said the first.

Lieutenant Higgins nodded, and then they were past. The two were older than Nate, perhaps in their late twenties. Both wore grubby looking overalls and had sidearms on their flanks, like so many of the crew on the ship. Between them they carried a large metal container marked with faded letters.

Just minutes before, they had been in the hangar, along with all the other military crew and civilians. Now they were marching behind the last remaining Navy pilot; all on the promise that the six of them could manage the controls of drone fighters, something none of them had ever actually done before. Each had played their part in the simulations, but the realities of combat were far from anything they might have experienced. Even the violent escape from the starbase was nothing compared to what they were being expected to do.

The marines had done all of the fighting, and so far Nate and his friends little more but run and hide. They were not soldiers or marines, and certainly not fighter pilots in the traditional sense. As they walked through the ship, Nate did his best to convince himself their promises could be acted upon. Memories of the contests with the Byotai pilots over the last few days were still fresh in his mind, but so were the number of times he had been destroyed in battle. They had done well, but rarely without losses. The stakes had just been raised.

*We can do this.*

He kept telling himself the same thing over and over, but none of that would hide the nerves rumbling inside his belly. The waiting was always the worst part, and now he felt he might vomit at any moment.

"In here."

Lieutenant Higgins stepped to one side and signalled for them to enter the sealed area. Rex was first inside, with Nate right behind. The Fighter Control Suite was a long, narrow room with a row of eight booths on each side. An open passage ran between the two sides so that a supervisor could keep a careful eye on things. In the centre of the corridor the space opened up to give way to a large hexagonal pit that rose out from the ground. Above it hovered a detailed three-dimensional model of the scenario.

"Wow!" Nate exclaimed.

The six cadets waited patiently while a single crewman activated the first six booths. As the man made his way from one to the other, the Lieutenant moved to the pit and indicated for them to follow.

"Relentless was converted to a training ship and drone carrier during her last refit. It's not a pretty system, but it integrates with the tech we have to hand."

The six spread out and looked at the model on display while Lieutenant Higgins activated the program. A model of a single carrier appeared that closely matched Relentless. He then turned away from the unit to look at each of them.

"I can operate the drones, sending them on prearranged waypoints and attack patterns. It is enough to scout an area, but any pilot worth his salt will blast them apart in seconds."

His eyes narrowed as though a bright light had just shone into his face.

"All I need you to do is show me you can handle my birds. Follow my commands, and deal with any situations that arise. Succeed, and you'll get a field promotion to acting lieutenants in the Navy. Anybody not interested?"

All six waited in silence.

"Good. To your pods and get ready."

Each of them turned away and moved to their allocated units. Billy was the only one that paused for a second.

"Lieutenant Higgins, what rating are we playing against?"

Nate settled down into the comfortable seat and pulled on the straps before glancing back to his friend Billy.

*The Lieutenant won't like that.*

"Rating? Son, this is a combat simulation, the same one used for first year officers. All safeties will be off, full gravitational model and limitations.

Overload the engines...and boom. Pull too many gees, and you're out."

Billy was like a dog with a bone, though, and would not let it go.

"But we are simulating drones, aren't we?"

The man shook his head and laughed.

"If you succeed, then yes. For now I need to know you know the limitations and strengths of a manned fighter. You'll show me you can fly manually before I even think of letting you try the Avengers."

He then pointed to the allocated pod, and Billy moved away, clearly chastened by the experience. Nate would have laughed had the situation not been as dour and serious as it actually was. He looked back at his displays and then pulled the helmet from its mount to his right.

*This is incredible!*

In front of him was perhaps the most complex set of equipment he'd ever been given access to. Directly ahead lay a bank of black curved displays that gave a slightly distorted, wide-angled cockpit feel to the booth. Below these were a series of small panels that should have displayed everything from mapping data, fuel status, and damage monitoring, as well as weapons handling and status. Nate looked back to the Lieutenant.

"Uh, Sir, nothing is..."

The man chuckled.

"Your helmet, son."

He had completely forgotten to pull it on, even though the unit was still resting in his hands. He pulled the device down over his face, and it instantly connected to the simulation unit, syncing with the controls and data feeds. Overlays popped up, giving him access to even more information, while the device actually placed imagery onto the panels using a beautifully encoded augmented reality system. To Nate, it now looked as though he was inside a fighter. He reached out to the colour controllers and found that inside his helmet they had come to life.

"Wow!"

He was truly stunned. With the screen and the overlays, he had access to more flight data than he'd ever seen before. Gauges and columns of data popped up everywhere, and he was immediately buried in far more data than he could ever hope to manage. The public version of Star Crusader was vastly simplified compared to this, and even the system used with the Byotai had been half as complex.

"Now, as you can see, the simulation system is configured to be compatible with both the internal layout of the Lightning Fighter, as well as a remote unit for the Avengers. One moment, and I will configure the system," said Lieutenant Higgins.

He moved along the line, checking each system was on-line.

"Good. Now we will switch to Lightning simulation mode. Get ready."

Nate kept his eyes open even though they started to become uncomfortably dry. Then half of the screens disappeared, and the cockpit transformed to match the layout of the classic Lightning fighter. Masses of data vanished in a second, and suddenly everything felt that much more manageable. Outside of the cockpit were large metal panels that completely blocked the view.

"Very good. Any questions before we begin?"

Nate shook his head, but this time kept his attention firmly forward. The beeping inside his helmet served as a constant reminder that the fighter was sealed and ready for launch. It was there so that he remained alert and waiting for the launch. He twisted to the left, but when he looked back inside the training suite, he could see nothing but the bulkhead walls of the hangar deck.

*Just like the real thing.*

"Yeah, I have a question."

The Alliance officer walked along and stopped next to Jack.

"Yes?"

He twisted around as far as he could go, but was stopped by the straps and harness unit.

"How do we win?"

Lieutenant Higgins laughed at the young cadet, a great disingenuous roar that filled the room with noise. Nate already felt uncomfortable as he adjusted his harness, and this did little to help. When Lieutenant Higgins finally stopped, Jack had turned back to look at his forward view. Lieutenant Higgins moved to the overview console hovering above the pit.

"This ain't no game, and there are no winners. You will be flying a combat operation, and you will defend my carrier. You have a job to do, and that is your only objective. Understood?"

"Yes...Sir!" came back the chorus of responses.

"Good. Now, get ready for launch. It's time for your milk run."

Nate closed his eyes and took a single, deep breath. Words repeated in his ears, and he listened carefully.

"Relentless has a damaged core and is undergoing repairs. We are unable to leave this sector until it is repaired. Our engineers estimate twenty minutes if they are left to work. Only four turrets are functional, so it is up to you to provide a defensive curtain around the ship and buy them the time we need. With six fighters, and the point-defence weapons of the ship, you'll have what you need."

He paused, waiting for them to make whatever notes they needed.

"Remember, the objective is to buy time and let the carrier withdraw to safety. Loss of the carrier is a failed mission."

Each pilot acknowledged his short brief, and as he spoke their radar scanner and tactical overlays updated. ANS Relentless was in the middle of a sparsely filled asteroid field, and there were at least a dozen large dust clouds that proved almost impervious to their scanners.

"Buoys have been launched and positioned to provide a one hundred kilometre dome around us. Wait..."

It might only have been a simulation, but it was already beginning to feel very real to Nate. This was not being played for points, or even a position in the team. This was an actual mission to decide whether they could help in the coming fight, and if they passed, he and his friends really might be all that stood between Relentless and certain death. It was a lot to think about, so he did what he always did in such a situation, he ran through the checks once more.

"It's confirmed. We have four bogies, on approach at fifteen hundred klicks, course one-thirty and moving fast. The computer identifies them as Khreenk mercenary fighters. The fighter chassis carry the signatures of a group responsible for the destruction of a Helion bulk transport. One is carry a payload of two thermonuclear warheads, and it has been armed."

Nate had only met a handful of the Khreenk, and all of them had been traders. The Khreenk Federation was one of the many known races in the galaxy, and they were the ones that confused him the most. Though perhaps the most advanced of the known races, they were a scattered and disparate people, made up of multiple independent star systems that traded as often as they fought with each other. The Federation might have formed a loose arrangement with the Alliance to trade weapons technology for economic assistance, but as far at Nate was concerned, they were not to be completely trusted. Rumour had it that they were actually a territory based upon the rejects and exiles of the others, an odd mixture of bipedal beings that had become obsessed with improving their physical bodies to increase their strength and prowess in battle.

"You are free to launch."

He opened his eyes, and there before him was space. The exterior blast doors were open, and his fighter was ready and waiting on its launch rail. He looked left, and then right, checking everything was as it should be. There was the checklist, and he mentally ticked them off.

"I'm taking the lead on this one. Follow me!" said Rex, "Go, go, go!"

Nate didn't like the idea of Rex taking command, but with time limited and so much at stake, he decided to play along.

*Better to have leadership than dissent.*

It was something he'd heard back home, and although he was not entirely convinced, he could also see that starting an argument right now would be a guarantee of a complete and utter failure. For all of Rex's faults, he was still an outstanding pilot, and in their last simulations he'd been consistently ranked the highest scorer of them all.

*Here we go.*

All it took was a single button press, and Nate was away. The frame running along the inside of the blast doors vanished, and he was still accelerating. For the tiniest of a fraction, he actually thought he was flying a Lightning fighter, but he quickly remembered that ANS Relentless was not in a battle, but in fact hurtling through space to their destination. If they had just launched from the ship, they would never be able to join up with Relentless, let alone the rest of the fleet.

"I'm with you. Billy, form up on my wing."

It took less than twenty seconds for the six Lightning Mark IIA fighters to form up into a V formation, with Rex leading. At his right-hand side was Jack, just as they always were in the simulation. Nate and Billy took the left flank, and Cassandra and Matilda took the right. One of the first lessons they had learnt back when first starting with the public version of the simulation was to pair up. It was deadly to be caught out alone in a fighter, and two pairs of eyes were always better than relying on just one.

"Okay, looking good Crusader Squadron," said Lieutenant Higgins.

As the man spoke, an image of his face appeared to the side of the helmet-mounted display. The feed was direct from Relentless, and the only real reminder that this was a simulation, and not an actual flight. The lighting behind the Lieutenant was red, and if he hadn't known better, he could easily have been persuaded that this truly was a real scenario.

"You've made it out, and you can manoeuvre your fighters. That is a good start but not enough to protect our passengers. There is more to fighter combat than just flying the ship."

Dots appeared on the floating radar tracking system, and Nate began making a mental note of how many hostile targets were present. At the same time, the onboard computer began to plot their course, velocity, and specifications.

"You have multiple inbounds. Defeat the fighters and protect the carrier."

Rex took the lead and altered his forward course.

"Okay, Crusader Squadron, you heard the man. We'll play this by the numbers. Check your weapons and change your course to...one-six-nine."

Nate scanned the status indicator of his weapons, making sure the guns were warmed up and ready. The cold of deep space was forever a problem, and it was imperative the kinetic weapons were kept warmed and ready for use. One of the two guns had a minor fault, and he quickly activated the warmers to resolve the issue. He then turned his attention from the guns to the wing hardpoints. There were two on top of each wing to carry short-range Sea Lance missiles, and another large hard point underneath to carry one of the deadly 60mm railguns normally only fitted to the Bulldog Mobile Gun vehicles. These weapons were powered by the fighter's internal powerplant and loaded with a hundred-round cartridge per gun. The resulting package was a small but deadly attack fighter that could take on other fighters, as well as small capital ships.

"Crusader Three ready," said Nate.

His voice was dry and croaky, so much so he had to swallow and then repeat himself. One by one the others joined in with him until all six confirmed their weapons were ready and so were they.

"Activate burners. It's time to end this."

Nate keyed his intercom.

"What about the carrier? Another fifteen seconds, and we'll be unable to protect her other sectors. We should split up. One group flying circuits of the carrier, the rest on an intercept vector."

Rex must have been busy doing something else because he didn't answer, so Nate repeated himself, and this time put forward a proposed route for them to take. Nate felt quite pleased with himself until he received a curt reply from Rex.

"I heard you the first time, Crusader Three. Stay on course, and focus on the mission. Our orders are simple; defeat the fighters and protect our carrier. And that, my friends, is exactly what we are going to do."

The next few words were blocked out by something, and as they returned, a few odd sounds muffled the audio. Nate selected the electronic warfare suite and activated the scrubber mode. It took a couple of seconds for the system to do its job.

"They're jamming our comms. Make sure you activate your scrubbers and switch to the alternating encoders."

This time Rex must have been at least partially happy with what he was saying because he said nothing until Nate completely finished. They activated the units and then he spoke.

"Good. We'll use missiles first. Lock on designated targets and prepare to fire. It is critical that we down the bomber first. The rest is secondary. I want three missiles per fighter."

Nate found his target, the fighter off to the left and now already starting to alter its approach vector. Using nothing more than his retina, he selected the craft. Older weapon systems would normally require locking onto the target signature using heat or radar tracking, and often a mixture of both. The new system on the Mark IIA was far more sophisticated, and at this range, entirely optical. The trackers would only revert to a different targeting mode if the target object changed substantially in mass, or ejected countermeasures.

"Coming into range, get ready."

"Alert. Atomic warhead detected," said the computer.

As always the computer's voice was calm and collected, completely unaffected by the seriousness of the situation. Nate checked the data from the fighters and spotted the flagged fighter. He tagged it and keyed his intercom.

"One is carrying heavy ordnance. I've tagged it."

"I see it," said Billy.

Rex then tagged the others as low priority targets.

"I want the bomber brought down, then hit the rest with our remaining missiles."

"But what if..." started Nate.

Once more Rex interrupted him, and this time his tone was much harsher.

"Cut the chatter, Crusader Three. Target the fighters and wait for my command."

Nate was now entirely focussed on his prey. The computer brought up a detailed model of what he faced, and he quickly recognised it as one of the Khreenk fighters commonly used in the last war. Though of a similar size to his craft, it was slower but also much more agile, due to its rotating engine mounts.

"We need to hit them first; those things are deadly up close."

"That's enough chatter," Rex snapped back at him, "Focus on your targets. Open fire!"

Nate depressed the launch trigger, and away went one of the state-of-the-art Sea Lance missiles. At such a high closing speed, it didn't take long for the range to drop below a hundred kilometres. He held his breath as the missile moved close and then exploded as it reached just a few metres from the target.

"Scratch one!" he yelled excitedly.

More flashes marked the impacts, and the fighters rushed ahead to examine their defeated foes.

"New contacts," said Lieutenant Higgins, "A heavy stealth frigate has been detected at close-range. She's arming particle beam weapons."

Nate looked at the radar-tracking screen but could see nothing ahead. The scanner could pick up all manner of units, leaving only the possibility of computerised reflective panels, cooling units for the engines, and no crew. It was something discussed back in school, but so far none of these proposed vessels had been seen before, at least as far as he knew.

*Stealth ships. They could get close enough to fire their weapons without being detected.*

He looked down at the oval unit and spotted red markers right behind them. The shapes were small, but the longer they were present, the more detail the computer could show.

"I knew it."

He had intended to speak to himself, but in his excitement he broadcast his feelings to the rest of the squadron.

"That's great, Nate. Stay in formation and follow me."

Rex performed a high-speed course change, but it took time, due to their increasing velocity on the original heading. As they moved around in a wide, lazy circle, more information appeared on the target ship.

"Sensors show she is a renegade Helion frigate, and she's launching fighters. She's equipped with retroflective panels, stealth gear, and second-gen particle weapons. We need help, fast!"

Nate shook his head in irritation. Now it was all a simple matter of mathematics. The fighters could only accelerate so quickly, and by the time they were in range of the ship, it would already have fired its primary weapons. The frigate was manned by the humanoid race known as the Helions, a people with a very similar biology to humans. Their race was shattered in the Biomech War, and now they were little more than a shadow to be protected by the ever-growing Alliance. Of all the ships they might have encountered in a simulation, this one was right at the bottom of the list.

"Burners to war power. Use everything you have!" Rex ordered.

Nate flicked the safety toggle that removed the barriers to the engine unit. The core reactor now increased in power, past its normal levels and into the danger zone. Every second at this setting increased the chances of a fatal failure.

"How long until we're in range?" Nate asked.

"Target will be in range in ninety-four seconds," said the computer.

At that very point, a flash marked the impact of one of the deadly particle beam weapons. These devices were brand new technology a generation ago and now used on all kinds of heavy warships. In theory, the range was limitless, and they fired an invisible beam of energy that hit with explosive force. When the weapon struck a ship, it would literally explode the target with an impact far in excess of anything possible from a kinetic railgun weapon.

*Come on!*

The fighter shuddered as the powerplant was forced to vent excess heat. Warning alerts popped up, but Nate and the others knew what was at stake. This might only be a simulated mission, but it could just as easily have been the real thing. All that mattered was the carrier. Without it, all of them were already dead. The calm, yet clearly annoyed voice of Lieutenant Higgins returned again.

"We're on our own. Point-defence turrets are active, but we have no defence against particle weapons. Gods save us."

Nate swallowed the mention of a deity. Freedom of religion was practised throughout the Alliance, yet it had little place in public life these days. Faith was a private affair, and that philosophy was encouraged throughout the colonies to discourage arguments, as well as to keep the state out of the affairs of its citizens. The very mention of them served as a reminder to the danger of the position they were now in.

"We've failed," said Matilda, "Nate was..."

Rex instantly blocked her audio channel.

"It's not over till I say it is. Target the primary weapon systems of the frigate. Fire on my mark."

The six fighters were now trailing dust and debris, as the outlet vents of their engines became so hot sections of metal were now burning off and drifting behind in a shower of red-hot sparks. Nate twisted his head around and watched the left engine of Matilda's fighter catch fire. It only lasted a few more seconds and then flashed. The explosion vaporised the fighter instantly. Again the voice of Lieutenant Higgins returned.

"Matilda is down."

Nate shook his head in frustration.

*No way, we can't do it.*

"Stay with me," said Rex, "We have to protect the carrier."

Nate continued shaking his head in frustration, but this time kept his thoughts to himself. If these had been manned fighters, they would have just lost a pilot, and in less than five minutes into their first mission.

*We should have put a cordon around the carrier!*

The computer locked onto the target, the grouping of super-heated emitter ports along the front of the frigate. Another flash indicated where the carrier had been hit. This time a massive section of hull tore off. More flashes spread through the hull, and then the entire stern tore off in a bright white explosion. The forward view of the fighter automatically went dark, a throwback to the days when planetary bombers were required to carry nuclear weapons on board. It was only for a second and quickly reverted to the normal frontal view.

"Carrier has multiple breaches. Engines are off-line, fires throughout," said Lieutenant Higgins, "It's not looking good. I suggest..."

Rex cut the channel and overrode the voice of the officer.

"Stay in formation. After the attack, change to position Theta, and follow me, fire!"

With their missiles now gone, it came to their kinetic weapons. The mixture of medium and large calibre guns opened in a devastating storm of firepower. The hull-mounted guns were modifications of the heavier weapons carried by marines, but the new 60mm wing-mounted cannons were deadly. With all five fighters now blasting away, they punched hundred of holes into the bow of the ship.

"Theta formation!" Rex yelled.

The fighters spun in different directions, like an ever-widening star shape. At the same time, they spun about to use the sliding position and continued shooting. Each fighter was flying sideways and raking the frigate as they flew along her hull. The guns were far from capable of destroying the ship, but they were certainly able to inflict major damage on the sub-systems, weapons, and engines. Dozens of point-defence turrets tried to track them, but the pilots were experienced enough to dump countermeasures as they hurtled past.

"Reform and follow me."

The fighters passed the rear of the ship and then formed up into the loose v formation. At the same time, the few turrets aboard ANS Relentless were making short work of the enemy fighters. Only one remained, and Rex quickly despatched the final one with a single burst. He started speaking just as his fighter, as well as Cassandra's, vanished.

"Break formation!" Nate cried out.

The remaining three fighters pulled away from the position as the frigate fired again. The invisible energy beam was impossible to avoid, and by straying between the two ships, Rex had led them straight into the paths of the frigate's main guns. Nate spotted another flash as Relentless was hit once more, and this time not even her armour could save her. An explosion engulfed her entire hull, and then his vision went black.

*What?*

He then felt hands at his head and the helmet removed. In front of him was Lieutenant Higgins, and he didn't seem particularly happy as he examined Nate's face.

"Well, that was not ideal, was it?"

Nate pulled off the straps and slid out of the seat.

"No, Sir. We failed."

The man stepped back and nodded in agreement. By now the other five had done the same and joined Nate to listen to the dressing down they all expected from their one and only chance to pilot the drones. Rex spoke first and quickly tried to dismiss the scenario.

"We did what we could, but a cruiser and two squadrons of fighters was..."

"Silence, cadet."

Lieutenant Higgins lifted his hand over the central pit, and the three-dimensional models showed what happened in the battle. It started with the asteroid field and the carrier, and then to the arrival of the first enemy fighters.

"This is a class scenario, used to check the tactical awareness of pilots."

The imagery paused, and he selected the first group of enemy fighters.

"These are expendable fighters, sent on a decoy mission. They draw out the defences and leave the carrier vulnerable. Half of your fighters was enough to deal with them, perhaps even two, if the pilots were competent enough."

He continued the display. Though the battle had been short, this replay seemed to go on forever. When the frigate materialised, he paused it once more.

"Relentless is heavily damaged and incapable of defending herself, even against a frigate. Where are my fighters?"

Rex looked to the others, but all were silent. Rex appeared as if he was going to answer, but Lieutenant Higgins answered his own question.

"Like most raw recruits, you've got your eye on the target, and not the mission. Three or four escorts around the carrier could have dealt with this frigate in less than thirty seconds. The ship is only modestly armed against fighters, yet by the time you returned it had already crippled Relentless."

Nate knew what needed to be said, and he stepped ahead of the group.

"We screwed up. We wanted to prove we could be pilots, that we could fight when we needed to."

For the first time Lieutenant Higgins smiled.

"Finally, one of you takes responsibility. Yes, and you have proven to me that you can fly. Now you need to learn how to fight."

He moved his hard, penetrating look to the other five.

"Get some food in you, and then get back here. You have forty-five minutes. We have a lot to do, and not a lot of time to do it in."

The six cadets waited in stunned silence.

"Well? What are you waiting for, pilots? Get some chow, and fast!"

# CHAPTER SEVEN

**Alliance Armoured Assault Ship 'ANS Relentless'**
**Day 3**

The fighter had exploded, that much Nate remembered, but everything else was little more than a blur. The fighters moved so quickly that a mistake of even a split second would make the difference between victory and disaster. He closed his eyes again and tried to remember quite how the explosion had struck his fighter. No matter how hard he tried, he could find nothing more than the flashing white light and the exploding consoles.

*This is getting crazy.*

He watched Cassandra and Matilda describe a manoeuvre from the previous engagement. Gone were the pieces of equipment or advanced technology, and in its place they were doing what pilots had been doing for centuries, using their hands. While Cassandra described the manoeuvres in detail, Matilda seemed more interested in the specifics, the use of lateral thrusters, manoeuvring jets, or burners to make subtle corrections. She even brought up the detailed elements of the weapons, from the hardened slugs of railguns through to the power of the anti-ship missiles. The Lightning fighters might not have been particularly advanced, but they were relatively simple to fly, and very heavily armed; the perfect craft to train the cadets on in the simulation.

"You okay, Nate?" Billy asked.

He looked to his right to the round, but sympathetic face of his friend. The two had found themselves thrown together after the initial evaluation in the Alliance. While both were good pilots, when paired together they seemed to work as one. Nate was by far the more aggressive, but Billy was cautious. Separately these could be dangerous, but combined into a pair, and the strengths of Billy became obvious. He was a check to the often-excitable Nate. He was always there, the perfect example of a reliable wingman.

"Yeah. That last one hit hard. The explosion."

Billy rubbed his forehead.

"I know, tell me about it. My head still hurts as well."

Nate nodded. His forehead was throbbing, and still they were not allowed to stop. While the other newly pressed members of the crew went about their chores, the six new members of the air-wing were being put through their own training. Less than ten hours had passed since the failure in their first mission. Since then Nate had gone over what they could, and should, have done over and over again. And when he wasn't thinking about the mission, the six had then been grilled about avionics, weapon configuration, ranges, and performance. It had much in common with school, except this time it was for real, and surprisingly to him Nate loved it. Since he'd been a small kid, he'd grown up listening to stories about the wars, and of his late grandfather. Admiral Lewis was something of a legend in the Navy, and to his family a bitterly lost war hero. If people weren't talking about the Admiral, they were busy trying to emulate him.

*I still can't believe this.*

Nate smiled, and although exhausted from their work, he could still hardly believe his own luck. He imagined launching one of the drones and engaging Byotai fighters for real, and it sent a very real shiver through his body. Only then did he notice Cassandra watching him. As their eyes met, she looked quickly away and used her right hand to operate the Secpad on her left wrist. All of them now wore the same sealed PDS suit as Lieutenant Higgins, though the nametags had been removed and so far not replaced. The six were spread out around the pit and looking at the model of the most recent mission.

"Okay, what happened? Why did you just get wiped out by a small number of fighters?"

Cassandra lifted her hand to get the Lieutenant's attention.

"Go on."

"Well, Sir. The Biomech fighters used their speed and manoeuvrability to stay in close to our formation. At this range, it was difficult to hit them without striking our own fighters."

"And then?"

This time Billy spoke, "Nate and me dropped back to provide covering fire, and destroyed the first fighter. The second managed to evade, and one of us hit Rex's control system."

Lieutenant Higgs sighed.

"Exactly. Individually, you're doing fine, but you're still making mistakes as a unit. The two of you have to watch your fire. A clear target can become blocked in a fraction of a second. Cadet Hampel, watch your rear cameras. They were lined up for too long, and you said or did nothing. In a simulation you might be able to make it by losing a few pilots or birds."

He pointed to the walls of the room, "But out there, in the void of space you cannot take that chance. We have a finite number of birds, and when they are gone, we are dead. You will learn to function as a team, or you will die."

He straightened his back and groaned a little from his numerous wounds. Nate tried not to look, but the marks on his body, especially those on his forearms and neck, made it impossible not to. Billy stepped on his foot and quickly distracted him from looking.

"We've got just over two days till we reach the fleet. Who knows what we will find out there. I need all six of you combat ready by then."

He waited, and Nate wondered if they were supposed to say something. Rex and Jack were unusually silent, and he could only assume it was something to do with the fact they were all exhausted. Nate moved his eyes upwards to the timestamp on the video replay of their simulated battle. It was almost midnight.

"Okay. Get some rest and be at the hangar deck at six sharp. Understood?"

Nate looked to Billy and Cassandra, both of whose eyes were wide open at this. Matilda checked her wrist-mounted Secpad and then looked up at the officer with faded, tired looking eyes.

"That's six hours, Sir?"

Lieutenant Higgins grinned.

"Well done, Flight Cadet. You can crash my birds and tell the time. Outstanding, simply outstanding."

Jack laughed, and for his trouble received a withering stare from the Lieutenant.

"You find that funny, do you?"

Jack shook his head and quickly quietened down.

"You've done your basic training on the Lightnings. It's not perfect, but it's enough to move to the next stage."

He looked to each of them as they tried to work out what he meant.

"It's time you saw the birds up close and personal. Six hours to rest your bones, and then grab chow before meeting me on the deck. Don't be late. You'll see what you've been flying so far. Then it is time for your graduation to the real deal."

Nate and Billy looked at each other, but neither of them spoke. Instead it came to Cassandra whose face had lit up at the prospect of examining the aging fighters first-hand.

"Real deal?"

Lieutenant Higgins nodded slowly.

"Yes, Cadet. You've completed basic training on a simple space fighter like the Lightning. You won't be flying them, though. If you're to protect the carrier, you will need to learn to fly the Avenger drones."

Nate, Billy, and Cassandra looked to each other, and Billy's eyebrows lifted up in surprise.

"Finally," he said excitedly.

\* \* \*

The canteen was quiet, and until Nate entered the doorway was bathed in darkness. The lights flickered on, apart from one in the centre that persisted in flashing intermittently.

"Yeah, that's not going to be annoying, is it?" Rex grumbled.

Rex and Jack pushed past and headed for the line of sealed metal containers at the far end. To the right were three cylindrical units, each connected to a tap.

"Man, am I hungry," said Billy.

Nate's friend wandered off, and Cassandra followed close by, giving Nate only a cursory glance. Matilda moved to his side and looked back at him while rolling her eyes. With her wide-framed glasses she had to lower her head to get a better view of him.

"That's not going to work with her."

Nate lifted one eyebrow in confusion.

"What?"

Matilda laughed to herself and then walked past him to join the others, leaving him alone at the entrance. He was about to follow when he heard footsteps coming closer. There was nothing to be concerned about, not when travelling at such vast speeds through space. Nonetheless, after everything they had seen so far, he found it impossible to be at least a little concerned. Unlike the rest of the crew, the six of them were completely unarmed.

*Stay back.*

Nate took three steps away from the doorway and then turned back to face whatever was approaching. The noise of footsteps stopped, and then in came a single individual. To his surprise it was the Byotai officer, and a single marine with him. Though fully armoured, the marine moved relatively casually and carried a carbine in its mount on the side of the body. At seeing Nate, the Private stopped and deactivated the helmet visor and faceplates. Each piece melted away to reveal the smiling face of the marine he'd last seen during their flight from the starbase. She nodded politely towards the new insignia on the tight-fitting PDS clothing.

"Flight Cadet Lewis."

"Private Valentine."

The mention of her name seemed to piqué her interest.

"Who told you my name?"

Nate tried to play it coy, but he clearly failed because she burst into laughter. The others heard the commotion, and Nate spotted Cassandra looking at her before turning away with an exasperated look on her face. Private Valentine moved in closer to him.

"Ouch. That's gonna hurt."

Private Valentine waited near Nate as the alien officer moved away to join the others in getting food. Rex and Jack already had theirs, and upon seeing the reptilian creature they moved well away and sat at a table at the far end, five tables from the food. Cassandra and Billy were a little less obvious, but even they moved, leaving just Matilda. Either out of curiosity, or foolishness, she tried to speak with him. Of the six of them, she was the only one that had mastered even the very basics of its language. Nate listened carefully as Matilda struggled with her pronunciation.

"Hvernig ert þú?"

At first the Byotai seemed not to have noticed. But then he turned around and lowered his head politely.

"Ég er góður. Þakka, barn."

The words were slow, and Matilda moved her head as she tried to translate each of the words. It took her a moment but she seemed to finally understand. The two continued, with the Byotai often repeating himself.

"Wow," said Private Valentine, "We were told your group was special, but I thought they meant you were the kids of some rich diplomats or something."

She looked at Nate, her eyes seeming to burrow deep into his skull. He could see faint signs of light brown hair, slightly curly, and pushed back behind her head.

"What's your special skill, Nate?"

"I...uh..."

Valentine laughed.

"Talking to women isn't one of them, is it?"

Rex had wandered over, but Nate had no idea quite how long he'd been there. Any confidence he might have been able to build was immediately lost with Rex, and finally Jack nearby.

"Private. What's going on here? This place is for Alliance officers only."

The happy expression on the very lightly tanned skin of Valentine vanished in an instant. Though they were not technically in the military, their provisional posting was classed as a battlefield commission, each the equivalent of pilot officer in the Alliance Navy.

"You should be saluting me," said Rex.

Any pleasure at seeing the group had already completely vanished in the presence of Rex. Private Valentine shook her head in frustration.

"No, Flight Cadet. Rules in the Alliance Navy are clear on saluting, but since leaving the starbase that has changed."

She looked to Nate, who did his best to offer a sympathetic expression.

"More than half of our crew is now civilian. Rules on saluting have been relaxed, for now. This kind of Naval discipline is not something that can be attained in a matter of days. These changes are temporary, just like your rank."

Rex's nostrils flared at the rebuff from the marginally older woman. He moved closer to her and then nodded towards the drink dispenser tanks.

"I'm thirsty. Get me a drink."

Her eyes narrowed and her facial muscles tightened.

"No. I'm on duty to provide an escort for our guest. You will have to struggle to the drinks unit yourself."

Rex opened his mouth again, but now Cassandra had reached him and pulled him away. She spoke in angry tones while he began to argue back at her. Nate waited until he was gone before speaking again to Private Valentine.

"I'm sorry. Rex can be..."

Valentine lifted her left hand and shook her head.

"Forget about it."

Her friendly demeanour had gone, and in its place the cold efficiency of an Alliance marine. All kinds of topics flooded into Nate's head, but to bring any of them up now seemed petty and insignificant. A noise from near the food containers made him turn around, and he began to speak without even thinking.

"What happened to him? The criminals on the starbase wanted him dead."

Private Valentine exhaled and did her best to relax.

"His name is Captain Dreuc, and he's a retired instructor from the Imperial War Academy."

Nate continued to watch as the alien sipped from a plastic beaker and continuing his conversation with the intrigued looking Matilda.

"I never saw him before the attack."

Private Valentine smiled.

"Oh, you wouldn't have. He doesn't teach lowly pilot cadets like you six. He's a fleet instructor. Rumour has it that he was a heavy cruiser captain back in the last war."

The alien finally finished speaking and walked back towards the marine, still holding the beaker.

"We go now."

His voice was dry and uncomfortable to listen to. Nate had heard many of his race speak before, but even his untrained ear could pick out the subtle differences between the way he spoke and the Byotai cadets. He was so busy listening he hadn't heard Matilda approaching his side. He glanced over at her. She had a smile drawn across her face, something of a rarity for Matilda. Unlike the others, she was a serious student of almost every subject. She was a competent pilot, yet an exemplary engineer, tactician, and researcher.

"He's one of the ruling castes and speaks the dialect of the patricians. You can pick it up with the inflections and the lack of colloquialisms."

Nate sighed quietly to himself.

"Matilda, what are you doing training to be a pilot? You should be with the intelligence or research division. You're wasted flying fighters."

Matilda pulled her head back in feigned surprise.

"You can't have a brain and fly a fighter?"

She then leaned in and whispered in his ear, "There's nothing like the feeling of combat, that's why. It's just the machine and me versus whoever faces me. You think they'd let me join the marines?"

Nate was speechless. Here he was thinking Matilda was little more than a tech nerd, when in reality, she wanted nothing more than the blast and destroy the enemy; just like the rest of them. Captain Dreuc made for the doorway, but as he reached the frame, he stumbled. It wasn't much, but it immediately betrayed the wounds he'd sustained. Only then did Nate spot the metallic frame attached to his lower legs where rods had been pinned directly into the bone.

"He took seventeen bullets in the firefight. His left leg was shattered, and he still managed to make it back with us."

Private Valentine glanced back into the room but focussed her attention on Nate in particular.

"Another time."

She then moved back into the passageway.

"Cadets."

With that, the two were gone, and just the six of them remaining inside the canteen. The silence was broken by the angry sound of Rex's voice.

"I don't care what he says, the Byotai cannot be trusted."

He then pointed to Matilda.

"You'd better watch yourself. Remember what they did on the starbase. One minute they were our friends, the next they stuck the knife in."

Rex stepped in front of Matilda and slightly to her left.

"Really? I hadn't noticed. I seem to remember this Byotai took it just as badly as we did. You saw his leg."

Rex had already turned away and was heading out of the door, with a bread roll in one hand and the other gripped tightly around a plastic beaker.

"Yeah, I saw. Just watch it. If anybody comes at me from behind.."

He lifted his left hand to strike, but with both hands full he was immediately frustrated in his plans. He grunted and then threw the beaker at the wall, splattering the battleship grey paint scheme with the red fluid.

"You'll what?" Cassandra called after him.

Jack and Rex were now far off in the passageway, but they could still hear the voice behind them.

"Throw juice at them?"

Billy stepped out and looked at the fluid dripping down the wall. He walked back inside, pulled a cloth from the rack unit on the wall, and ran it under the water container. He walked back out and began sponging down the wall.

"What are you doing?" asked Cassandra.

Billy scrubbed again, bending down to rub at the stained metal.

"Somebody has to do it, and we're kind of lacking in crew."

Nate moved back inside and grabbed another cloth, joining his friend to help clear it. Soon Matilda and Cassandra were there, and in less than two minutes, there was little sign that the drink had been thrown.

"There," said Billy, "Just like new."

As they admired their handiwork, none of them noticed the figure of Lieutenant Higgins far off into the distance. He was back to the sidewall and partially obscured by the shadow cast from the wide bulkhead. He waited until the cadets had finished, nodded silently, and then vanished as quietly as he'd arrived.

* * *

**'ANS Relentless', Combat Information Centre**

The massive warship accelerated through space without a sound to mark her passage. With her course laid in, there was no way to make any meaningful changes. Space travel at these great distances was a complex affair, but there had been few advances in human space travel since the early colonisation of the planet Mars. Only through combining the technologies of multiple races had the secretive scientists at Taxxu produced something more advanced. This technology was currently only used by the elite Interstellar Assault

Brigade, as well as the small number of explorer vessels.

Deep inside the many rooms and bulkheads of the ship, the CIC buzzed with the sound of scanners and computer systems. If the ship were fully crewed, it would have been filled with officers. Now there were so few it looked almost empty. The single most significant source of light was the vertical display, but more than a dozen other small units flickered as they brought up pages of critical data on the running of the ship. It was reaching the end of its forward flight and would soon perform a one hundred and eighty degree rotation, ready to begin an eighteen-hour deceleration period.

Captain Galanos looked hot and tired, something quite obvious due to her baldhead glowing with perspiration. The engines were being pushed hard, and though the internal life support system was doing its best, the system was still struggling to disperse the excess heat from inside the main power unit. She moved closer to the vertical display and looked carefully at their destination. White shapes marked the known celestial bodies, with particular emphasis on the largest asteroids in the XX Field.

"So, this is to be our new home."

She looked to the Byotai officer.

"Even if just for a matter of days. We will need time to replenish our food, water, fuel, and weapon stocks. If we're lucky, we might even get some fighter crews and drones back aboard."

She concentrated on one part and let out a slow, long sigh. The imagery showed the barren region, known simply as the XX Field in the Alliance mapping system. Millennia ago multiple star systems had collided, leaving the entire territory a shattered wasteland. At its heart was a single black hole, itself orbited by massive discs of swirling rock and ice; all that remained of the planets, moons, and even stars that were once there. At her side was Lieutenant Higgins, as well as Captain Dreuc of the Byotai Imperial War Academy. He spoke, and the ship's computer translated on the fly so that anybody in the CIC could hear.

"I assure you, Captain. The Imperial Fleet has no permanent facilities in this sector."

Captain Galanos ran her right hand along her chin. Though doing their best to be discreet, the pair of marine guards at the door were a constant reminder of the danger the ship was in, both to external threats, as well as the potential problem of having a Byotai officer aboard.

"As far as you are aware. Nonetheless, the Deadlands as you call it, is still part of Byotai territory, is it not?"

The Byotai listened carefully as the Captain asked her question. He might look slow, but when he spoke, his own words poured out at quite a rate. The computer system stalled, and it took a full four seconds before finally translating his words for a frustrated looking Captain Galanos.

"That is correct. Our ships frequently patrol the border between the nine quadrants and the Deadlands."

He lifted his right arm and immediately winced. He ignored the discomfort and pointed to a series of icons on the display.

"It is a wasteland, but it also houses rarely used Spacebridge connections to the Ninth Quadrant, as well as the core stars systems in the Trinity."

Captain Galanos moved some of the celestial objects out of the way on the screen, and then pointed to one circular icon now taking up the bulk of the middle of the unit.

"And this sector? According to my data, it is home to a Spacebridge to the disputed warzone you call the Tenth Quadrant. Is this accurate?"

The Byotai appeared surprised she knew this. He opened his mouth twice, letting his body cool before answering.

"Yes, there is a third Spacebridge to that warzone. A regional security force guards it, as well as a small force of border patrol ships. We have only limited control over them."

He looked upwards.

"Since the mutiny, there is no way to know what has happened there. All I can tell you is that it is the main route to smuggle troops and resources to the separatists in the Tenth Quadrant. Their allies took control almost a month ago."

134

Once more Captain Galanos ran her hand over her chin. The network of Spacebridges that allowed instantaneous travel between star systems was far from complete, and it could take days, sometimes even months to reach the entry point of a Spacebridge. They had only a short time to prepare, and the more she knew about the area the better.

"Will we find allies or enemies in the Tenth Quadrant?"

The Byotai officer made an odd sound, one that might equally have been laughter or choking. He glanced back to Lieutenant Higgins and then to the Captain.

"It all depends who you find. General Makos has vanished, along with the remainder of his fleet. If you run into rebels, or worse the Anicinàbe, then you can expect no mercy."

The two spoke for a little longer, all the while Lieutenant Higgins waited patiently. He'd been summoned twenty minutes earlier, and so far not one question had been levelled at him. By the time Captain Galanos actually spoke, he barely even noticed.

"Lieutenant, did you not hear me?"

He cleared his voice and racked his brain for the words that had not even registered. He was tired, and the pain from his injuries was still causing him trouble. None of that was a reason to have drifted off in a briefing such as this.

"Apologies, Sir."

The words were there, and just another moment and he had them.

"Yes, the cadets."

Captain Galanos nodded impatiently.

"I know, I asked the question. Are they ready?"

Lieutenant Higgins shook his head.

"No, not yet."

There was much more to say, but he knew from experience that if the Captain wanted to know more, she would ask. She turned back to the display and examined the rendezvous location for nearly ten more seconds. Just as the Lieutenant began to relax she looked back.

"Will they be ready when we arrive?"

This time Lieutenant Higgins nodded.

"Yes, Sir, they will be ready."

The Captain seemed satisfied with this. She moved her hand in front of the display and brought up a live feed of the ship's hangar decks. There were crew out on them now, as well as several civilians, presumably those with technical or engineering crews. She started to speak, but this time kept her eye on the screens.

"According to my data, we have only half of the fighters ready for operations, not the ten you described on the deck. Please explain."

She looked at her last remaining pilot and waited for him to speak. The Byotai officer also looked, though it was hard to gauge either his interest or emotion from his face.

"That's true, Captain. The Four Lightnings need ten hours, perhaps twelve to get them functional. Without pilots, they are less than useful. Instead, I've had the work crews strip weapon systems and relevant parts from them to get the Avengers ready."

The Byotai officer said something, and the computer followed shortly afterwards.

"Drone fighters. Can you rely on them?"

Lieutenant Higgins glanced to the Captain, and she gave him the nod to answer.

"Yes, they can be relied upon. Our drones can now only be used when slaved to a control package. Even if connections are severed, they will follow the default program."

"Which is?"

Again he checked with the Captain before answering.

"If undamaged, to return to base and land. If too badly damaged, then to auto-destruct."

The alien seemed satisfied by that and looked back at the many screens of data. Captain Galanos was still there and had brought up the video feed from the canteen where the cadets were just leaving.

136

"Six rookies, all fresh out of military school. You know none of them has applied for entry to the military after they graduate, don't you?"

Lieutenant Higgins shook his head.

"No, Captain, I did not know that."

She looked at him for a moment, trying to assess the man.

"Lieutenant, in ten hours we will begin reserve thrust. After that, it's a done deal. We will arrive at our destination in little over a day. There could be an Alliance fleet waiting for us, or a Byotai battleship. Just tell me straight. What is your assessment of them? Do I need a new plan for our arrival?"

Lieutenant Higgins remained upright, and his expression hard and uncompromising.

"The six are a mixed bunch, but together they have the potential to be as good as any squadron I've led. By the time we arrive, they will be ready to pilot all of our Avengers. They are practicing reconnaissance, escort, and bombing runs, and they will do what needs to be done."

"Very good. Let us hope they won't be needed."

She looked back at the screen, focussing her attention on the spacecraft lined up inside the hangar bay. One in particular stood out over the rest.

"Your Mauler. She's the single most powerful spacecraft in our inventory. What is her status, and more important, can you fly her?"

Lieutenant Higgins eyebrows rose as he listened to her questions.

"Mongoose took one hell of a beating in the fight. The engineers have repaired her, but the cockpit is too badly damaged to be pressurised, same for the rest of her."

"Understood."

"As for the guns. The secondary turrets are gone, but the forward weapons are still functional. With a gunner she'd be workable."

"And you, Lieutenant. I know you have substantial injuries from our escape. But right now, I don't have much of a choice. I need every asset at my disposal ready and able to fight."

Lieutenant Higgins did his best to stand up as tall and straight as the pain would allow.

"Captain, if I'm needed, I'll fly her."

For the first time in what felt like months, the Captain actually smiled at him. She was not the kind to show much in the way of emotions, and that was more disturbing to him than anything else he'd seen so far.

"Good work, Lieutenant. I will leave you to continue. Please keep me notified of any changes."

"Sir."

He turned and made for the door where the guards waited, as always. Once outside he almost ran into Sergeant Popwell, his gunner from the last mission.

"Sir."

The Sergeant's hand came up into a smart salute, and Lieutenant Higgins responded.

"How are your marines?"

The Sergeant winced at the question.

"Not brilliant, Sir. Half of my people were forced to redirect to Gorgon. Now they are either dead or prisoners of the Byotai rebels. What with major injuries, I'm down to eleven combat effective."

"And Gunnery Sergeant Perkins?"

"He's good, Sir. Since we made it back, he's reorganised the remains of our unit, and taken on a group of the younger civilian volunteers."

"What for?"

"Logistics, first aid, and fire duty. They're receiving basic fire drill training as well. It's not much, but it's better than nothing. They'll be handy in a fight, and it's not like we're lacking in spare firearms."

"Very true. Can you do something for me?"

The Sergeant shrugged.

"Of course, Lieutenant."

"Make sure you are available as my gunner when we reach the rendezvous. I'll also need a single experienced fireteam on standby."

"Understood."

The Sergeant began to move away but looked back.

"Sir, are we expecting trouble?"

Lieutenant Higgins laughed.

"Trouble? When was the last time we weren't in trouble?"

# CHAPTER EIGHT

**Alliance Armoured Assault Ship 'ANS Relentless'**
**Day 4**

Relentless was silent, a ghostly vessel bereft of crew and passengers. In the past she may have been filled to bursting point with officers, crew, and pilots, but no longer. Nate had travelled aboard many ships in his life but never on such a large vessel with so few people aboard. They were already halfway to the hangar deck and still he'd seen not a single soul outside of their own group.

*This is too weird.*

He entered one of the many junctions, instinctively checking both directions before crossing. It was big enough that he could expect to make it through without bumping into people, but after the bloodbath on the starbase, he was taking nothing for granted. There were blackspots throughout the ship, and they had been warned to stay together and well away from them. As he continued to make his way through the passageway, his mind filled with images of space fighters. Since humanity's expansion into space, they had fought many enemies, including factions from within, aliens, and even the dreaded biomechanical machines of the last two wars. All he wanted was take command of one of the fighters and do his part, like so many pilots before him.

Cassandra walked in front and Billy at his flank. Their boots made a clunking sound, and though incredibly tired, Nate found that for the first time in days he was starting to relax. It wasn't that they had nothing serious to think about, but he was actually beginning to feel comfortable controlling the fighters. What had seemed complex and confusing was quickly becoming second nature, and Lieutenant Higgins must have noticed it.

"Hey, Nate. Do you think he'll let us actually sit inside one of the active Lightnings? I've only been in one of the Mark I models in the military museum on Terra Nova."

Nate looked at him, and although he'd heard the words, they were just sound, nothing more. He looked at his friend for a second as he tried to gauge what he was saying. Normally, Nate would have loved to listen to more stories of Terra Nova. He'd spent his entire life on Kerberos, and even though it was one of the most advanced planets in the Alliance, it was still never going to match the prestige of either Proxima Prime or Terra Nova. His mind was far from thoughts of those planets, though. Seeing armed spacecraft was quite the distraction, but then so was the odd sound he could hear. He kept walking but tilted his head to listen. It was a knocking sound, like somebody on the other side of a door hitting it with a wrench.

*Weird.*

It stopped as quickly as it had begun. He shrugged, lifted his foot, and took another step forward. It returned, but this time it was a jarring sound like rough metal being dragged along a flat surface. As his foot touched the floor, the entire ship shuddered violently. It wasn't enough to make him lose his balance, but he did reach out to make sure he didn't bump into Billy or the wall.

*Not good!*

Nate regained his balance and then came another series of thumping sounds. The ship shook three times in quick succession, and at that exact moment the lights went out. As darkness filled the ship, it was followed by a series of loud banging sounds, each one louder than the rest. A single last booming one sent a shockwave like a thunderclap through the ship. The blast was so great Nate felt it rush through his clothing. He couldn't see what was happening, but the noise level increased as if a tornado was ripping through the shafts and passages.

"Brace yourselves!" yelled somebody off into the distance, "Here it comes!"

Nate instinctively lifted his hands to his face, and it wasn't a moment too soon. He struck something hard and metal at speed. His fingers pulled back, but not enough to cause damage. He reached out, found something strong, and held on. There was no way of telling if it was a hatch cover, grab handle, or a loose piece of equipment, and at that moment, Nate didn't care. All he wanted was to live.

"It's an attack! It has to be!"

Nate recognised the panicked voice of Jack immediately as he cried out loudly to whoever was nearby. Without light, the interior was completely black, not even a pinprick of light to show the way. Something flashed, and then Cassandra's arm glowed blue, along with her face. She moved her fingers to access systems, and a single light at the end of the passage flickered and then stayed on. It wasn't much, but it at least illuminated the rough shape of the corridor they were currently in.

*Secpad! Use it, you fool!*

Nate had completely forgotten about his own bracelet. He pulled closer to the wall and ran his right hand over the unit. With a single pulse it activated, and the blue hue appeared. Once functional, he looked back into the passageway. A long groan sounded as if the spine of the ship would crack at any moment. It was unlike anything he'd ever heard before, and it filled his heart with terror.

"Stay where you are...wait for the..."

The low level lights came on one at a time, filling the passageway with a subtle red glow. It was a fraction of the normal lighting but more than enough to make out the shape of the passage. Nate didn't want to see the damage, but curiosity, tinged with a sense of self-preservation, forced him to turn around. Billy was nearby and holding onto one of the many rungs. Blood had leaked out onto his face, growing into a small patch that refused to drip in any particular direction.

"You okay?"

Billy nodded quickly.

142

"Yeah. I'm okay."

He lifted his left hand to his face, rubbed the blood, and then looked back to Nate. The smeared blood was still there, and instead of improving his looks, he now actually looked far more injured.

"Sorry about that. I...I panicked."

He grinned at his friend's embarrassment.

"You don't say!"

Nate then pushed out, but kept one hand on a rung so he could look further into the ship. The other four were spread out, with Cassandra helping Rex position a temporary field dressing. She spotted him watching and nodded at Rex.

"Lacerations to the forearm, nothing serious."

A great weight pulled on his body, and he moved down to rest on the ground. The pull increased, and then as quickly as it had left, artificial gravity was back to normal. The loudspeakers fitted everywhere crackled to life.

"This is the Captain. We have intruders at engineers. All marine and militia units report for duty. This is not a drill. I repeat; we are under attack. Communications and networked devices have been hacked. All other personnel are to follow breach protocols. Do not use your mobile communications."

Nate swallowed uncomfortably. The breach drills had been practiced twice so far, and each time had made him feel sick. His eyes blurred, and he suddenly felt nauseous. A pulse of what must have been electromagnetic energy rushed through the ship, and he was sure he could feel the affect on his body. As it moved through him, his Secpad data link vanished as though the ship's main computers had just shut down. In an instant his device turned into a disconnected computer. He looked to his comrades. Matilda reacted the quickest.

"Into the nearest compartment, now!"

Nate had made it four steps and was heading in the same direction when the shooting started. It was impossible to tell how far away it was, but the vibration of the guns could be felt through the floor. He looked ahead at

Matilda activating a security door. The thick metal door slid open, and she signalled for them to get inside. The entrance was nearly ten metres away, and just across from a crossroad in the passage.

"In here, quickly!"

It was a small door, large enough just for one person to enter at a time. Rex and Jack were already inside and Cassandra was next. Billy stepped across the junction, leaving Nate as the last of the group. He moved to the open space and spotted movement far off to his right.

"Run!"

Billy was blocking his path, as well as leaving himself completely vulnerable out in the passage. Nate pushed him hard but stumbled, falling face down to the ground. He looked up and saw Billy looking back at him, three metres away. His friend reached out, but a streak of thermal energy rushed past his face from the right. He'd seen it before, back on the starbase.

*Byotai weapons!*

Nate wanted to move forward to join his friends, but two more blasts narrowly missed him. These were not the minor flashes of pistols, but the powerful blasts of military grade firearms as used by marines. He pulled back as a third struck where his head had just been.

"Nate!" Billy yelled.

An arm reached from the small doorway, yanked Billy inside, and then a great thud marked the shutting of the door. One moment the group were making their way through the ship, the next he was alone, and with an enemy force nearby. In game simulations, he would have leaned to the left, fired a few shots, and jumped back, but this was no game. Nate and his friends were unarmed, and their Naval issue PDS gear was not designed for the rigours of combat, merely to protect against debris, heat, and flash burns.

*Keep your head, and stay alive.*

He stayed low and crawled backwards to where he'd come from. Only his head now stuck out, and though his gut told him to keep going, something persuaded him to roll his head to the right. Then came the sound of voices and the figures of four heavily armed Byotai soldiers. He had never seen such figures in the flesh before, and they were a terrifying sight. Bulkier than a man, they were covered from head to toe in layered plate, not the smooth finish so prevalent among the PDS Alpha armour. Nate had seen pictures of Byotai soldiers from the last war, and these were very different. The thick plating and great size of the bulky carapace plates made them look massive.

"Dræb ham!"

The words were shouted with a loud, guttural roar unlike any sound emitted from a human. Nate had no idea what it meant, and with one last push moved backwards. At the same time, a powerful blast of heat struck the ground and burnt a hole as large as his fist. He lifted up to his feet. The sound of the soldier's footsteps became louder and louder.

*Run, you fool!*

He turned and ran back. The passage was not the longest on the ship, but on this particular occasion, it felt like the greatest distance he'd ever travelled. Just as he reached the end, it turned away to the right. A heat blast struck just centimetres from his left and put a long black scorch mark on his PDS suit. Then the shapes of three armoured warriors appeared in front of him. He was moving so fast he crashed into the first and sent them both to the ground.

"Get back," said a stern voice.

Nate was still on the ground, but he looked up. Three marines were aiming their carbines off into the passageway. The L52 Mark II carbine was a deadly weapon, but when faced by the massive shapes of the Byotai, it somehow seemed puny in comparison. The marine on the floor was now back on his feet and glanced over to Nate. At the same time, the visor plating slid back.

"Cadet, you in trouble again?"

"Private Valentine."

Nate tried to sound confident, but he was already out of breath. His chest was pounding from the exertion and unexpected arrival of the Byotai. Private Valentine looked away from him, and her visor clamped back into position.

"Contact!" said one of the others.

The first marine spun about and then crashed to the ground, a burning hot projectile embedded in his face and still hissing away. Blood dripped from the wound and made a foul sound as the heat from the projectile made it crackle, like oil in a pan. Nate turned from the scene of carnage and vomited on the metal deck. He choked twice and then staggered towards the wall.

"Open fire!"

Private Valentine had already lifted her carbine and activated the unit. She was exactly where the first marine had died and taking aim. Her comrade may have just been killed, but her training and instincts were to move back to the firing line. Nate could see the marks on her armour where it had been penetrated by the projectile in the previous battle. It had been repaired, but the mark was easy to see.

"Stay back."

The marines fired a volley from their carbines as soon as they spotted the shapes of the first two Byotai. Nate pulled himself backwards but still managed to see the glint of shining metal as the rounds struck armour. Sparks and flashes flickered all over them, and then they returned fire. The marines had the edge in terms of training, but the Byotai had the element of surprise, as well as the thick armour plate that seemed perfectly suited to beating off attacks from the carbine.

"Fall back."

This time Nate recognised Sergeant Perkins. The marines moved back but kept their fronts to the enemy, putting down such a withering hail of defensive fire they managed to make it to the next junction without suffering a single loss. Sergeant Perkins took the right and signalled for Private Valentine to take the other. She then signalled for Nate.

"Get behind Valentine, and keep your head down."

The corridor now effectively looked empty, each marine waiting at a side of the crossroads. Sergeant Perkins moved his carbine out around the corner and took aim. Few might know, but the carbines were designed to send video feeds directly from their sights to the visor of the carrier. It was a

146

simple mechanism and allowed the marine to fight safely from behind cover. Then Nate heard a sound behind him. He turned around and found a single civilian. It was a man in his late forties, and he was falling. The man hit the ground hard, his knees striking the metal surface with a cracking sound. He tipped over and landed face first. Nate took a step closer and then stopped upon seeing the dark shape of a Byotai soldier coming right at him.

At this range he had the perfect view of the monster. Though slightly bigger than the average human, the Byotai were often bulkier, and with this new armour they appeared even bigger. He was fascinated to see the plating was clamped on top of existing armour like reptilian scales.

*Now what?*

He twisted around and called out to Private Valentine, but it was too late. As he opened his mouth, a great roar filled the passageway. The bright light floodlit the marine so well he couldn't even make out her features. Nate flung himself to the wall and was stunned to see Private Valentine was safe. She turned around, took careful aim, and then fired. Nate glanced back. The Byotai soldier was already down on one knee, hit by gunfire from in front and behind.

As he dropped to the ground, Nate found the figure of Captain Dreuc with an old-fashioned Marine Corps L48 rifle in his hands. The weapon fired again, sending an intelligent warhead at the back of the enemy soldier. The shell exploded with a bright yellow flash, and then he was dead. The body lay silently on the ground, as if it had always been there. Private Valentine immediately bent down, and for a second Nate thought she was about to attack the fallen warrior. But she grabbed his thermal carbine, checked the safety lock, and tossed it to Nate.

"Take it."

He reached out and caught the weapon awkwardly. In his hand it seemed massive, yet the ergonomics matched his physiology surprisingly well. The stock was longer than he would have liked, and when he tried to lift it to his shoulder, he found it caught at his armpit. It was front-heavy, and the curved ridge at the front warm to the touch.

"Keep it under your arm, and don't shoot unless you're sure it's an enemy. Got that?"

Nate nodded and started speaking, but the ship's internal speakers growled loudly. Much of the audio was muffled, and occasionally alien-sounding words would completely blot it out. Finally, a few made it through before it cut completely.

"...aboard...breached networked systems. Marines, activate Protocol Seven...Go Dark."

The two marines looked at each other at the mention of this.

"Seven," repeated Private Valentine.

The audio system crackled, and then a long, continuous tone activated, drowning out any other sound. Private Valentine grumbled, jumped up, and struck the speaker with the back of her armoured fist. The worst of the sound vanished, but it was still faintly audible from other, much more distant speakers. Nate tapped her arm.

"What is that?"

He had a terrible thought that the protocol might mean evacuation of the ship. But as her visor slid open for the briefest moment, he could see she remained calm and confident.

"They've block our comms, may even be monitoring it."

Nate shook his head while resting his newly acquired weapon under his arm. It made him feel powerful even though he'd never used a firearm in anger before.

"Protocol Seven. What is it?"

Sergeant Perkins leaned in and spoke.

"It means we're in serious trouble, son. The Byotai must have infiltrated us before we escaped and waited till we were tired and vulnerable. Now they're heading for propulsion. The other routes have been blocked. The only way through is this corridor and pass us."

Captain Dreuc moved up to them and then double-checked his L48. Nate had no idea where he'd got the old Marine Corps weapon from, but neither of the marines appeared bothered. One of them spoke via their integral translator, and Nate was left listening to the guttural sounds of the two speaking. Finally, they stopped, and Captain Dreuc placed one of his hands onto Nate's shoulder.

"Komdu meth mér."

Nate shook his head.

"What?"

Private Valentine laughed grimly.

"Go with him, and watch his back. He'll take you to the others. Tell the Captain we have them pinned. We'll keep them occupied, but they need to be hit, and hit hard. We don't have much time."

"What about you?"

The Private's visor hissed shut once more, and she pointed off into the distance.

"Go."

The two marines moved around the edge of the corridor and opened fire. Both were using the low-power settings on their weapons, a mode that increased rate of fire at the expense of damage and penetration. Nate had little doubt the reason was to limit the damage to Relentless as much as possible. The last thing any of them wanted was a breach in the outer hull.

*Look at her!*

For a brief moment, Nate was entranced. He watched Private Valentine fire burst after burst and then pull to the one side. A thermal round struck the nearest bulkhead and showered her in red-hot sparks. The marine leaned to one side and returned fire, never once flinching from what had to be done. The entire episode played out as though in slow motion. Then everything began to speed up, with a mixture of screaming, gunfire, and shouting.

"Run!"

Nate had no idea who was speaking, but needed no further encouragement. Captain Dreuc was already moving, and he followed right behind. As they rounded the first bend, he threw a quick glance back at the furious firefight. The two marines were outnumbered, yet neither was giving ground, and then they were gone. Nate and Captain Dreuc moved through an array of corridors, and to his surprise they found every single secondary hatch and seal locked. As they moved back, he stopped at any of the remaining passageway blast doors and locked them as they went through.

*What are we doing?*

After what seemed like an age, they rounded a corner and directly into another marine, as well as Captain Galanos herself. Like the marines, she also wore full PDS Alpha body armour, and in her hands she carried the venerable L52 carbine. Her first words were to the alien, and then to him.

"Cadet. So, the Byotai are engaged. Can they hold?"

Nate licked his lower lip.

"For now, Captain. Private Valentine told me they needed you to hit them, hard and fast, Sir. Her words."

Captain Galanos grinned.

"I intend on doing just that."

She then nodded at the Byotai weapon in Nate's hands.

"Take the safety off. Can you use it?"

Nate could have shouted at himself for being so stupid. This particular Byotai weapon had a time-sensitive safety unit. If it were unused for more than five minutes or so, it would revert to its safe state. He had actually deactivated it the moment he'd been handed the weapon. The small bar near the trigger had pushed out and emitted a faint, barely perceivable glow. He pushed it in, and a gentle hum echoed through the unit.

"Yes, Captain. I can use it."

Captain Galanos remained impassive as he made the weapon ready for battle.

"Very well. Come with us."

The two PDS armoured warriors moved into the next passageway and towards a closed blast door. This part of the ship was less often travelled and a much narrow section barely wide enough for two people side by side. The door opened as they approached and gave access to a small cylindrical room, itself leading to additional doors. The three moved inside, but as Nate entered, the other two stopped.

"Ready, Captain."

The Captain glanced at the weapon and gave him a brief smile.

"Good work, Cadet."

The two were now waiting, and Nate stopped once he was in front of the hatch entrance, assuming they would enter first. The first marine had moved his head inside, but Captain Galanos pulled him back and shook her head.

"No, he can go first."

She then looked to Nate.

"Take the lead, Cadet, and keep your head down."

Being the smallest of the three, he was much more suited to the narrow passage. Even so, he stopped to check with the Captain.

"Sir, are you..."

"Cadet Lewis. The passage is narrow. You can enter without making much noise. Check it is clear. We will follow."

Nate moved into the darker passageway and turned sideways. He might have been smaller than the other two, but it was still quite a tight fit. At least twice his back scraped along the wall, and each time he almost panicked at the sound it made. He could not see the Byotai from here, but the sound of battle was definitely close. He looked down at his own weapon and suddenly felt incredibly vulnerable.

*Where are they?*

He looked to his left and saw the armoured face of Captain Galanos looking at him.

"Keep going," she said quietly.

Nate took another long breath and moved another six metres before clambering out of the narrow gap. The main lights were off, and only a secondary light flickered in the distance. The passage was tall and narrow, with the ceiling filled with pipes. Every two metres a pair of bulkhead sections pushed out, narrowing the space even more.

*Don't stop now.*

Nate moved one foot at a time, working his way through the section until finally reaching the halfway point. The bulkheads were narrowest here and gave a view of two new corridors. A light flashed to the left, followed by shooting. He pulled himself to the bulkhead and peered around the side. There was nobody there, but off into the corridor were shadows, and multiple flashes just like there had been near Private Valentine.

*It's them.*

Nate looked back. Both PDS armoured marines were looking back at him from the other side of the narrow section. He crept back to them, doing his best as before to make little noise. He pushed his head inside and whispered.

"It's them, Sir. The Byotai are to the left, at the end of the corridor. I can hear them talking."

The two warriors looked to each other, and then Captain Galanos began to climb through. She paused and lifted her left arm, pointing ahead. Compared to Nate's, her hand was massive inside its armoured gauntlet.

"Wait at the end. Cover us."

Nate needed no encouragement and headed back to the end of the long section and waited. Unlike the marine issue PDS Alpha armour, his lacked the sensors and tracking equipment. Once there he had to rely upon his own sight and hearing. He had run through Marine simulations a few times before, but he'd always been kitted out with the latest issue gear. He'd never felt quite so vulnerable as he did right now. A quick glance around the corner at least confirmed that the Byotai were not about to kill him. The hairs rose on the back of his neck, and he twisted around as Captain Galanos pulled herself forcibly through the gap. Her armour screeched as she twisted and turned, and Nate felt his chest pounding, expecting the enemy to appear at any moment.

*The gun!*

He looked down and checked the gun for the tenth time; the ever-real fear of being confronted by an enemy and then failing, all for the simple reason of forgetting to take off the safety. Unknown to him, the safety only reactivated when a hand was removed from the weapon. It was still live, and the gently green glow was just enough to help calm his nerves. He exhaled at the exact same moment an armoured hand touched his shoulder.

"Good work, Cadet Lewis. Follow us."

The group of three moved through the gap and into the primary shaft. The more heavily armoured marines moved first, and Nate quickly forgot that one of them was actually the Captain. She moved little differently to the marine, and he began to wonder if at some point in the past she had been one of the rough and ready marines, like Sergeant Perkins or Private Valentine.

"Clear," said the marine.

Captain Galanos indicated with her left hand to move on.

"Continue."

All three moved at a fast walk, but with their weapons lifted and ready to fire. They were now in the passageway, and it was much bigger than the previous one. It curved gently to the left where it followed the same path as the cooling pipes. The ship might have been old, but she was very well maintained. Even this far from the main passages, the deck was clean, and every single compartment and storage locker correctly sealed. Cables were fitted up out of the way and wrapped around the many clamps fitted throughout. Nate spotted several more drawings, each carefully drawn, using thick paint that was still visible to the touch. He made a mental note to come back to look at them, if and when they were victorious in their battle.

"Stay focussed," said the Captain.

As they rounded the last part, they moved into an oddly shaped hall with a thin railing running along the right. A drop of three metres on the other side led into a chamber filled with locked doors and a pair of airlock doors. One led off to the right, and the other to the left where a furious firefight was going on. Captain Galanos moved to the ledge and took aim.

"Aim," she whispered.

Nate moved up alongside her and took aim with his weapon, remembering to check the timed safety once more. He looked down. There were two Byotai soldiers off to the left, constantly ducking back from the corridor where they were being hit by incredible firepower. From here it might seem an entire squad was shooting, but Nate knew it was actually only two marines, Sergeant Perkins and Private Valentine.

"Wait," said Captain Galanos.

Off to the right were another pair of Byotai, but they were partially obscured by a tall bulkhead pillar. As one moved into view, Nate saw it was positioning a motorised gun platform. It was substantial in size and already blocked line of sight to most of the warriors. Behind the platform was the fourth of the group. As well as the wheels and primary weapon, there was a thick shield plate mounted on top of the gun platform. The unit made a screeching sound as it dragged along the floor, and then for some reason, it stopped. Nate's finger moved over the trigger, but he still waited for the signal from the Captain. Her hand lifted up in a hold position.

"Not yet," she said quietly, "Look."

The large doorway into the chamber flickered with light, and two more Byotai rushed in. Coilgun projectiles clattered around them, and one glanced over the last soldier's armour.

*Valentine.*

Nate had no idea how they were doing it, but somehow the two of them were keeping the Byotai at bay. Another staggered into the chamber and howled with pain. It grabbed a shoulder plate, tugged at it, and cast the broken section to the floor. It then moved further back into the chamber into a position along the side of the weapon platform. Nate could see the caterpillar tracks had locked up on the one side, making it difficult to move, but already they had stopped and rotated the unit to point in the direction of the footsteps.

*They're going to ambush Valentine!*

Nate altered his aim a fraction and pointed the weapon in the direction of the main gunner. As soon as it was in his sights, one of them stopped what it was doing and looked up in their direction. It grunted something, but it was already too late. He began to spin the weapon platform around so that the barrels pointed up at the ledge.

"Fire!" said the Captain.

154

The coilguns shuddered as they unleashed powerful blasts of projectiles. Unlike the others, Captain Galanos was taking no chances and used the high-power setting. Each time the trigger was pulled, the carbine accelerated three solid slugs together and fired them in a dense pattern at the target.

*Shoot!*

Nate squeezed the trigger, and the weapon snapped back under his arm. The shot was wide, so he fired three more, but only by the fifth did he hit the weapon platform. Each round sent a shower of hot sparks over the target. At least two Byotai were cut down by the time the platform was pointed up at them, and then it opened fire. All three threw themselves to the ground as it tore up bulkheads, doors, and panels with ease.

"Stay down!" Captain Galanos shouted.

The clattering and thudding of the gun went on for an age. It then stopped to be followed by shouting and a myriad of other weapon sounds. Nate lifted his head and looked over the ledge. Two marines were in the chamber, and all but one of the Byotai soldiers dead.

"Chamber's secure, Sir. Looks like we've got a prisoner."

Nate recognised the voice of Private Valentine immediately. He watched her manhandle the soldier from behind the weapon. The Byotai was much bigger than the marine, yet she lifted him as though he was little more than a heavy child. When she looked back up, her visor was open and she smiled. Nate was sure it was towards him, but Captain Galanos was already giving orders. He watched in silence at the scene of the bloodbath. More crew had arrived and were helping to move the bodies; two more helped carry away the corpse of the dead marine.

*That could have been me.*

Nate couldn't be sure he'd even hit the Byotai, and as he watched the bodies taken away, he hoped he hadn't. A quick glance to his weapon showed it was deactivated. He moved his hand to check. Captain Galanos was looking at him.

"Well done, Cadet."

Nate tried to look confident.

"Thank you, Sir."

She then extended her hands to take the weapon.

"I suggest you join your comrades and take an hour. Get some food, and try and calm yourself down. I think you all deserve it."

Nate was a little confused at the request.

"Food, Sir?"

The Captain turned completely around and pulled at the seal on her armour. The helmet clicked, and she removed it to reveal her baldhead.

"Yes, Cadet, food. Trust me; based on what Lieutenant Higgins has prepared for you, you'll need it. Three hours, and then you'll be back to your duties."

"What about the..."

"Byotai?"

Captain Galanos looked back to the scene of the fight.

"Only six of them revealed themselves. We'll search Relentless from bow to stern to see if we have any more stowaways."

She gazed at the young cadet, realising in that instant how serious the effect of the fight was having on him. She was tempted to send him to the counsellor, but then, of course, there was no counsellor anymore.

*Any chance of having somebody on board to help him was lost when we blasted away from the starbase. Now he will have to manage on his own.*

"There will be a time to reflect on this, Cadet Lewis, but that is not for today. In forty hours we will reach our destination, and I need Relentless ready for battle. Can you do that?"

Nate licked his lips, straightened his back, and nodded quickly.

"Yes, Sir, I can do that."

"Good, very good."

Captain Galanos felt a pang of guilt. She didn't know whether Nate had noticed, but the shot that killed the second Byotai soldier had been a thermal bolt, fired from a Byotai weapon. She saw him looking at the carnage and stepped in the way.

"For now your job is done, Cadet. You are dismissed."

And as quickly as that, Nate's first experience of combat was over.

# CHAPTER NINE

**Alliance Armoured Assault Ship 'ANS Relentless'**
**Day 4**

Nate wandered onto the hangar deck much more quickly than he'd intended. After all the excitement of the gun battle with the Byotai, his pulse was still racing. This part was well lit and showed a pattern of large red shapes on the ground, each marking positions to move ordnance and spacecraft. The paint was well worn, and parts used so much little of the red paint remained. Yellow and black chequered outlines marked areas not to cross under any circumstances.

He was moving so fast he almost crashed into Billy who was standing there speechless. The other four were waiting, as well as a small group of marines, all of whom were stripped down to their training fatigues. Nate nodded politely towards Private Valentine. She gave him a barely perceivable nod. He'd tried to find her after the battle, but he'd only found Matilda, and she wouldn't stop talking about their ordeal in the locked crew compartment.

*Great work, Nate, great work. Now who looks like an idiot?*

"Now that you're all here, I'll begin."

Nate twisted about. Lieutenant Higgins and the Byotai captain were present. Both were back in their normal uniforms, and gone was their body armour. The other cadets looked nervous around the Captain, but not Nate. It wasn't that he was now suddenly close to her, just that after the encounter with the Byotai, he was still pumped up on excitement and adrenalin. Captain Galanos started to speak, and her powerful voice boomed through the ship.

"We just survived a major breach by the Byotai. We lost lives, but survived the attack."

Her words were slow, yet every one dripped in the seriousness of the situation.

"In four minutes, Relentless will perform a last rotation, and then start the final deceleration phase towards our objective. That means we have less than thirty-six hours before we arrive, and when we do, I will need fighters on call. Without fighters, I just have an old carrier with limited ammunition and supplies."

The news was not surprising to the group of six. They had all talked about it during breakfast, especially as the Captain had sent out a briefing to all of them via their Secpad devices. There was not much information other than their estimated arrival, and that all had to be ready. The Captain looked directly at Nate.

"All of us, you included, have suffered great trauma; the violent battles on the starbase, our escape, and now this sabotage attempt by the Byotai. I'd like to say the worst is behind us, but I cannot. What lies ahead is uncertain. What I do know is that when pressed, you worked as a group. You have the skills, and over the next day you will gather more experience."

She looked to Lieutenant Higgins, and they exchanged a few quiet words. The Captain reached into her pocket to touch something and then walked out in front of the cadets. Nate noticed her hand come back out empty.

*What was that, a relic, some kind of superstition?*

"I've seen your status reports, and I believe you will do what needs to be done. As of today, the Crusader Squadron has been activated, under the command of Lieutenant Higgins. You will be the eyes and ears of Relentless, and I expect each of you to do whatever is required to keep my ship, and my people, safe."

All six cadets called out in unison.

"Yes, Sir!"

Then the Captain moved along the line.

"Work hard, and I promise you, the name of Crusader Squadron will be

159

remembered."

She turned and walked to the nearest wall. Above her were a series of windows fitted with thick, multi-layered material to protect the inner compartments in case of breaches. The deck team used it to handle flight operations in wartime. The Captain stopped and took something as big as her hand from inside her tunic. She held it up and then slid the electronic tag plate to the sliders on the wall. It slid into place without a sound, flashed, and then lit up with a new name. Nate looked at it, and no matter how hard he tried, he could not hide his smile.

*1st Crusader Squadron!*

The name was not of their choosing, and in fact taken from their tournament name in the Star Crusader simulation. Each team needed a name, and of them all, the Crusader title had potentially been the least exciting name used. Now it had become permanently associated with the cadets and taken on a life of its own. Captain Galanos left the deck. Within a few more seconds it was just the Lieutenant, six cadets, and a pair of deck crew who moved off into the distance.

"So far you've trained on the Lightning fighters. That's all well and good, but you will not be climbing inside these fine old machines. We have only the four, and there is a lot more to flying them than just the simulators."

He sidestepped and pointed to the back of the hangar deck. Unlike the section nearest them, the rear was pitch black. In a spacecraft, the only possibility of seeing an object was through artificial light, and all of that was being projected towards the group of cadet pilots.

"These are your fighters, and I want each of you to treat them like they are your family."

One by one a series of lamps switched on. At first just a few ceilings lights activated, and they cast odd flashes and shadows onto the fighters. Then more came on and revealed the gleaming shapes of the deadly Avengers.

"Relentless is rated to carry manned fighters. The Avengers are here as part of the training detachment, and now they are yours."

160

Nate looked at the shapes, and the Lieutenant's words faded from his mind. He'd seen a few of them when they came aboard the ship. Back then most were covered to protect them from dust. Now all six had been brought out into the light, and he truly felt he'd never seen anything quite as beautiful. At first it wasn't obvious, not until Nate pointed to the nose of the nearest fighters. One of the civilian workers had clearly been busy, and the imagery of an ancient warrior, cased in metal armour and bearing a sword ran along the nose.

"The Crusaders."

Nate didn't mean to say the name quite so loudly, but in the silent space of the hangar deck it seemed to echo throughout the great space. He looked back, but the other five were not interested in what he had to say. Rex had moved to the guns, Jack and Matilda were examining the opposite side of the fighter. Cassandra and Billy were close by and fascinated by the paintwork.

"I wonder who painted this?" Cassandra asked.

Lieutenant Higgs joined them and touched the side of the drone fighter.

"Two of the civilians pulled from the starbase were artists. They've been helping in the canteen, but when they heard about the Squadron they were...well, let's just say they preferred painting the artwork than preparing another meal."

The quality of the painting was exceptional, and even Matilda seemed impressed by the detail and colour. Lieutenant Higgs pointed at the nearest fighter, one where the helmet bore different colours to the others.

"The Squadron is more than named for the six of you."

Nate and Cassandra turned their attention from the craft and to the officer.

"It is something that gives everybody in this ship hope. The civilians see the fighters as the one thing that will keep them safe, and my crew see you as the payment for the costly evacuation of the starbase. Crusader Squadron is the culmination of all of our efforts, from the engineers, artificers, and mechanics up to the cooks and deck crew. Everybody has something invested in the Crusaders. None of the others seemed to know what to say, but Nate had no such qualms.

"Sir, we will not let them down."

It wasn't much, but it seemed to be enough for Lieutenant Higgins. He gave Nate a short nod and then grabbed onto one of the vertical rails currently raised in the hangar.

"Rotation completes in seven seconds. Hold on."

Each cadet knew what was coming and had experienced the odd feeling multiple times before. They moved to the many grab rails fitted throughout the ship and waited for the inevitable. The fighters, and all loose tooling and equipment were already tied or strapped down. The main engines had been deactivated nearly ten minutes earlier. On a less sophisticated ship this would have meant the complete loss of gravity, but not on Relentless. Like so many older vessels, she had been refitted multiple times to bring her up to something approaching modern specifications. Gone were her old short-range engines, and in the brand-new, long-range pulsed Ion engines with boost extenders. The main powerplant had been changed to the same core used on the powerful Crusader class warships.

More important to the crew than engines or new weapons was the installation of the first generation artificial gravity generators. This one piece of technology made long-duration operations bearable, as well as allowing the crew to stay in top physical condition; more important when accommodating large numbers of marines for tactical deployments. Though the new units were incredibly powerful, even they suffered in the initial bursts of acceleration when engines activated. The ship was technically facing backwards, not that it could be noticed from inside unless one was near a window.

"Now!"

The great ship groaned as her engines activated and then increased in power. They would run at full burn for thirty-six hours, a feat possible only through the use of high-efficiency engines and powerplants. As the groaning sounds settled down, the Lieutenant released his hand on the grab rail and looked to the cadets.

"Okay, then, the die has finally been cast."

Matilda almost snorted at that, but Nate and the others looked none the wiser. Lieutenant Higgins sighed and shook his head before looking along the group.

"So, then, who can tell me the specifications of our state-of-the-art fighters?"

Billy lifted his hand, and the Lieutenant gave him a quick nod.

"They are X57 Avengers, Sir. This is the Mark III, the final development model before the drones went into full production."

"Indeed it is. Twelve months ago the X57 Avenger was put into service as a standard front-line fighter in the Alliance Navy, with the attack drone designation of..."

Matilda lifted a hand slowly. He paused, perhaps wondering if she really knew what she was looking at. He was a pilot of the old school and learnt to fly on the old generation training equipment. He could only imagine what they had seen on the Star Crusader simulation.

"Sir, the Avenger has to use the same nomenclature as all other vessels in the Alliance military. It has now entered service as the MQ-5 Avenger, Sir."

"I see. What else can you tell me about its name?"

"Sir, the M is for its role as a missile carrier, and the Q signified an unmanned drone platform."

"Good. Very good."

The Lieutenant walked back to the drones and signalled for the others to follow. The spacecraft were much bigger than they looked on a computer screen. He stopped on reaching the rear of the first pair.

"I can only assume you have come across these units in your simulated engagements?"

Matilda and Cassandra both nodded in the affirmative at the same time.

"Good. Well, one thing you might not know is that the configuration of the Avenger has been kept something of a secret. Only the first generation specifications were allowed in the simulation. Later models are much...improved."

He indicated to the nearby drone.

"What we have here is the most sophisticated and powerful robotic spacecraft ever used in the Alliance. I'm told that we're coming close to the capabilities of our old friends, the Biomechs. Maybe we are, and maybe we aren't. All I can tell you is that this represents the nest generation in space combat."

Nate looked to Billy and found his friend's mouth was wide open. He would not even have been surprised if he'd been drooling.

"Each Avenger drone packs a single powerplant with eight CVTC Anthros engine outlets."

Nate's eyebrows lifted up. He was all too familiar with the specification in the simulation, and he knew from memory that the Mark I fighters were equipped with only four outlets for flight control. He now began to wonder quite what else might have changed.

"This model develops a total of more than two hundred kilonewtons of thrust. That's adequate for a light manned fighter, but for an unmanned drone it gives you incredible power. Each outlet can be controlled individually to give you manoeuvrability unlike any other spacecraft, and is directly integrated into the flight control computer."

He moved along to the short, bat like wings and reached out to touch them. The overall design strayed greatly from the more traditional design of the Alliance fighters.

"Six eternal pylons, and enough internal space for another fifteen hundred kilograms of ordnance."

Billy bent down and looked up at the tightly fitted bays. They were only visible due to the black lines running around the outer frame, and the small letters and symbols that marked where the locking clamps were installed. Nate moved closer and reached out, placing his hand on the smooth metal. It was much colder than expected, and its surface rough, like an incredibly thin paste had been applied.

"Is this.."

Lieutenant Higgins grinned.

"Nanocrystalline Cellulose paste?"

Nate nodded. "Yes, Sir."

"That's exactly what it is. All four of our birds have the test version. It's thicker than the production model and not as efficient. It will still give you extra protection against fragmentation weapons and shrapnel."

He then grinned.

"Like I said, the final models of the Avenger are rather different to what you've seen before."

Lieutenant Higgins was already moving along the flank of the craft and resting his hand on its fuselage. His fingers moved along the newly dried paint, stopping as they reached the fearsome muzzles of its primary armament.

"All of these weapons are useful, but you must always remember that when it comes to the crunch, there's little out there that can beat quadruple barrelled high-velocity cannons."

The combined barrels took up as much space as his head and protruded out from the fuselage. The muzzles were covered in small circular hinged plates to protect them from dust or other substances. Lieutenant Higgins watched the six cadets run their eyes over the drone's smooth lines.

"These guns are not far off the power of the attack variants of the Lightning, and all combined into the Avenger drone package."

He turned away from the craft and placed his hands on his waist.

"So, all I need to know is this. Is Crusader Squadron ready for drone combat training?"

They looked to each other, and for the first time Nate noticed even Rex seemed excited at the prospect. Only Matilda seemed able to control her feelings, yet she still smiled at this opportunity. One by one the cadets said what he wanted to hear. Satisfied, he pointed back to the noses of the drones. They were lifted up high on their sleds so it was impossible to see quite what he was pointing at from there.

"Each carries your name on its nose. This particular drone belongs to Flight Cadet Rex Hampel. You will learn to fly her and bring her back in one

165

piece as though she was a part of you."

He pointed to another drone and then another, until finally to the one with a massive two-handed sword running along the front flanks. The design was striking and gave the impression the drone was pointing a sword point directly at an enemy.

"This is yours, Cadet Lewis."

The conversation continued, but Nate's mind was in one place, and one place only. The drones were all the same bar their paint scheme, yet this one had taken on a life of its own. By placing his name on its body, it felt more like an avatar than a machine, and he couldn't believe it. Finally, the introduction was over, and the lights switched off until the bulk of the hangar deck was shrouded in darkness.

"So..." said Lieutenant Higgins, "We have one and a half days to get ready. So let's get back to the Fighter Control Suite. We have multiple missions to run, and you need to get familiar with the differences between the fighters and the combat drones. When we arrive, you will no longer be fighter cadets."

He waited as each of them looked back in silence.

"You will be combat pilots."

* * *

ANS Relentless was one of the few ships in the Alliance Navy still equipped with a fully functional brig. It was a modest affair, but with enough space to hold six separate prisoners. Each was tiny, and the outward facing wall composed of a thick cross-section of reinforced steel. A narrow passage in front of the cells was blocked at both ends, with a single narrow door leading into a battered looking foyer. Against the far wall was a transparent security station, now manned by a single marine. There was no way for a prisoner to even move without being observed by those in the station.

The Marine guard stood smartly to attention as the security door leading into the rest of the ship opened. In walked a Marine Sergeant and a

Byotai officer in his off-duty regalia. Both were armed with weapons on their flanks.

"Private," said Sergeant Popwell. He moved up to the security station and stopped, "Here as arranged to speak with the prisoner."

The marine checked a display unit, and then looked to the Sergeant.

"Your sidearm."

Sergeant Popwell moved his hand to his weapon. The guard instinctively reached for his own and waited for the weapon to be handed over.

"And him?"

The Private nodded at the alien. Sergeant Popwell looked to Captain Dreuc and nudged him. The Byotai officer grunted and then reached for his own weapon, before handing to the Private. Both weapons were placed in a sealed unit to the side and then locked.

"Through the security seal."

The Private moved from his station and to the side of the door. With his right hand on his weapon, his left put the series of codes into the panel. The door then slowly opened.

"Inside please."

Both guests entered through the doorway and into the corridor on the other side. They now had the perfect view of the six cells, all but one of which were unoccupied. Sergeant Popwell moved in front of the sealed cell door, but it remained closed until the door leading back to the security station was correctly sealed. The Private was already back at his post and activating the security protocol.

"Five...four..."

With a clunk sound, the security bars moved into position, and the two visitors were locked out from the rest of the ship.

"Just say the word, Sergeant, and the area will be cleansed."

"Understood, Private. We'll be fine, just fine."

He moved to the cell door and hit the access panel. The bars slid off to the sides, as well as a thick section that slid down into the floor. The door then opened outwards, revealing the tiny space inside, along with the prisoner.

"Well, hello, my little friend," said Sergeant Popwell.

The cell lacked anything that could be used by the occupant, all apart from a small shelf to sit or sleep on. Neither guest was interested in the facilities, but only in the bulky form of the Byotai warrior. Based on the colouring on the face, it was clearly male, and a thick metal plate had been clamped over a field dressing on his upper arm.

"We're here for a little chat," said the Sergeant.

So far the marine was speaking in his own language, and he knew quite well that there was almost no chance the Byotai understood him. The many races of the Helion Nexus had been in contact with humanity for little more than a generation, and so far nothing even close to a lingua franca had developed. He looked to his right and nodded for Captain Dreuc to enter. The wounded officer moved through the doorway and garnered an immediate reaction. The Byotai soldier remained seated, but as he turned his attention back to Sergeant Popwell, he looked up, opened his mouth, and let out a long hiss. Sergeant Popwell ran his right hand over his Secpad bracelet and activated the translator circuit. As he spoke, the unit recorded the strings of text, translated them, regurgitating them via its external speaker hole in the Byotai language.

"I take it he's not happy at seeing you?"

Captain Dreuc glanced at the Sergeant and made an odd sound at the back of his throat. He looked to the soldier and moved closer. The two exchanged angry words for almost a minute. Finally, Captain Dreuc turned his attention back to the Sergeant.

"Well, explain."

Captain Dreuc spoke, and the Secpad based translator did its job.

"He is part of the Crimson Company, and he wants to die."

Sergeant Popwell looked surprised.

"The what?"

"The Company is one of the many agitating groups among my people.

Most are young, looking for changes in our society."

He looked back at the other Byotai.

"He will not tell me his name, but I can tell from the way he speaks that he is another of the plebiscite movement. They want to destroy our way of life, break up the great households of the Patricians, and redistribute our resources."

Sergeant Popwell lifted his hands.

"Okay, slow down. I don't need to know any of this. All the Captain wants is to know why they were here, and what they know."

Captain Dreuc waited for the translation, and then nodded in the way he'd already learnt from the humans.

"Very well, give me ten minutes, and I will have what you require."

He stepped fully into the cell, looking back at the reinforced security door.

"Close it behind me, and do not enter under any circumstances."

Sergeant Popwell hesitated but pressed the button to start the locking procedure. As soon as it clunked shut, the Captain lurched at the prisoner, put both hands around his throat, and lifted him up from his seated position.

"Hvers vegna rathast a menn?"

The prisoner said nothing at first, but Captain Dreuc was having none of it. He gripped even more tightly and thrust the wounded soldier to the wall. The very bones of the soldier began groaning under the pressure until finally his will broke. The soldier answered a number of short questions, and in less than ten minutes, the entire affair was over. Captain Dreuc signalled to be let out. When the door opened, he walked out. Sergeant Popwell noticed the clenched fists and the taut muscles. The colour of his dry skin has become much darker, with almost black patterns showing on the lighter sections. The door clunked shut behind him, and the prisoner slid bitterly to the floor. Captain Dreuc looked back at the prisoner and said just one word. He returned his gaze to Sergeant Popwell.

"We have a problem, Sergeant, a very big problem. I need to speak with Captain Galanos, immediately!"

The CIC was dimly lit, the majority of the light coming from the displays and computer monitors. For the first time in many hours the place was quiet. With Relentless hurtling through space, there was little need for most of the senior officers. Captain Galanos knew how long they had until they arrived at their destination, right down to the second, and she was using that time to rest her crew as much as possible. She remained on the bridge, along with two junior officers to monitor the systems. Opposite her were Sergeant Popwell and Captain Dreuc.

The silence was broken as the Captain let out a single, long breath. Captain Galanos looked at the Byotai officer with an incredulous look on her face. She'd heard all sorts of stories and rumours, but nothing had quite prepared her for what he had just put forward. She turned her gaze to Sergeant Popwell, but as she was about to speak, Lieutenant Higgins appeared.

"Apologies, Sir. I came as quickly as I could."

Captain Galanos didn't seem particularly bothered and waited there, shaking her head. Lieutenant Higgins looked throughout the CIC and then back to the Captain, waiting for her to speak. It may have only been for a few seconds, but the mood and tension was palpable.

"Lieutenant, it would appear we have found ourselves in the middle of a massive and violent revolutionary movement throughout the Byotai Empire."

Lieutenant Higgins was not entirely surprised at this news.

"Yes, Captain, that makes sense. The demographic on the starbase was made up of all castes, bar the patrician caste."

The Captain shook her head and cut him off, as though irritated by his very words.

"No, you do not understand."

She walked to the vertical display and wiped off everything, replacing it with a single map of the Helion Nexus. At the centre were the Helion Star

Systems, and connected to them the empires of the various different races. On the top right was the vast region known as the Byotai Empire. She placed her hand there and pointed to the region directly opposite it.

"A revolution has been declared from within the ruins of the border worlds of the Tenth Quadrant. As you know, both the wandering tribal fleets of the Anicinàbe and the settlers of the Byotai have been fighting there for more than a decade."

She moved her hand in front of the display and drew a wide blue oval shape that encompassed both massive regions, and then turned to face Lieutenant Higgins.

"If our Byotai guest is correct, and the information he just extracted from the prisoner is true, then we are in serious trouble. And I'm not just talking about this ship."

She shook her head in astonishment.

"Very big trouble."

"I...uh...I don't understand, Sir."

The Captain continued to shake her head as she explained. Her tone was completely at odds with the words, and she was clearly having great difficulty in understanding what had occurred. This intrigued Lieutenant Higgins even further.

"The prisoner is a soldier from the so-called Crimson Company, a paramilitary group originating in the Byotai industrial sector. They've joined with hundreds of other groups, from tradesmen and miners to engineers and diplomats. Apparently, most of the shipping workers and large numbers of ship crews have also joined."

Captain Galanos stopped and looked back at the vertical display. She shook her head and spoke quietly to herself. Lieutenant Higgins had never seen her this way, but he was just as surprised to hear the prisoner had been so free with the information.

"This information, Sir. Is it verifiable? Can it be trusted?"

Captain Galanos shrugged.

"No to both of those questions, and right now, I do not see how it would make any difference. The only facts we have are that the Byotai have betrayed us, and that the majority are from the plebiscite movement. They have turned on us and killed where they can. This boarding party waited until the perfect opportunity before striking. If they had been successful, we would be adrift and vulnerable to attack, perhaps even destroyed."

"Sir, the boarding party was a suicide raid?"

Captain Galanos shook her head.

"No, they were here to slow us down. I suspect to buy time for our pursuers. The Byotai do not want us sharing what we have found. As I suspected, they will close access to all Spacebridges, and that will give us little choice on what to do next."

Lieutenant Higgins had one last question, but Captain Galanos didn't appear to notice. She looked at the vertical display and the dispersion of the different star systems.

"If what the prisoner is saying is true, then Anicinàbe tribes and members of the plebiscite movement among the Byotai are joining forces. Between them, they have the numbers and resources to bring down both territories."

Captain Galanos rubbed her forehead in frustration.

"This is an auspicious day for all of us. The Anicinàbe and the Byotai have a chance at unifying under the dictatorship of this new revolutionary movement, and if they are successful, they will be able to create a regional power unlike anything we've ever seen before."

She looked to them and smiled, doing her best to provide hope.

"None of this matters to us today, though, does it? We have a job to do, and it is a simple one, to escape the clutches of the Byotai and rejoin the fleet. To your stations, and make sure you're ready. We arrive shortly."

# CHAPTER TEN

**Alliance Armoured Assault Ship 'ANS Relentless'**
**On final approach to the Arnos Cluster**
**Day 6**

The powerful engines of ANS Relentless increased in power as the ship began the last stage of its trip. Their journey had taken days, and in the haste to escape the Byotai, the ship burned its main engines four hours longer than intended before rotation. This subtle alteration in the flight-plan meant they would overshoot their target, even with their engines running while travelling in reverse. The solution was a simple one, but it had put the old ship under a great deal of strain. Now the engines were burning fifty percent more than normal, all to decelerate in time to reach their objective. Every few seconds the coolant units would send a shudder through the ship as they vented heated gas to the void. To any external observer it would look as the though the ship was on fire and leaving a trail behind her.

Captain Galanos was at her post in the heart of the CIC, surrounded by those officers that remained. Gone was her executive officer, killed in the bloody attack as they escaped the starbase. She looked at the timer once more and then activated the intercom.

"This is the Captain. We arrive at the Arnos Cluster and our rendezvous with the fleet in T-minus forty-six minutes. Have your stations ready and check in with your deck officers. We don't know what to expect, but we will be ready."

The Captain looked at the vertical display. It was partially obscured by the countdown clock. Normally, it was a lot smaller, but as they reached the last hour, the significance of those minutes had grown. She looked to her assorted group of officers. There were also two civilians, both taking over the communication and engineering stations.

"There are no replacement bases, starbases, or Spacebridges within a week's travel of this location. What it lacks in facilities it more than makes up for in raw resources, and in safety. Once within the Cluster, we will be shielded from any attempts to locate us. I'm relying on each of you to do your job. Be ready, and stay alert."

* * *

**Alliance Armoured Assault Ship 'ANS Relentless'**
**Fighter Control Suite**
Nate had been waiting in the control suite for fifteen minutes, and the tension was palpable. All six of them were there, but still no sign of Lieutenant Higgins. For the first time, Rex appeared nervous, but it might just as easily have been he was too busy thinking about what was to come. Billy, as usual, tried to change the mood of the group, with little success.

"Well, looks like it's time, doesn't it?"

Jack was at Rex's flank, just as always, and shook his head in the direction of Billy.

"Of course it's time. That's why we're here."

Nate looked to Cassandra and at her pale face. Her long blonde hair was smart and pulled back, though where she found the time to do that he would never know. She lifted her left hand to brush a hair from her brow and spotted Nate looking at her. Normally, she would have been harsh towards him, or at the very least attempting to assert herself. Based on previous experience that was what he would have expected. This time she actually smiled, and that one act put him immediately off-guard.

"You okay, Nate?"

Each word slowed him down, and it took several seconds before he was able to reply.

"I'm okay. A bit nervous about the mission."

The door opened as Rex began to laugh at Nate. The sound of laughter quickly dissipated as the upright form of Lieutenant Higgins entered the suite. The cadets faced him and stood upright to attention.

"As you were, Flight Cadets."

It was only a single extra word, but the addition made all the difference to the six of them. Gone were the days when they were lowly cadets, whose only significance to the ship was that they had been rescued, and at great cost. Now the six were known as Crusader Squadron and the effect on the passengers and crew had been substantial. ANS Relentless had been a ship without pilots. Now she carried a squadron, however untested they might be.

"We will arrive at the rendezvous shortly, and it will be down to all of you to do your part. The last simulations were successful, but you will have to work closer together than ever before."

He focused his attention on Rex.

"Of all six pilots, you are the most gifted."

Rex loved this kind of attention, and he glanced at Nate.

"Your skills at piloting all fighters is exceptional, and the Avenger is no different. You are the best qualified to take on and engage enemy fighters."

He lifted his right hand and pointed at the cadet.

"But just remember, on your own you are nothing. Without your team, you will die as easily as any other pilot."

Next came Jack. Though the smallest of the group, he was ever the angry looking one.

"Aggression is your strength...and your weakness. Control your feelings and concentrate on the mission, above all else. Combined with Rex, you are a formidable combination."

Matilda looked to Cassandra when the Lieutenant turned his attention to her. Your flying is adequate, but your attention to detail is exceptional, as is your strategic understanding. I expect great things of you, one day. For now, I will expect you to lead Crusader Squadron with the skill you have demonstrated in the simulations."

Matilda nodded politely, watching with interest as Lieutenant Higgins hobbled along to the last three. He stopped in front of Cassandra.

"Like Flight Cadet Hampel, your skills are in your flying. There is little to tell the two of you apart in combat, and the competiveness has no place in battle. Curb this and concentrate on the mission. Listen to your flight leader."

That left just Nate and Billy, and the Lieutenant looked at them both, speaking to them collectively.

"Individually, the two of you have strengths and weaknesses, but together you are the best pair in the squadron. Flight Cadet Lewis, your flying is by the book, technical and of a high quality. You would make an excellent flying instructor. What you lack in flair you make up for in consistency."

The man's eyes barely moved as they turned to Billy.

"Flight Cadet William Mitchell. Your background inspires little confidence, and I've seen the report on your...incidents at your previous college. Your scores are low in mathematics, engineers, and even strategy and tactics."

Rex chuckled, and Lieutenant Higgins spun around to face the sneering teenager.

"Yet this cadet is the single best wingman of the six of you. In simulations, he has stuck with his partner, no matter the danger. Your eyesight and observational skills are above average, and you give the Squadron additional backbone."

Lieutenant Higgins twisted his back a moment, doing his best to avoid the pain running up through his spine. The injuries from the starbase assault were going to be with him for the rest of his life, and the painkillers, combined with the anti-inflammatory drugs, could only do so much. With a final movement, he stepped back to look at the group. Though hardly an old man, he certainly felt it as he looked across to the group of six cadets. They were no older than he was back in his Academy days, but for some reason they seemed so young.

"Your birds are fuelled. The deck crews have sent them topside to the launch deck. There's no faster way to get into action, and it will allow the

176

hangar doors to stay sealed. Now remember, we only have the six, so no fooling around. I want each of them back in the same condition you found them in. Understood?"

All six acknowledged immediately, and he nodded back at them in satisfaction.

"Six pilots, and six Avengers. Today is a special day for all of us, but especially for you. Crusader Squadron is loaded and armed for reconnaissance and escort duty. So watch those triggers. You'll have the firepower to crippled Relentless if you make any mistakes."

Billy looked to Nate with wide-open eyes that betrayed his excitement. They'd been playing the Star Crusader simulation for so long now neither could remember the first time. Yet, after all those sessions in the simulators, they had never once been able to actually fire a live weapon. Even more pertinent, the only thing on the line had been personal glory and the opportunity for advancement in the Academy programme.

"This time it's real, Nate."

"I know. Are you ready?"

Billy nodded slowly.

"You know something? I think I am."

Lieutenant Higgins moved to the pit and activated the unit. A model of the ship appeared in the centre and then shrunk away to show the surrounding area.

"We're already entering the boundary areas of the Deadlands. We cannot scan the interior at this range."

Nate looked at the others. Cassandra's eyes were looking right back at him. As they met, she quickly looked away. Normally, Nate would have done the same, but something felt different. They were dressed in the Naval issue PDS gear, their nametags displaying both their names and the newly christened squadron. At close inspection, the text was rough and had been put together by a volunteer on the ship. Much more important to Nate, it made them feel they were a valued part of the ship's crew.

"Cassandra. Are you up for this?"

Again she gave him that nervous smile.

"Oh, yes, I'm sure of it."

Lieutenant Higgins nodded at the seating positions.

"Okay, then, it's time to mount up. Run through your final checks and prepare for launch. We've got little over half an hour, perhaps less. We need to be ready for whatever might happen. Are you with me?"

Each of the cadets, even Matilda and Rex seemed excited.

"Yes, Lieutenant!"

* * *

The Arnos Cluster was one small part of the Deadlands, yet its total space still larger than the combined territories of Proxima Centauri and the old worlds of Sol. The Cluster was the largest and most dangerous part of the Deadlands, and contained more than fifty percent of all matter in the Deadlands. The Arnos Cluster swirled around a single black hole that busily consumed anything coming close to it as it slowly removed everything around it. Every year the Black Hole reduced the integrity of the Arnos Spacebridge, a celestial phenomena that allowed instant travel to the disputed Tenth Quadrant, an area now a bloody warzone.

ANS Relentless plunged into the heart of the Cluster at great speed, her engines burning brightly. From the outside all seemed well, but inside the powerful klaxons played their grim song, as the mighty warship unleashed a final burst of power. This was more than four times the standard, and a desperate attempt to end their journey nearly a million kilometres from the destination. Such an emergency halt was unprecedented and placed enormous strains on the engines, powerplant, and even the hull of the massive vessel. More modern ships, such as the venerable Liberty class destroyers, would suffer under such high levels of energy. As each second passed by, a series of pipes burst, seals blasted open, and electrical circuits disintegrated, yet still the engines roared and sent great gouts of flame ahead of the ship. To a third party it might look as though it was actually in the process of landing on a planetary body, rather than desperately trying to slow down.

ANS Relentless was already through the outer regions of the Deadlands, a place that could prove deadly to a ship in unfamiliar territory. The entire region was littered with the remnants of old stars, moons, and planets; the name apt for something often described by the Byotai as the graveyard of worlds. The situation had changed for Relentless and her crew as the sector altered beyond recognition due to the ever-shifting landscape. The plan was for the ship to continue on this current course while decelerating over an additional ten million kilometres before finally cutting the main engines. But the complexity and density of the debris field forced the Captain to cut their journey short and bring them down to conventional speeds much further away than intended.

At this point in the Arnos Cluster, the debris was sparse but consisted of massive asteroids, some of which were easily big enough to form small worlds on their own. The target location was hidden almost a full astronomical unit away, deep inside the cluster of dust and small rocks that made the use of sensors almost impossible. As the final burst of power subsided, the ship groaned, the sound and vibrations being noticeable anywhere in the vessel. The primary engines cut, and the great warship rotated into its standard position. The helmsman looked over to Captain Galanos and nodded.

"Captain, we're under standard drive, one quarter speed, and on approach to the designated coordinates. Estimated penetration of the inner fields in four minutes."

"Very good."

She looked over her right shoulder to her new Chief Engineer, an older man known as Martin Newman with a background in shipbuilding and starship engine management. He still looked uncomfortable in the CIC, yet he remained calm, and his knowledge of engineering matters was as good as anything she could expect to find in the normal officer corps.

"How long until our scanners can penetrate the field?"

The man checked the computers for almost ten more seconds before answering. Normally, this would have caused quite a ruckus in the CIC, but he was being careful, and making sure the information he obtained was up-to-date and accurate.

"Captain. We will need to breach the inner wall of debris before any of our sensors will have much of a chance. I've never seen anything quite like this. We will have to make our way carefully inside. I estimate that once we're through, it could take anything from thirty minutes to an hour at this speed."

Captain Galanos looked back at the screen. She'd anticipated getting much closer to the target, but a single piece of astronomical flotsam had disintegrated in the last few days and had now completely altered their angle of approach. She spoke quietly, more to herself than to anyone present.

"This site was chosen more than four months ago as the regrouping location for any ships in this sector. And now, for some unexpected reason, there has been a major shift."

Her hands moved quickly, tagging various objects for the crew to assess, while constantly checking the route through the debris. Even she was surprised at the density of the Cluster.

*It is certainly ideal as a discreet location for a fleet rendezvous. Assuming anybody else made it.*

Captain Galanos looked back at the external feeds and watched a large chunk of matter drift by. None came to within even a hundred kilometres of their ship, but in space that was effectively point blank range. What confused her was why so much had changed since the Alliance survey ships made the same trip. She ran her hands on the approach path and shook her head.

"Wait a minute."

A quick twist of her neck brought her around to face a smaller display. In the middle was a list of known ships in the area, their last recorded location, and the projected routes they would take to reach the Arnos Cluster. Two in particular should have travelled through this exact same location. Even as she looked, a sickening feeling crept up into her stomach.

"You'd think something new and violent occurred out here before we arrived. Like a..."

It became immediately obvious to her, and for a few seconds, she was unable to speak as the magnitude of what might have happened occurred to her.

"I want all sensors on. Give me a full tactical and chemical assessment of the immediate area. What exactly as we moving through?"

The small cadre of officers returned to their systems and began the painstaking task of setting parameters for the myriad of sensors. Using them would announce their presence to any ship in the area but would also find anything hidden, right down to the size of a human-sized object. Object penetrating radar could even provide the detailed shape and makeup of the most damaged and irregular shapes, and then each piece would be crosschecked and analysed by the computer.

"Anything?"

The ship continued on its course, the helmsman making constant corrections as they past the drifting field of debris. Captain Galanos looked at the vertical tactical display in silence. The secondary screens showed objects in all directions, none appeared more than rock or ice. Then Engineer Newman spoke, and everything changed.

\* \* \*

**Alliance Armoured Assault Ship 'ANS Relentless'**
**Fighter Control Suite**
Nate sat in silence waiting for orders. His five comrades were in exactly the same position, but there was no talking or idle conversation. Nate was busy running through the checklists for the fifth time in a row. There was a lot to manage with the drone, from power usage and armour settings, through to fuel burns rates and trim controls. The majority could be left on automatic, but the last thirty-six hours had shown even a few minor tweaks could make the difference between adequate performance and victory.

The drones had been in this position for only a few minutes when the klaxon sounded. An image of Captain Galanos popped up in the corner of the video overlay.

"This is the Captain. Brace for immediate deceleration. Our target destination has experienced a change in dispersion pattern. I repeat, brace for immediate deceleration."

The image vanished just as quickly as it had arrived, and once again Nate was on his own. Strapped into the seat, it was almost impossible for there to be any kind of an issue for him, no matter how hard the deceleration was. The inertial system was coupled to the gravitometric generators, and that would take the sting out of the enormous pressures against the ship's hull. Even so, there was still the chance the immense energies could throw the flight cadets about.

Lieutenant Higgins' voice returned, and for a moment, Nate did not even realise the man was speaking, so entranced was he by the amounts of data coming at him from all directions.

*Wake up, you fool! Get with it.*

"Pilots. As you heard, we are slowing down, and it's happening fast. Make your final checks and wait for my command."

Nate licked his lips with anticipation. They could be just seconds away from a launch now, and as he waited, he imagined the myriad of scenarios that could occur upon leaving the ship. Images of dogfighting with enemy fighters through to capital ship engagements appeared and vanished with equal speed. At the same time, he went through the checklist, just as requested by the Lieutenant. It was all second nature now, but he forced himself to reread every section. Routine bred laziness and could result in mistakes, and they had been reminded time and time again what would happen if they got anything wrong.

*Waiting, always waiting!*

Nate had heard that was always the worst part, and now that he was ready for combat, he finally understood what they were talking about. Sitting inside the drone, and with no access to the outside world, was becoming frustrating. With his helmet fitted and the computer active, he was completely cut off from the interior of the ship. Unless he thought hard about his situation, it was easy to visualise himself sitting inside the drone, as though he was the pilot of a Lightning fighter.

The wait went on for seconds, and then minutes. The forward display through the virtual cockpit showed nothing outside of the fighter other than dorsal hangar doors leading out onto the flattop launching deck. When fully equipped with a full quota of spacecraft it was useful to have multiple launch and landing points. It would be possible to conduct both launch and resupply operations from the exterior of the ship, on what looked like a conventional flattop. The flank hangar doors could then be sealed against possible attacks.

Four of the Avenger drones waited inside the ship, sitting patiently on their ramps, but not these two. The fighters controlled by Nate and Billy were on the interceptor ramps, just waiting for the signal to launch. Each fighter was fully fuelled, as Lieutenant Higgins had promised, and loaded and armed for combat. Then the face of the Lieutenant popped up once more, and this time his expression had changed. At the same time, the outer doors opened up to reveal the blackness of space. At least that's what Nate expected to see. Instead it was a collection of shapes rushing past at great speed. It was as though they were hurtling through a dust cloud.

"We're heading through a thick curtain of dust, ice, and debris. I need two of you to guide us through. This is for Crusader Three and Four."

The mapping orb updated to show the objects around the ship. Nate moved his eyes and tagged various objects, quickly orientating himself. He could see the path they were taking and the nearest large objects. It was a much denser field than they were told to expect.

"There's something else," said Lieutenant Higgins.

Nate knew that tone even after the few days he'd spent aboard the ship. The officer rarely showed any form of emotion, but this was one Nate had seen during their final escape from the Byotai starbase, an event that now seemed months or even years ago.

"Scanners show ship plating debris of unknown origin. There appears to have been combat here at some point. It could be a coincidence, or the sign of something much more serious."

"Sir," said Nate, "Is it wise to continue to the destination vector under these circumstances?"

Lieutenant Higgins looked just as pained as he answered the obvious question.

"Son, we have no choice anymore. Relentless is down to twenty percent fuel reserves. We were only half fuelled at the Mognathus 7 Starbase. Expenditure during the escape, as well as leaks from the battle, has left us weakened."

A number of icons flashed up, one large one marking the final destination of the carrier. A dotted line moved back to the ship, along with multiple course corrections required to make it through while avoiding the many objects in the path.

"We need the replenishment ships and pilots. Moreover, if we're to have any chance of reaching the Spacebridge and getting to Alliance space, we will need to obtain every single ounce. Don't forget, the replenishment ships include mobile refineries."

The lights came on one at a time, and each identified how close Nate was to launching out into space. He might have been locked away securely in the Flight Control Suite, but at that very moment, his mind told him he was in the fighter, and every part of his body believed it.

"I've prepared a series of waypoints. It's a standard zigzag pattern, just like you've practised. Clear the field, and make sure we have a safe route through. I'll be watching your back from here."

"Yes, Sir."

The final red light deactivated and was replaced by a flashing amber one. Nate counted down mentally, and then it turned green. His heart lurched with anticipation. In that brief moment, he knew his life would never be the same again. The final doors slid open quickly, their powerful motors performing the entire action in less than a second. Nate was greeted with the view of the wide flattop deck. The large section was marked out with flashing lights, and it instantly took him back to playing with toy ships as a child.

*A real carrier!*

A beaming grin appeared on his face, and his eyes raised and looked out into space.

"Launch!"

There was no physical stimulus from the launch into space, but he still shuddered as the drone was blasted off the ramp via the electromagnetic launch rails. There was no sound as the drones exited the ship, and the fighters' engines didn't even activate until they were a hundred metres from the outer hull. As they moved away, the launch sleds slowly retracted into their waiting state inside the ship. Both sliding outer doors moved back to their closed position and within a few more seconds, the ship secured.

None of this mattered to Nate. He was out of the warship and in space for the first time, and he already knew he loved it. A quick glance to his right showed the shape of Crusader Four, Billy's designation for his Avenger drone. They were barely a hundred metres apart, and already it was proving difficult to make out the features on the other drone's hull. The only illumination came from several nearby stars, as well as the navigation lights on the drones.

"Crusader Three. I am clear of Relentless and on approach to waypoint one."

Billy also reported in as the pair of fighters accelerated out in front of the assault ship. Nate activated his onboard sensors, as well as starting the electronic countermeasures unit. The drone was equipped with a variety of defensive measures, one able to project false magnetic patterns around them, effectively creating ghosts for enemy sensors.

"Reconnaissance mode activated. We're starting our sweep."

Eight bright flashes marked the position of the Anthros movable engine outlets. Each accelerated the drones well away from the ship in a matter of seconds. With no physical crew on board, they could accelerate without fear of impacting on the biology of the pilot. It took only twenty-three seconds for the fighters to make it to the first waypoint, at a position one hundred and fifty kilometres ahead of the ship. As soon as they passed through the virtual marker, the computer beeped and brought up the next two in sequence.

"We're in position. Area looks clear. Deploying recon buoys...now."

Billy formed up a kilometre away and above Nate. In this position, he could keep an eye on his lead fighter, while being far enough away to avoid making them both easy targets. His computer detected the buoy as it exited a flap on the upper side of Nate's fighter. With a small burst of gas, it vanished from view as the device targeted the nearest asteroid. The unit was fully autonomous and would attach using its integral harpoon unit.

"Moving on," said Nate.

A quick tug on the controls, and the Anthros outlets changed direction and spun the craft around. The speed was astounding, made even more impressive by the corkscrew manoeuvre Nate performed. He was accelerating away as the craft settled on a path to travel through a belt of forty plus objects. Billy came in close behind, with both jinking from side to side to avoid collisions. Every object they passed was scanned by the multiple sensors on board and then tagged as safe. It was a laborious process, but as each minute faded, the number of secure targets increased.

"Nate, are you seeing this?"

Both had spotted the object far off to the left of their present course. While ANS Relentless was making her way ahead, a massive cloud of rock blocked off a large area to the right.

"Yeah, let's check it out."

The two drones flipped over and boosted their engines. Streaks pulsed from the outlets as they accelerated past the rocks and towards an odd-shaped asteroid as big as a space station. Large sections extended out in a bizarre series of towers and spikes. They were forced to separate as they moved in closer, like a pair of skimmers moving through a rugged desert canyon.

"Yeah, stay close and watch your corners. This could be...interesting."

As Nate rounded the first tower, he found himself staring at something odd. There were, of course, all manner of strange rock and ice formations in the Deadlands, but there was something about this particular object that caught his eye.

*Artificial, it has to be.*

He brought his Avenger in closer and skimmed past the surface, running a series of detailed tests. After he passed the section, he no longer needed the computer. Directly in front was the back half of a Byotai cruiser, and it was embedded into a large structure that could only have been a station of some design. For a second he was lost for words, as more of the shape became apparent. Rock and metal had fused together into a sickening collection of destruction. Another large spiked mountain appeared in front, and a quick blip of power spun him around to move into a safer position.

"Crusader Leader, we've found something."

The communications system made a painful squawking sound, followed by the clear voice of Lieutenant Higgins.

"I have your feed here. It looks like the remains of an outpost."

Nate spotted the shape of Billy's Avenger as it used its multiple engine outlets to alter its position. Both were now moving in a fixed position, allowing them to observe the damage at their leisure. With the flick of a single switch, the forward lamps activated and floodlit the immediate area. Billy did the same, and between them they moved along the surface, checking details as they did so.

"Yes, Crusader Leader, I concur."

Nate then tagged multiple sections and waited as the computer ran through its database. It didn't take long.

"Sir, the computer has identified Byotai components. Looks like there was trouble out here, and the Byotai paid the price. I have no idea how long ago this happened."

"Understood. Drop a buoy and move to the next waypoint. We're moving through the final layer and to the rendezvous. Don't hang around. We need you there, and fast. I'm deploying Crusader One and Two to watch our rear. I don't want anybody sneaking up on us."

"Understood, Sir."

Nate waggled his wings and then spun about, performing a one-eighty spin before activating all of the eight engine outlets. Billy followed right behind as they travelled between asteroids, still continually checking for possible signs of danger. It wasn't just wreckage or even ambushing ships; there were also possible mines or defence turrets left behind by other ships. With Relentless so low on resources, they could take no chances.

"Here we go, follow me."

Nate burst out from the dust cloud that found him looking out into a large open space, surprisingly clear of debris. Far off into the distance was a massive asteroid upon which an entire space station had been constructed, and a short distance away several vessels.

"Wait, we've got something."

Nate tagged each of them, but this time Billy's computer finished first.

"Alliance ships, we've found them!"

Nate shook his head with surprise. One by one the computer identified the silhouettes and then the individual parts of the ships. At first the possibility of a match was only marginal, but with each moment passing, the percentage chance increased until finally reaching a hundred percent.

*Alliance ships! I never thought we'd find them out here. I really didn't.*

"My computer confirms Crusader Four's assessment. It's the fleet. I am detecting a navigation beacon in the area."

Nate looked backwards to see the distant shape of ANS Relentless moving through the final wall of dust and debris. This far away it was like she was pushing through a waterfall, even though little of the dust was anywhere near her. Powerful lamps fitted all around the ship activated. The units switched on and then swivelled about to highlight anything nearby. As he turned back, he spotted Billy wagging his wing.

"We've made it, Crusader Three. I can't believe it."

Nate smiled while still shaking his head. He looked ahead and at the shape of four ships in a holding pattern next to the station.

*Yes, we did, Billy. Yes, we did.*

A slight movement against background betrayed the position of Rex's fighter. Nate altered his viewing mode. The other two fighters were far off to the right, slightly behind Relentless. He might not have been a great fan of Rex, but knowing he and Jack were also out there gave him a warm glow inside. It was something akin to confidence. He grinned and imagined an enemy fighter trying to come near them.

*Let them just try it. We're ready.*

# CHAPTER ELEVEN

**Fleet Rendezvous, Arnos Cluster**
**Flight Control Suite, Two hours later**

Lieutenant Higgins watched the holographic model floating above the command pit. Coloured shapes showed the positions of all the different vessels in the area. Though Captain Galanos commanded the ship from the CIC, he'd been forced to take on the role of drone commander as well as CAG. Luckily, the high-speed internal communications system rendered the difference in distance to be unimportant. As he looked over to the occupied pods, he realised he was effectively alone. It was a lonely job, but right now that didn't particularly bother him.

ANS Relentless was now less than a thousand kilometres from the Alliance ships, and he was beginning to feel uncomfortable. There was still no contact from them, and with every second that passed, their escape became more difficult. Fuel supplies were at the limit, and in theory they would be hard pressed to travel for even a few more hours. The last deceleration had burnt much more fuel than intended. This should not have been an issue, but after escaping with limited supplies, they were now at breaking point. He activated the communications unit, and the image of Captain Galanos appeared in the middle of the pit.

"Captain. We've confirmed the area is unoccupied by Byotai forces. There are no mines or active weapon systems in the area, and no sign of active scanning equipment."

He moved his hands and rotated the view of the ship. The position of the drones shifted accordingly. The asteroids were by far the most significant objects, but the bulk of them remained in the unusual ring around the starbase.

"I have four Avengers in the field, two on recon and two flying close escort. Two remain in reserve. All are loaded in case of trouble. Mongoose is operational and on the deck also."

"Good work, Lieutenant. Your pilots have not disappointed us. I am, however, more than a little surprised at the ships."

The Alliance vessels flickered red as the Captain tagged them.

"Are you certain there is no sign of life aboard them? What about the navigation beacon that brought us here?"

The Lieutenant shook his head, his disappointment clear to see.

"Crusader Squadron has performed three flybys so far, as well as deep scans. They show no signs of damage aboard the transports, but their powerplants are cold and their systems off-line. It's like they all just walked out and left. The beacon is near the escort ship and still active."

Captain Galanos looked away and spoke to somebody else for a second. The image blurred before her face returned.

"Very well. I am bringing Relentless in close. We need to secure those replenishment ships as fast as possible."

Even Lieutenant Higgs was taken aback at this haste.

"So soon, Sir? Shouldn't we..."

The Captain shook her head while answering.

"No, Lieutenant, time is not on our side. I have enough fuel and ammunition for one small skirmish. Any more, and we'll be reduced to hurling rock ice at them."

She tried to laugh, but it ended up being little more than a grimace.

"We cannot leave this sector until refuelled and restocked. Rotate your fighters. I want full coverage during this operation. We can salvage whatever supplies they have via the automated loader aboard Relentless."

"Understood, Captain."

For a moment, it seemed Captain Galanos had finished, but she continued to speak. Her face was tight, and the stress of their predicament clearly showed on her brow.

"Deploy six recon drones along the length of the ships. I need supplies brought on board quickly. I want Relentless fully fuelled and resupplied within the hour. Leave nothing to chance."

All major warships were now fitted with replenishment equipment. The gantries and pipes would extend out and connect to the ports fitted to the replenishment vessels. The system was designed to be as automated as possible so that it could be performed if necessary in the middle of battle. Even without crew on the ships, it would be possible to suck out fuel, water, and coolant from their storage holds. Assuming any still remained.

"And the abandoned Byotai research station, Captain?"

The Captain's face vanished from view, and the rest of the hologram distorted to noise before she came back into focus.

"Lieutenant. You've already deployed two recon probes to the base, and they confirm there are no weapons and active sensors. Are there not?"

He nodded slowly in agreement.

"Very well, Lieutenant. We don't have the manpower or the spacecraft to perform a full investigation. Not yet. The base can wait...for now."

He opened his mouth to protest, but the Captain kept going.

"The only priority is to get Relentless back into fighting form. I need food and water for the crew, ammunition for the guns, and fuel rods for our powerplants. Without these, we are as dead in space. We cannot fight or flee until this is done."

"Yes, Sir."

The signal cut, but it left Lieutenant Higgins with the uncomfortable realisation the Captain's description of their plight exactly matched the position faced by the four dead ships.

*What if they suffered this exact same problem?*

There was, of course, little point in worrying about this. He had a job to do, just like the others. There were only so many options available to them, and at this moment in time, they had neither the fuel nor ammunition to do otherwise. It was frustrating, and even if they could fight, they were hardly in good shape for it. His pilots were still to be tested.

*We need to restore our combat capabilities. Then we can start worrying about everything else, not a moment before.*

Lieutenant Higgins knew this was the sensible approach, but it didn't stop a shiver run down his spine as he imagined the worst. He looked over his right shoulder at the two occupied pilot pods. Nate and Billy were locked down, with their helmets over their faces. Of the other four, two were watching the imagery feeds above Nate's position, while Matilda and Cassandra waited nearby.

"Flight Cadets. Your assessment, if you please."

Both turned from Nate's displays and joined him at the pit. Cassandra extended her arms and moved the models about in front of her. The computer made subtle adjustments based on the movement of her arms.

"The ships have been moored in a safe orbit around the base. Nate has already identified the clear orbital path, and it is the one taken by our comrades."

Lieutenant Higgins nodded.

"That is correct. What does this tell us?"

Matilda now rubbed her forehead. Although only a little older than the other five, she seemed to have aged considerably in the last few days. Her long, straight auburn hair hung over her shoulder in a mess, and she'd resorted to wearing her glasses, giving her an even older, sterner look. She tried to smile, but as usual it came off as more of a grimace.

"They've been captured or killed. The energy field in the starbase is blocking most of our deep scans. The ships are undamaged, so there is a possibility a weapon was used to kill those on board."

Cassandra listened intently and began nodding as Matilda reached the last few words. She lifted her hand while continuing to nod.

"Yes, yes. That's very true."

She then moved her hand in a circle around one of the ships.

"If the ship's magnetic energy fields were disabled, it would be possible to attack the crew with direct radiation."

"Exactly," Matilda agreed, "It would be like a solar flare ripping through the ship."

She pointed at the same place as Cassandra.

"Without radiation protection, the crew could be killed. There are rumours of neutron weaponry with the Byotai, aren't there?"

Lieutenant Higgins smiled.

"Good work, Cadets. Damned good work."

He then turned around and looked in the direction of Nate and Billy.

"Get yourselves ready. You'll be launching in a few minutes. I'll pass on your thoughts to the Captain."

The two cadets looked to each other as they acknowledged his orders, and then made their way towards their small cubicle units. The mirror screens were operating and showing the same views the pilots would see with their own eyes. It was an easy way for a third party to watch over the pilots. Lieutenant Higgins moved the model of the starbase forty degrees to give him a better view of the ships.

*Is that what happened? Were you ambushed and hit with direction radiation weaponry?*

The very thought of such a fearsome weapon made his skin crawl. The idea had been used in the past in the development of neutron bombs, but few now existed in the Alliance. Such weapons were classed as genocidal and outlawed by all civilised people. They were generally designed to unleash a burst of neutrons that would be intentionally allowed to escape as a weapon. These were capable of hitting a target with more than 14 MeV, a dose of radiation that was lethal to all known life forms. Even worse this radiation could penetrate every level of a warship unless properly shielded.

"Sir, drones are ready and on the rails," said Matilda.

The two flight cadets were both ready, their helmets fitted and straps automatically locked in tightly. With all of their senses now cut off from the ship, they were just as attached to their drones as Nate and Billy were.

"Very good. Continue your checks and wait for my mark."

As they ran through their long checklists, Lieutenant Higgins moved his attention to the ships. There were now five Alliance ships in the immediate area, including ANS Relentless. Four were transport and replenishment ships of the Alliance Navy Auxiliary, and the final a late generation Furious class light frigate. Introduced after the war, the Furious was the standard escort ship. It combined the combat abilities of pre-war cruisers as well as small hangar mounts to carry drone fighters. In total, it was a considerable array of ships, but lacked the one thing critical to survival in enemy territory, capital ships. Relentless was by far the largest and most capable of them all, and more important, she was only one that currently bore any signs of life.

*I don't like this, not one bit.*

He reached forward and tapped the icons for his pair of fighters. Crusader Three and Four were a long way from Relentless and currently following a figure of eight flight path over the silent ships. The response from them was immediate.

"Crusader Squadron. What's your status?"

\* \* \*

The view from the drone's cockpit was glorious, and Nate could have sat there to admire it for hours, perhaps even days. The rocks of the Arnos Cluster paled into insignificance next to the great chunks of ice drifting slowly about. Some were as big as moons, and glinted as his front flood lamps scanned from left to right. Positioned amidst the flotsam of space were the Alliance ships, and as each minute drifted past, they became more and more worrisome. To his surprise, the beacon had not been transmitting from the ships, but from inside an ice formation.

"We have made four complete passes. There are no signs of damage on the transports. I'm picking up strange readings throughout the frigate, though. None are responding to our hails. Either they are unable to respond, or they are unwilling."

This was not what Nate or the others had expected. Deep down there was always the chance the ships would not have made it, but they were here,

195

and so far there was nothing active anywhere near them, with the exception of the automated beacon that lay a short distance from the frigate.

*This is all too weird.*

The scanners detected yet another large section of rock, and he tapped the controls to move around it. This one was much smaller and little bigger than the drone. It was almost impossible to see, and he was now completely reliant upon the high-resolution radar scanners fitted to the drone to stay safe.

*If we were doing this in the MK I Lightnings, we would have been killed hours ago.*

It was an odd feeling to know how close they could have been to death, more so because neither Nate nor Billy were actually inside the Avenger drones.

"Understood, Crusader Three. What about the escort ship? I notice she's further away from the starbase than the transports are. Can you see any signs of combat damage? What about the evacuation lifeboats? Why are they not responding to your hails?"

Nate gave the engines a gentle boost and moved closer to the Alliance vessels for yet another pass. Since arriving, he'd expected to assess the entire area, but all his attention had been focussed on the dormant Alliance ships. With each metre he moved, the more confused he became. According to the computer, there were four of them, yet none of them was responding to his hails. He had flown past four times now, and the last had brought him to within ten kilometres. Captain Galanos forbade going in any closer in case of traps or hidden debris. Nate's arms were beginning to cramp even though he'd only been at this for little more than two hours.

"I'm passing the frigate now. The markings on her hull say she's ANS Cyclops, a Furious class ship. The computer identifies her as part of a joint border patrol unit with the Byotai."

Nate shook his head angrily as he read that. Until this violence had begun, the Alliance and the Byotai had been on good terms. The two had worked together in the war, and though different races, they seemed to share so much. The massed trade fleets of the Alliance had already established trade links with dozens of Byotai worlds. And now all of that was smashed by

196

whatever insanity was ripping apart the ancient and noble race.

*I don't understand it, none of it.*

He blinked twice and then focussed on the frigate. The ship was very different in design to ANS Relentless, especially with her thin armour, more streamlined appearance, and sunken weapon mounts. If he didn't know any better, he'd think it was a hybrid ship based on the alien Helion designs. Nate found looking at these ships to be a mesmerising experience, and it took a great deal of effort to tear his eyes from the view.

"I see some light scoring to the hull, and a number of puncture points on the left flank."

He altered his course a fraction and neared the ship's rear quarter. At this range his flood lamps were able to pick out substantial amounts of detail. A gentle tap of the controls, and he spun about.

*What is that?*

One tap on the thrusters, and he moved even closer, his lamps penetrating deep into every crevice of the ship. Then he spotted it. At first it looked like little more than a shadow, but as he drifted further to the right, the shadow shifted, giving a perfect view into the hull. It was a crack, big enough to fly a ship inside.

"Sir. I have a major breach in the hull. Scanners show it penetrates through to the inner decks. I'm also detecting a major radiation spike."

The computer isolated the multiple sources and flagged them on his navigation orb. Nate examined them carefully while keeping an eye on the ship, as though it might spring to life at any moment.

"The computer shows multiple radiation sources throughout the hull. Most of the decks are irradiated."

He opened one of the hatches on the drone's hull and launched a small probe. It was small, little bigger than a man's hand, and contained only a modicum of fuel for its ion thrusters.

"Deploying recon drone now."

The tiny device entered the breached hull and continued onwards in the innards of the ship. Its internal pulse scanner fired every five seconds, each burst penetrating the vessel and sending data back to Nate's computer. With each pulse, the picture of the ship became even clearer. After the first six, the fate of the ship was obvious.

"Probe confirms that Cyclops sustained multiple heavy external impacts that breached the hull. Impact areas indicate asteroid or rock ice strikes. I have at least eight penetrations, all containing rock ice that matches the material in this sector."

As he said the words, he tried to imagine what it would have been like as these objects struck the ship. At the same time, his eyes were drawn to the flashing beacon on his navigation orb. He'd assumed it would have been used to help the other ships find the rendezvous point, but it quickly became obvious it had another purpose.

"The beacon, Sir. It wasn't to tell the other ships where to go. It was a warning. A warning to avoid the same fate."

He moved his drone backwards to get a better view of the entire ship. With its powerplant off-line, it was little more than a derelict, like so many of the ghost ships that filled yards throughout the galaxy.

"Understood, Crusader Three. Continue your sweep and then come home. Crusaders Five and Six will take your place."

"Yes, Sir."

Nate passed on the next waypoints for the sweep to Billy, and then increased is forward velocity. Only then did he realise quite how long he'd been out there. His limbs were unaffected, but his mind and his back both ached.

*That's the longest mission I've ever been on. The longest Star Crusader scenario was the Siege of Titan battle. And we were done in little over an hour. This is insane.*

He shook his head and immediately felt a little wheezy. There was a marked disconnect between how he felt on board Relentless, and how he expected to feel inside the weightless environment of the Avenger drone fighter. Nate glanced to his right and checked Billy was at his wing. For a second he lost sight of his friend, but then the white diamond shape picked out the tiny object. The Avenger fighter looked menacing but incredibly small, when compared to the monstrous shapes of the capital ships nearby. He might have been able to see Billy in the cockpit, but there was nothing of the sort in an unmanned fighter. There was a darker section that gave the impression of where a pilot might be, but that was a decision made for aesthetic reasons only.

*What's that?*

An icon appeared over the Byotai starbase that they had given only a cursory look at so far.

"What about the base?" Billy asked, "Maybe they left the ships and are down there. That, or the crew are still on the ship."

Nate nodded to himself. Although neither of them had said it, the meaning was clear. If the crew were not somewhere else, then they were on the ship, and dead. The very idea of the ship filled with bodies made Nate shudder.

"Good point."

He contacted Lieutenant Higgins directly.

"Sir. There is no sign of the crew out here. We..."

"Understood, Crusader Three. Perform another flypast and then return to base. In the meantime, we are preparing a survey drone for the base."

Nate paused, considering his answer. He felt he knew this small part of space quite well now. With their two fighters they had performed a full scan, as well as having personally examined the ships from every conceivable angle. There was still an area they had been told to avoid, and the longer they were out there, the more important it seemed to investigate.

"Sir, I request permission to run a close-range flyby of the starbase. It appears undamaged, and my sensors show fluctuating power levels deep inside its structure. Better to expose a problem now than leave it too late."

There was a much longer pause this time before Lieutenant Higgins answered. His voice was slower and more considered.

"No closer than ten kilometres. Unlock your weapons and be ready. A single flyby and then return to base."

"Understood, Sir. Moving into position."

Nate didn't need to pass on the orders to Billy as both were receiving the audio. Nate took the lead, with Billy trailing behind and at a slightly raised position above him. They left the four unmarked Alliance ships and made for the station. According to the limited data previously gathered by the Alliance survey teams, this part of the Cluster was occupied only by a small group of research stations. There were at least five more similar locations, with many over a month's travel away in any direction. Even the Spacebridge to the Tenth Quadrant was days away and protected by an unknown number of Byotai guards of dubious loyalties.

*Take it slow and keep your eyes open.*

In gaming scenarios, this was exactly the situation where an enemy would likely be hiding. The station was vast and protected by huge extrusions, some natural and even more being completely artificial. Long docking arms reached out into space, and curved rib sections bent out to clamp around any ships currently moored. It was very different to anything Nate had seen before, and clearly constructed a very long time ago by the Byotai. Only a small portion of it was visible; the rest presumably buried deep inside the larger asteroid.

"On approach. Ground penetrating scans confirm internal landing bays and substantial development below the surface. I'm having a hard time reaching below fifty metres."

A quick change on the sensors, and the onboard computer began a detailed assessment of the facility, but as before, the system was unable to penetrate past that one point, as if it was being protected. A smile formed across Nate's face when he noticed the unusual pattern.

*No way!*

It took a fraction of a second to connect through to Lieutenant Higgins.

"What do you have for me?"

"Sir. There's a shield unit blocking our scans. I think there are people deep inside the base."

"What makes you say that?"

"There are a number of life signs right at the periphery of the shielded area."

Even as he talked, the sensors detected fading signs before they also vanished.

"They are gone, Sir."

For a moment Nate thought he wouldn't be believed, but this was not the twentieth century, and Lieutenant Higgins could also see everything he saw. More important, every piece of information sent from the drone to Relentless was being stored and analysed.

"I saw it, and I think you're right, Crusader Three. They picked up your scans and have moved further back. There's something alive on that station. Drop a buoy and activate the holding pattern. I need to speak with you both."

"I've got something!"

Nate checked his overlay, but he already knew the voice was Rex.

"What is it?"

Rex was much further away from the buoy than Nate, and he could only surmise he must have been monitoring the scanner feed at the very moment the craft entered the system.

"Multiple contacts moving towards the inner debris field. Our perimeter buoys just picked them up. Two targets, both converging on the beacon."

Nate swallowed as he checked his mapping data. Rex and Jack were at least double the distance from the buoy as they continued their sweep. Lieutenant Higgins tagged Nate's fighter and then issued new waypoints.

"Move into position and observe the new group. Wait there and activate silent running."

"Understood, Sir."

Lieutenant Higgins then selected the two fighters commanded by Cassandra and Matilda.

"Same for you two. Move into position and observe."

Nate had already punched in the new data, and both he and Billy were moving away at high speed. Neither used the burners, for fear of creating a heat bloom that could be easily traced back to this region. He could see the other two pairs of fighters moving to their new positions, and it was quite clear Matilda and Cassandra would be too far away to be able to assist him if he ran into trouble.

"Sir, I recommend placing Relentless' defence systems on standby. We could be looking at a pincer movement, and our space defences are...well, just us, Sir."

"Already done. Crusaders One and Two will remain to provide CAP while you two pairs can scout for trouble."

"Yes, Sir."

Nate began the process of disabling systems to reduce his heat signature and electronic emissions.

"What are our rules of engagement? There's a possibility that Byotai ships could arrive, but do not attack us first."

It was a simple question, but one Nate had to ask. They couldn't just open fire, even if the new arrivals appeared to be enemy craft. They would have to be certain they were the enemy, and that they were a threat. The consequences for attacking, and possibly destroying harmless Byotai ships, could cast the Alliance into a massive war.

"Standard ROE, Crusader Three. Fire if fired upon, or if you find yourself in mortal danger."

Nate increased the boost of the engines and watched carefully as the inner rim of debris came ever closer. On the other side were the thick layers of rock and ice, as well as the remains of some battle from an unknown age. According to the scans, there were three craft, plus something a little larger heading their way.

"Sir."

"I'm bringing Crusaders One and Two back to Relentless. They can run CAP. Keep your eyes open while we continue replenishment operations. Estimated time to completion is thirty-three minutes."

The two fighters continued on their lazy arc towards their final destination. As they moved towards the last few kilometres, Nate activated the stealth operations panel. Though intrinsically stealthy spacecraft, there was one major issue with drones. For them to remain effective, they had to stay in direct contact with their control ship at all times, or revert to the risky autonomous operation.

"Billy, you ready?"

Nate's friend acknowledged almost immediately.

"I'm dropping the comms drone...now."

The small unit was the size of a missile, but this was no warhead. The unit drifted in space, in effect another piece of debris in the vastness of space.

"Okay, switch to piggyback line of sight communications only."

Both activated the unit at the same time. It was a subtle change, but it would make the next part of their mission much safer. ANS Relentless would continue to communicate via direct laser targeting to the communications drone. The unit would then send microbursts to the two Avengers, using its own targeting matrix. Any lag or lost data would be overridden by the Avenger's built-in safety protocols to avoid collision, detection, and combat where necessary.

"I'm in silent running mode. Switching ship only communications," said Billy.

One unusual consequence of commanding the two drones was they could speak with each other just fine actually inside Relentless, without the need for risky audio communications in space.

They were now at the inner-rim of debris, and both pilots took full control of their Avenger fighter drones. The larger sections were relatively stable, but there were still large amounts of smaller junk flashing about, and any one of them could rip apart their fighter in a single strike. As Nate darted in and out, he noticed the odd piece of distortion on his display.

*Signal quality is failing this far away.*

It wasn't serious, not yet anyway. But the further they travelled from the communication drone, the worse it was going to get for them. Nate checked his mapping data and the projected route for the new arrivals.

"They'll be here in under a minute. Take cover..."

Nate led Billy away from the main route and towards one of the large ring-shaped asteroids. It was massive, at least a hundred kilometres in diameter, and surrounded by a thick cloud of smaller segments. Nate came in close so that his craft was hidden deep inside the layer of material. Billy followed shortly afterwards until they were hidden from view.

"Now what?" Billy asked.

Nate turned his attention to the forward view. He couldn't see them yet, but he did have their electronic signatures showing up on his main display. The computer had already isolated a number of key patterns, one of which confirmed they were all running Byotai military issue powerplants.

"We wait. Keep your weapons on safe. The LT wants us to collect detailed intel, and that's exactly what we're gonna do."

The two fighters were almost impossible to spot where they waited. Nate spoke quietly, completely forgetting they were on board Relentless, and that it was impossible for anybody out there to hear them. His onboard navigation lights were off, and with all but the most basic systems now off-line, the drones would let off very little heat. It was another of the benefits of taking people out of the spacecraft.

"Look," said Billy.

Nate moved his eyes about, and it took a moment until he found the small formation. For a second it looked insignificant, but then he realised what he was looking at.

"I see them."

He tagged each of the craft and glanced down as the computer analysed their silhouettes. The Alliance database was detailed, but still contained gaps where Byotai military hardware was concerned.

"One small command and control corvette, plus three heavy escort fighters."

He shook his head.

"They are running a patrol around the ships. And if they find Relentless, they'll call for help."

"You're sure? What help? There's nothing out here?"

Nate might have laughed had he not been well aware of the dangers before them.

"Of course. This group is a short-range patrol. They must be operating from a base or mother ship nearby."

As he said the words, he realised how precarious their position had just become. Relentless had come here to meet with the fleet and to resupply. Now it looked as though they might have arrived right after a major assault, and in an area where the enemy was already strong. A flashing light filled the corner of his view with a gentle pulse. Nate deactivated the warning, but looked across to check on the issue.

"Targeting computer."

"Billy, they're scanning for targets. Do not move, not under any circumstances."

On went the group of Byotai spacecraft, and as the seconds ticked by, he had the perfect opportunity to examine the craft in more detail. They were much bigger than he'd expected. As the statistics came in, it was clear they were closer in size to an Alliance Mauler than the Avengers drones. Each was constructed in a bizarre three-segment shape, much like the body of an insect. It was bulbous, with only small pods extending on the flanks to house four retractable landing skids. Vanes reached out from the rear segment to create small wings. The lower nose section was taken up completely by a launch tube assembly.

"Nate, the computer says they're Komodos."

Nate had heard the name before, but he'd never seen one. He brought up a side scan of the passing ships and matched it to the database himself. A list of statistics popped up alongside the model, and he began to shake his head.

"These things are...insane."

"I know," replied Billy, "Seven crew, four engines, and enough guns to take on a small ship."

Nate kept nodding in agreement, as he ran through the numbers. Much of it was mere speculation, but he suspected there must be some truth to it all. According to his computer, the spacecraft were classed as heavy bombers, each carrying eight 12.7mm pulse cannons, a lightweight variant of the particle weapons used on capital ships. The single tube array under the nose was used to release a variety of ship killer weapons, a hypothesised high-speed missile with the explosive potential of a frigate-class torpedo.

"Crusader One, do you read?"

Rex's serious tone came right back at him.

"Here."

"I've got a single command corvette and three Komodos. They are all heading your way."

Nate checked the position of the four craft before continuing. The computer concluded that the small group was taking a direct route to the beacon, and presumably to the derelict spaceships. Another indicator activated, and it was followed by the sound of Matilda's voice.

"It's a ghost signature at our waypoint."

*A diversion!* Nate thought.

"We've changed course and are coming back to Relentless, ETA eleven minutes."

Nate looked at the mapping screen and quickly realised their predicament. A third of their fighters were now too far away to help, and this new force was getting closer by the second.

"I see them. What's the plan?"

Nate felt that pang of nerves that seemed so commonplace today. He was not the official squadron leader, but out here with his eyes on the target, he knew best what was happening.

"The command ship will be in direct contact with the enemy commanders. We need to eliminate them, and fast. I doubt even our jammers could stop her sending a signal back in time."

"But what about the three bombers. Don't we need to destroy them before they can hit Relentless?"

Nate knew they could hit the corvette, and quickly, but so far the Byotai ships had done nothing particularly offensive. He had to speak with Lieutenant Higgins, but at that very moment, the warnings inside his fighter came on.

"Billy, we've got multi-band radar emissions. They've spotted Relentless!"

The formation began accelerating away, their engines pulsing with energy. All three heavy bombers were making their way to the target and the tiny escort waiting to stop them, while the corvette changed course to move back in the direction it had come from.

*They are out of range. They must be. That's why they are turning back...to send a warning.*

"Jam them!"

Billy's face grinned as he looked at his friend via the image overlay to the right.

"Already done."

"All fighters; break and attack!" Lieutenant Higgins ordered.

This time the officer's voice had lost some of its natural calm. With just a handful of drones in the area, there was relatively little to protect Relentless against such firepower.

"Affirmative, we're on the way."

Nate gave the signal, and both drone fighters detached from the asteroid and formed up in a tight formation above the Byotai corvette. The ship was little bigger than a Mauler and covered in antenna and dishes. There were only a small number of turret mounts fitted along its bulbous hull, and as the Alliance fighters closed in, they tracked about, each looking for signs of a hidden enemy.

"The bombers have acquired Relentless," said Rex, "Inceptor course laid in."

Nate saw the first missiles leave the bomber a fraction before the warning alarm sounded inside his fighter. It was the final signal they each needed to move from a stealthy course, to one of action.

"Weapons free!"

At the same time, he spotted the line of white and yellow flashes as Relentless activated her own defence grid. The computer would control the point-defence turrets in groups, and use them to create an overlapping field of fire towards the enemy. Their missiles streaked towards the corvette, but its defence turrets were too quick and blasted the missiles apart in seconds.

"Switch to guns and shoot! Shoot now!"

The two Avengers bore down on the corvette and opened fire with their quadruple-barrelled cannons. At this range, their weapons had little chance of missing. Both emptied the initial box of armour-piercing, explosive slugs through the top plating of the ship. Explosions ripped through the ship, yet still its crew fought on. Sparks flashed from bow to stern, and an entire segment tore off and drifted away into space, trailing sparks.

"Don't stop. Keep hitting it!"

As they moved closer, they activated their burners and accelerated away in opposite directions while dumping three countermeasure units each. The turrets chased them, with each battery of guns firing a powerful volley of small-calibre projectiles. Several pierced the left wing of Nate's fighter as the corvette's powerplant overloaded. The entire ship ripped apart in a massive blue explosion, sending metal, ammunition, and equipment in all directions.

"Form up."

The two fighters moved close together and then raced around to chase after the three bombers. In the twenty-six seconds since the start of the fight, the bombers had covered a great deal of ground. Even with their burners on full, it was going to be difficult. Nate connected to Relentless.

"The corvette is gone. Just the bombers."

"Understood," replied Lieutenant Higgins, "Pursue and engage. Do not let them hit Relentless, no matter the cost."

Nate lined up on the bomber and let the computer do its work. In less than a second, it had performed a full and detailed analysis of the entire craft. It continued to wobble as it tried to avoid the stream of defensive fire from ANS Relentless. Several rounds struck the left hull and sent a shower of small sections behind it, along with a cloud of sparks.

*Shoot it!*

Nate depressed the trigger, and the forward guns opened up with a mighty roar. The drones shuddered violently, and the forward view might have been completely obscured, had it not been for the gyrostabilised camera mounts. Sparks ran along the craft's hull as Nate inched closer and closer. From here he had the perfect view of the bug-shaped bomber. The turrets were now facing him, and long bursts of fire struck near him.

*Dodge, evade, and shoot.*

Months, perhaps years of video gaming had instilled reactions in him that he barely knew existed. As he spotted the flashes of light, Nate hit the strafing controls that gave a boost to the lateral thrusters. With no pilot present, he used the maximum setting that quickly shunted the fighter nearly a hundred metres to the left. Gunfire whistled past him, and then he was back, the bomber in his sights, and the guns fired.

"Nate, I'm..."

*Billy!*

Nate glanced to his left, but the other bomber was much too far away to be visible. He activated the cameras, locked onto his position, and magnified the area. Both Billy's fighter and the bomber had disappeared, and around them, the explosive ordnance of ANS Relentless continued firing for several more seconds. Nate shook his head bitterly. Crusaders Five and Six were still heading back to ANS Relentless, but even at their speed would have little chance of intercepting the bomber, let alone any ordnance it released. Flak exploded around the Byotai craft but still it came on, ignoring the minor damage and even the fires now burning through its starboard engines.

*One down, five of us left!*

# CHAPTER TWELVE

**Fleet Rendezvous, Arnos Cluster**

The initial volley of two high-speed missiles was already three quarters its way to Relentless when Nate spotted Rex. He was moving at a similar speed to the missiles and heading right at them. To split the defensive fire, the two bombers had broken formation, heading left and right. Nate tagged the one to the left.

"I'm taking out bogey alpha. Crusader One, take out the second."

The Avenger drone rolled to one side and pushed its burners to maximum. As Nate followed after the enemy, he noticed that Rex and Jack were still heading directly at the missiles.

"Crusader One, alter your course," said Nate.

"I've got them. Just another second..."

The missiles kept going, the bright white flame behind them marking the powerful thrusters that pushed them on to incredible speeds. They were big missiles, and the computer had already detected the low-yield neutron atomics inside them.

*If they hit, they'll knock out the electronics and burn the crew from the inside out.*

It was a horrific idea and for a second, there was every chance the missiles would succeed. Nate watched in amazement as Rex and Jack launched their own missiles, and then opened fire with their guns. Two Byotai missiles evaded the approaching warheads, but it was not so easy to avoid the hardened railgun slugs. Their guns quickly knocked one out, but the second used manoeuvring thrusters to jink out of the way at the last minute. There were just seconds to go before impact, and Rex was moving too fast to adjust his course. He increased his power to beyond the safe limits, and warnings spread throughout his cockpit. In a last second manoeuvre, Rex slipped past the missile before he could fire. Jack followed behind him and found he was also moving too quickly to alter course in time.

*Idiots!*

By moving so quickly, they had removed almost any chance of now chasing the third and final missile. Rex must have realised this, as he used every last ounce of power to push his fighter up and towards the Byotai bomber. He began to spin his fighter about so that it would be able to keep shooting when it flew beneath the missile. His guns blazed away, but with so little time, he succeeded in only damaging the incredibly tough torpedo.

*Too late, Rex, much too late!*

Nate launched another of his missiles, but even if it managed to lock on correctly, it would still strike too late to make any difference. So busy was he in assessing the fight, his brain barely registered the impact. Rex ran nose first into the remaining ship-killer missile, destroying both in a single moment. The warhead must have triggered because it emitted a massive pulse that reached out nearly a kilometre in all directions.

*Watch out!*

The blast's wake expanded outwards, and Nate made a last minute course adjustment to stay well away. It was only a subtle change, but he made it to safety just as the ring of deadly radiation subsided.

"Nate!" Lieutenant Higgins said.

The officer now completely ignored their official squadron names.

"The neutron blast has managed to breach our shielding. We're undamaged, but it has temporarily knocked out our targeting matrix on the port side. We're down to manual gunnery only. Take out the bomber, and fast!"

It was a lucky hit for the Byotai, and Nate could only assume the damage had been caused earlier, perhaps during their first escape. All Alliance ships were shielded against radiation and magnetic weaponry, but only so long as their hull shielding remained fully sealed. A grey shape flashed in the distance, and Nate tagged it, tracking the fighter via his tactical overlay.

*Jack, he's still alive!*

Nate had no idea how he'd managed it, but Jack had somehow managed to avoid the impact, but only just. Nate glanced to the right and watched him vanish off into the distance, now too far away to assist. There were no signs of contact from the drone's computer as it vanished off into space.

"All fighters. The remaining bomber is priming additional missiles. Stop them, now!" Lieutenant Higgins ordered.

Nate dived after the last bomber. It had used the short moment of confusion to try and get away, while the turrets on board ANS Relentless unleashed their deadly firepower against the bomber. Nate ignored the turret fire and moved the craft into the sights of his guns. With automated targeting off-line, they were far less accurate, and the flak was as likely to damage him, as it was to hit the bomber.

*Almost there!*

From Nate's cockpit it looked like cascading rain coming down towards him, but this was gunfire, not water. As quickly as that, he was on the tail of the bomber and could see the detailing, markings, and powerful engines. The nose was filled with gun barrels, and all of them were blasting away towards the assault ship.

*Come on, Nate, you can do this.*

Either by luck or judgement, he managed to hit something vulnerable. At least one of his hardened projectiles struck just behind the cockpit. At the same time, a large chunk of flak debris wedged against his left wing and knocked out the bank of Anthros thrusters. He entered a spin just as the Byotai bomber broke up. It must have been firing its missile because a secondary explosion ripped it apart, embedding hundreds of small chunks of metal in his hull. The alarm sounded, but Nate at least had the satisfaction of knowing he'd ended the threat.

"Good work, Crusader Squadron. Five, return to Relentless. Crusader Six, I want you to bring in our missing birds. I've lost communication with Two and Three."

*  *  *

Nate removed the helmet and shook his head. His short but scruffy looking hair had matted close to his scalp, and the helmet had left a line running around his head that would take several minutes to dissipate. After nearly two and a half hours in the cockpit, his head was swimming. There had been so much to take in, from the vastness of space, to the myriad of data and controls critical to the flying of the drone. Worse was the feeling of being one with the machine, that even an accidental movement one way or the other could spell disaster. The drones could stay out there for hours, even days, but not the pilots. The visor cleared slowly, giving his eyes a few more seconds to adjust to the interior.

*Ouch, that is not nice.*

The lighting in the Flight Control Suite was radically different to what he experienced inside the claustrophobic interior of the Avenger drone. Where he had become used to the blackness punctuated by light blue and red lighting, he was hit by the harshness of the faded white lights. He blinked once, twice, and then three times before reaching for his harness. With a clunking sound it detached, and he lifted himself out from the seat. For a second it felt like he'd stumble, but with a little effort he righted himself and found he was staring at the uniformed and ancient looking form of Lieutenant Higgins.

"Good work, Flight Cadet, very good work. The area is secure, but your bird needs to be patched up. Looks like your inlets are clogged, and two thrusters are out of action. She's a no go for now."

He then looked off to the left where Billy had just removed himself from his seat. He took three steps, bent over, and retched violently. Lieutenant Higgins glanced back to Nate and tried to reassure him with a disarming smile.

"It's pretty common. Don't worry about it."

Lieutenant Higgins pointed at the display floating above the pit and signalled for Rex and Jack to join them. The four moved around the pit, while the two girls continued their missions aboard their untouched fighters.

"We lost two birds. One is not responding, and a fourth is out of action following that little skirmish. Until we get Crusader Two back on-line, I'm down to a pair of fighters, and that's not great."

He looked back at the display and pointed at the designated bays inside the ship. There were the old manned fighters, and the battle damaged Mauler known as Mongoose.

"The replenishment mission is not far from completion. As soon as it's done, we will be leaving this place. Captain Galanos doesn't want to stay here a minute longer than we have to. Every extra hour increases the chance the Byotai will find us here. That corvette has to have been from a nearby patrol, and we cannot risk being found."

Rex and Nate were busy looking at the shapes of the abandoned Alliance ships.

"What about the crews? They must have gone somewhere, and my guess is the..."

"Yes, I know," said Lieutenant Higgins, interrupting Billy once more, "Probes confirm there was major fighting aboard the escort. Inner scans show large numbers of bodies, presumably killed by the neutron blasts inside."

Lieutenant Higgins rubbed his brow.

"The other ships are undamaged, save for a few scorch marks to their hulls. I suspect the escort was knocked out early, and then shots were fired at the auxiliary ships."

He changed the view in the pit to show the starbase; specifically the long docking arm and the thick black walls that looked like vast shield walls.

"We've got just the one Mauler, and the Captain has asked me to send her down to the starbase while we finish supplying Relentless."

Nate raised his eyebrows at this.

"Captain Galanos wants to check if there are survivors. If there are, I'll find them."

He looked back to the pit, but kept talking. His voice was hard and stern, "And I will bring them home."

"Yes, Sir," said Nate.

The Lieutenant almost chuckled at seeing Nate had no idea what he was saying.

"Flight Cadet Lewis. Of all six of you, you are the one showing most promise in command. I want you to be the CAG until I'm back. Somebody needs to get our marines on the ground, and in one piece."

He then looked to Billy.

"You will assist him. It's a big responsibility. Understood?"

Billy nodded, but Nate shook his head and pointed to the tactical map over the pit.

"I've only done this in simulation. I'm not a tactical commander."

Lieutenant Higgins took a step to the left and groaned from the pain. His body was still weak from the bloody injuries he'd sustained in the initial escape. Nate glanced to Billy who was already shaking his head.

"Sir. I..."

Lieutenant Higgins cut him off in mid-sentence. He then turned his attention to the pit and tagged the returning drones. It looked like Billy's was once again communicating with the computers, and Matilda was towing back Nate's damaged fighter.

"Crusaders Five and Six. Once you've finished with the damaged bird, you will follow the pre-set escort pattern and watch Relentless' back. Replenishment will be finished soon."

He threw a quick sideways glance at the two of them.

"We can pump out what we need without even going aboard them. We'll send additional probes in to see if anybody is still aboard, but I'm not optimistic, not as the last unit breached the outer hull to investigate."

He could see Nate was not happy about his new post.

"Look, Flight Cadet Lewis. It's not ideal, but it's critical a pilot stays in the loop between the Captain and our birds. I'm not in great shape for this, but it's not like you can fly a Mauler, is it?"

Nate answered before even considering the question.

"Yes, Sir. I've flown the MK I and II in simulation."

Lieutenant Higgins seemed a little taken back. He knew the cadets were all experienced in flying a variety of different craft, but a Mauler was quite unusual. Most pilots for these vessels were usually those that had graduated after years of experience flying fighters and bombers in Navy service. The Mauler was technically granted the same status as the small patrol ships and sloops in the Navy, and even bore the ANS moniker, in just the same was a cruiser or frigate.

"Really?"

He moved in closer to Nate and looked him directly in the eyes. The officer's gaze was so powerful it almost seemed to burrow into Nate's brain. He nearly stepped backwards; so uncomfortable was the feeling.

"A Mauler is no drone, Cadet."

He said that one word with a tinge of ice to his tone.

"You'll be packing a lot of weight, heavy engines, and the most valuable cargo on my ship. Our marines. Don't mess me around now. Can you do it, or not?"

Billy tried to intervene, but Nate remained adamant.

"Yes, Sir. I've run the Karnak simulation and put down marines under fire. I don't claim to be a Mauler pilot, but I do have the experience, and the flight qualification to do it."

Lieutenant Higgins had no desire to see a young flight cadet take the helm of Mongoose. She was the only functional Mauler aboard ANS Relentless, but he was also acutely aware of two problems. First, he was the most experience flight officer on the ship. If there was going to be trouble, he should be directing the fighters and controlling the battle. Second, he was far from healed, and a long way off the top of his game in terms of piloting a spacecraft into battle. He pointed at Nate.

"Take Flight Cadet Mitchell with you. If anything goes wrong, he can help out. I don't want any heroics. Just get the Mauler to the base and land our marines. You'll take orders directly from the field commander, Sergeant

Perkins. Understood?"

Nate nodded as he answered. As his body moved, he realised just what he had done. Up until now his role had been to command robotic drones, but now he faced the chance of flying something real, and filled with combat ready marines. It was a massive responsibility, and the mere thought of sitting in the Mauler rendered him almost speechless.

"Yes, Sir. Sergeant Perkins has operational command, and Flight Cadet...Mitchell will co-pilot with me."

"Very well. Get to the hangar deck fast. The marines are waiting for you."

Nate took in a deep breath and felt his entire body shudder at the thought of his new mission. He wanted to tell the others, but the four were strapped into their units and controlling their own drones. As he walked past, he could see the imagery of their craft. Only two were now in space and patrolling around the ship. He paused, but only long enough to see that two were waiting near Relentless, moving in lazy circles around the ship. He looked back to find the Lieutenant looking at Rex and Jack. The two of them didn't look angry. Instead, they appeared disappointed.

"Sir, what about us?"

He smiled in reply.

"I've got a few jobs for you, don't you worry."

* * *

Billy waited nervously outside the Mauler as the marines filed inside. He'd assumed only a few would be going, but there were six of them, including Sergeant Perkins. The other five marines waited on the deck, Sergeant Popwell amongst them. The two Marine Sergeants spoke for a moment, and then the older of the two led his group back inside the ship. Sergeant Perkins glanced towards Billy who almost stumbled backwards. The marine was a hard man, and Billy felt like a child in comparison. Then the man's expression softened a little.

"You'll be taking us in. My squad is counting on you."

Billy tried to speak, but words failed to come out. He moved back to the side hatch and banged on it. Almost immediately, Nate's face appeared and looked out at him. He then spotted Sergeant Perkins looking at them both. Behind him were two more marines with their visors open. Nate saw Private Valentine, but either she was too busy to notice him or had her mind on other things. She said something to her comrade and then climbed aboard the Mauler. Nate moved his attention back to the stern looking Sergeant.

"She's good to fly, Sergeant. Are your marines ready?"

Nate moved his eyes a tiny fraction to look over to Billy. His friend was still lost for words, and Nate might have laughed had the situation not been quite so tense and serious.

"Very well, son. Good luck," said the Sergeant.

With those few words their look separated, and Nate could let out a long, yet almost silent sigh. He grabbed Billy and pulled him to the hatch.

"It's all fixed now. Are you ready?"

Billy nodded nervously.

"Uh...yeah. Let me inside."

With a loud squeak, Nate opened the exterior door, and the tiny hatch swung to the side, giving just enough space for Billy to climb through. It was triple-layered, and there were multiple marks where gunfire had previously struck it. Nate had gone in first, but the hatch had jammed upon climbing through, and for almost a minute it looked as though the mission might have to be aborted.

Billy was halfway through when the loud voice of Sergeant Perkins echoed through to the cockpit.

"Okay, marines. You know the deal. Get inside!"

Though neither of them could see what was happening, the constant clunking of armoured boots on the metallic flooring of the Mauler gave it away. Billy checked the door was shut for the second time, and then hit the seal button. Metal rods moved into position from the top and side, locking the plate securely into position.

"That is seriously over engineered."

Nate was already in the right-hand position and sat down in the large seat. It was carefully moulded to hold its occupant firmly in position. He pulled the straps tight across his body and then glanced over to Billy.

"It's as I told you. The Mauler is like a flying tank. You'll not find thicker armour outside capital ships. You heard the racket when we came here in the first place."

Billy didn't seem particularly reassured by that memory. It was only a few days earlier they had made their first and only ever journey aboard this very Mauler. For all Nate's posturing about its toughness, there were still signs of the violence all around it, from the patched up bodywork, to the scorch marks and dents.

"We might have made it, but you saw the state we were in when we landed. A few more hits, and we would still be out there."

Nate pressed several more buttons, and the computer system sprung into life. He leaned to the side and pulled on a wheel to slightly adjust the height of his seat. Like Billy, he was a good half a head shorter than Lieutenant Higgins, and without adjustment, he was finding reaching some of the further controls a little difficult.

"Billy, the engineers have done their best. Not bad when you consider there's only twenty-seven crew left on the ship. I suspect some of the civilians might have lent a hand on this job."

Billy shrugged and moved past his friend and towards what remained of the shattered gunnery pod. Normally, it would have been the place for the co-pilot, but previous modifications had turned it over to gunnery tasks only. After their escape, it was in a much worse state and far from pretty.

"I'm supposed to sit here?"

Nate nodded quickly.

"Yes, its functional. Try it."

Billy did his best and groaned as he twisted and turned to fit inside the odd arrangement. To his surprise, the main seat and gun controls were intact, or at the very least had been replaced. He tugged at the straps and made sure he was in securely.

"According to the deck chief, all four of the forward turrets are operational. They're slaved directly to your control unit."

"I'm sensing there's a 'but' coming," said Billy.

Nate might have been able to hide it from anybody else, but not Billy. The two had spent a lot of time on the Star Crusader simulation since their victory in the original trials. After all those weeks, it was as though they'd been best friends for years.

"The tracking system is no longer connected to the targeting computer. You'll have to track and fire on manual."

Of all the things that could have been a problem, right now that seemed to be the least significant. Billy grunted and turned his attention to the panel near his belly. There was a myriad of switches, most now non-functioning. It took a moment until he found the replacement-arming switch and checked it was still disabled before finally relaxing.

"Okay, I'm ready."

Damage in the firefight during their original escape had left the Mauler riddled with holes. Patches covered up the worst of the trouble, but the gunnery pod was a mess. Parts of the strapping were gone, and in their place one of the turret seats from a stripped down Thunderbolt heavy-fighter.

"You're kidding, right?" Billy asked, "Where are the windows?"

Nate looked to his left and laughed.

"You never looked at the schematics, did you? There are not supposed to be windows on this ship. She's armoured for assault landings."

He pointed to the many controls throughout the cockpit. It was radically different to the advanced avionics system install throughout the Avenger drones. The Mauler was a much older machine and with a completely different brief. Simplicity, and the ability to absorb punishment were far more important than being controllable from another ship, or by remote.

"Everything is functional. Look."

With the flick of a single toggle, the displays came on. As with the drones, the forward view was facing outwards and at the final outer hangar doors. Red lights flashed continually, serving as a reminder that this part of the ship was about to vent the outer compartments into space.

"Everything okay in here? We good to go?"

Both turned around and looked at the face of Sergeant Perkins. Though young for his rank, he always looked stern and incredibly serious. His jet-black tattoo seemed to positively gleam under the bright lights still active in the cockpit.

"Yes, Sergeant," said Nate, "Mongoose is fully functional, and I have the destination locked in. We're fuelled and armed for combat. We're ready to go when you are."

The marine struck the inside wall of the cockpit and that activated his visor.

"Good work, Cadets. Get my people there and back again safely. I'm counting on you."

With those brief words he was gone, and the hatch shut behind him, leaving the two alone. An image of Lieutenant Higgins appeared on the secondary display, and he looked just as stern as the Sergeant.

"You have a clear approach to your target. Crusaders Five and Six will watch you in. Your target is three hundred kilometres away. Use the third landing platform, designated Zone Alpha. Don't forget, there is a gravity well generator inside the facility. Get the computer to compensate on your approach, or you'll crash and burn."

Billy's eyes widened as he listened, though he said nothing. Nate knew his friend hadn't even thought of the potential problem. They'd spent most of their gaming time working on fighter manoeuvres, formation flying, and paired tactics. Mauler scenarios were rare, and countering gravity wells during landings were even rarer.

"Get Mongoose down fast, and wait until the marines are ready to leave. Good luck."

His image crackled and then faded away, leaving them in silence. Nate leaned forward and began running through the complex sequence prior to launch.

"This is Mongoose, locks secure. We're ready for launch."

The designation was an odd one to Nate, and as he ran through the screens of data, it still felt as though he was in a simulator. Only when the alarms sounded, and the sound of the massive inner doors sliding shut, did reality kick in. After a few more seconds, the doors crashed together to protect the remainder of the hangar deck from the harsh void outside.

*Here is comes.*

Nate had dreamed of this, and flying the drones had been the closest so far. But as the outer doors opened just a fraction, he was granted a view of space from inside an actual spacecraft. Without windows, the view was actually provided by the display units, each positioned as if they were windows. Technically, he was seeing a view that was no more real than the one seen inside the Avengers, but this time there was one big difference. This time Nate was actually inside the craft, and he was about to take it into deep space.

"Okay. Fire up the engines."

He was speaking to himself as he activated the main power core. One by one the indicators flicked on, confirming everything was set as normal. It took another ten seconds before he was satisfied they were ready to leave.

"Disconnect clamps."

The physical clamps disconnected from the Mauler so that it was now connected to the launching rails by electromagnetic clamps only. Billy ran through the limited number of settings for his weapons and then checked the safety was still off.

"Turrets active and operational. Guns in safe mode, I'm ready."

Nate gave him a quick nod and leaned towards the release switch. As his fingers touched the smooth finish, he activated the internal speakers.

"Five seconds to launch."

The wait seemed an age, and by the time the five seconds had elapsed, Nate almost rushed to press the button. The capacitors fitted near the rails released a surge of power and pushed the launch sled out to the side of the ship. ANS Mongoose shunted into space, using nothing more than the sled to propel them. He felt his torso push back against the powerful push from the ship, and then it vanished, leaving him in the weightless environment of the drifting spacecraft.

"Here goes nothing."

Nate activated the main engines and tensed his body. There was always a chance that something could go wrong when activating engines. He had heard stories of fuel line leaks and faulty fuel rods, all of which could leave a spacecraft dead in space, or worse. The light came on, and a gentle force pushed him back into the seat. It wasn't much movement, and the abilities of the Naval PDS pressure suit absorbed most of it.

*We're clear!*

The Mauler left its position near Relentless and moved off towards the first virtual waypoint. The screens position around the cockpit gave a perfect view of the area near the assault ship. Nate spotted a minor glint to his right and then found the Avenger. Behind the craft was a thin pulse as it activated its main engine to stay in a wide formation with the landing craft.

"This is Mongoose. On approach vector, looking good."

As the spacecraft continued forward, Nate found a short moment to check on his friend. He suspected Billy would still be there, looking nervous, but he was wrong. Billy was moving his hands in front of the panels and checking the operation of the turrets. He spotted Nate looking at him.

"All good here, too. Four turrets moving at full rotation. Guns are functional, with one showing targeting imbalance."

"Excellent. Keep on it and watch for the Byotai. I don't like this."

The Mauler followed its pre-set course towards the target. The starbase was little different to any other, the bulk of its structure hidden deep inside the rock and ice. What did push out was a scruffy collection of gantries, docking towers, and loading arms. When he was within the one kilometre cordon, he felt the pull from the base. It was light, and according to the readout on the engineering display, it would be no more than a sixth of normal gravity at the landing point. That was still more than enough to throw him off and to crash the ship.

"Marines. One minute out. Target looks clear. Moving in now."

It was Nate's first time piloting a ship from the inside, and it felt as though it was already over. They traversed the relatively short journey in just a few minutes and moved in closer to the third landing platform, designated Zone Alpha. He followed standard procedure and performed a single orbit before moving in to land. The platform extended out from the single largest structure. At the far end was a sheer wall of what seemed to be gleaming obsidian. There were a number of deep lines cut into it, giving the impression of multiple doors and seals.

"Hold on."

Nate deactivated the flight assistance model and took full manual control. Four monstrous engines fitted in the corners of the landing craft powered the Mauler. Usually, a landing would be performed using just the manoeuvring thrusters. This time he needed the primary engines, due to the gravity assistance provided by the starbase's well.

"Proximity alert...Proximity alert," warned the navigation computer.

It was a sound Nate had expected, but for some reason known only to him, he'd forgotten to switch it off. The Mauler was fitted with a variety of auto-assistance modes, but none would ever be able to fully offer the same flexibility and control as the human pilot. He deactivated the unit and focussed his attention on the displays. As well as the forward view, he was also checking on the Doppler radar unit to estimate the distance to the landing platform. Metre by metre they dropped until it looked as though they should already be down. The number said fifteen metres, but the external feed made it look so much closer.

*Landing gear!*

Nate was convinced he'd actually deployed the landing gear, but the underside camera feed showed it was most definitely still safely locked inside the fuselage of the ship. Unlike civilian craft of a similar size and capacity, the landing gear on this craft was hidden deep inside armoured cupola. As an assault lander, it was critical the Mauler was as well protected as possible, and that even included the landing gear.

*How could I miss that?*

He still couldn't believe he'd completely forgotten after having spent so much time in the simulators. As he looked at the controls, he was sure he'd activated them during the initial landing pattern. The Mauler was a big vessel, and her landing skids would have to deploy unless he wanted his very first landing to be directly on his belly. More a crash than the soft, gentle landing that would have been expected.

It was the kind of mistake a rank amateur might make but not him, and not right now. There were not just the two of them commanding the Mauler; there was also the precious cargo of heavily equipped marines waiting inside the cavernous hold.

"Nate!" Billy yelled.

"I know."

Nate hit the release button for the third time, and still nothing happened. He then flipped open the backup panel and released the emergency hydraulics option. Secondary pumps attempted to move the heavy metal arms, but still nothing happened.

"The landing gear...it's not coming down!"

He pushed more power to the engines and halted the descent. The digital display showed they were just over three metres from the platform. Nate brought up the diagnostic screen and shuddered upon seeing the warning lights. There were six red lights and all related to the landing gear.

"Relentless, this is Mongoose. We have a problem."

Billy swung the gun control mounts out of the way and brought up his own display. Much of the data was duplicated straight from the pilot's position, as well as an additional and more complex engineering unit.

"There's a new rupture on the control pistons. I think I can get two of the four skids down...maybe."

Nate shook his head.

"No, we have four skids. Two will just bring us down at an angle. If we're going to land safely, it's three or more legs..."

Nate glanced ever so briefly at Billy.

"Or none at all."

As before, the image of Lieutenant Higgins popped up on the forward display and alongside the main view. He looked almost as concerned as Billy was.

"I see it. I've run the data against my diagnostics, and it looks like the gear motors are locked. The backup pistons have released too much pressure and locked two of the outer doors."

Nate swallowed as he listened to those words.

"So, what do we do, Sir?"

"You're going to have to go belly first. Take it slow."

The underside of the Mauler was completely flat, and unlike most spacecraft, heavily reinforced due to its combat role. There were occasions in the past where Maulers had crashed inside enemy capital ships and space stations to deposit their warriors. Right now, none of that gave Nate the confidence he needed.

*Stay cool. You can do this.*

Lieutenant Higgins continued speaking, but now his voice had softened.

"Just settle her down. The hull is easily tough enough. Remember, quick reactions but gentle movements."

Nate dropped the power back for just a moment. The Mauler started to descend and using microbursts, and he slowed the descent as low as possible. The distance shortened until finally the counter read zero. Nothing happened, and then the Mauler lurched violently. For that one moment, Nate nearly pushed more power into the main engines. His gut told him to react calmly, and he provided just a tiny blip of power. The vibration stopped, and everything became quiet.

"Billy, we made it!"

There was still work to do. With the gear locked up, there was nothing to keep the Mauler on the platform other than the severely reduced gravitational pull. Nate swung the main thrusters about and activated them on their lowest possible setting. It was very little thrust, but more than enough to ensure they remained connected to the pad. He then activated the speakers and spoke to his passengers. There was no way to contain his relief as he blurted out the words.

"We're down."

The reply was short and abrupt, "Good work, wait for us."

# CHAPTER THIRTEEN

**Alliance Mauler 'ANS Mongoose'**
**Fleet Rendezvous, Arnos Cluster**

Sergeant Perkins led the squad of six marines out of the Mauler and onto the landing platform. Private Valentine dropped down beside him and waited for her boots to connect to the surface. The magboots did not always provide a firm bond, and she had no interest in vanishing off into space. To an untrained civilian it would have been a terrifying experience, but to her it was little different to the scenarios they'd practised many times before. The landing platform was part of a long arm extending out from the main structure. The sides were completely clear, and there was nothing more than a low barrier, perhaps a metre from the ground to hold onto.

"Move on," said Sergeant Perkins.

The three pairs of marines continued forwards, each making small leaps before connecting safely to the metal platform. In less than a minute they cleared the length and were outside the jet-black wall.

"Cover formation, Cortez, get this thing open."

"Yes, Sergeant!"

Private Cortez moved to the front and positioned himself right next to the smooth structure. There were clearly multiple doors, and when he moved his arm in front of it, a panel flipped open and projected a small holographic model of an encoder unit. He might have been the shortest man in the squad, but his voice was by far the loudest, even when compared to the booming voice of the Sergeant. It took just over a minute, and every waiting second was agonising. Finally, the marine looked back and gave the thumbs up.

"Opening now."

Without a sound, the massive external blast door slid open to reveal a barren looking, layered loading bay. There were a pair of lifter suits clamped to the walls, and bright blue lamps floodlit the whole area. An odd haze hung around the open space, and Private Cortez extended his hand into the haze. He retracted it and shook his head.

"It's atmospherically sealed. There must be functional environment inside."

Sergeant Perkins checked the levels inside his visor and nodded.

"Keep moving. Fan out and check for traps. Our scanners are still being blocked."

The small group of marines spread out and approached the secondary doors. Private Cortez remained at the exterior blast doors and activated them. With a low rumble the large sections slid back into position. As soon as the seal was complete, a dull blue line appeared around the inner door.

"Looks like an all clear to me," said Sergeant Perkins.

He pointed to the middle of the door where a gently pulsing light seemed to show an activation panel. The marines waited while he reached out and tapped it with the butt of his carbine. The wall split apart, and two segments pulled away to create a large opening. It took a moment for the light levels to stabilise inside their helmets, and then they were inside.

"Two by two, and watch your corners."

This was just the kind of job the marines had trained for. Their internal sensors provided a detailed picture of the surrounding area, as well as heat blooms and radiation emissions. The interior was smaller than expected, merely a wide passage in a slightly oval shape. The space was broken up by cylindrical columns on the flanks and seating areas placed in clumps on both sides. Signage above them glowed faintly, with some of the units inoperative. Far off into the distance a single blue light flickered and flashed.

"Sergeant, I've got readings ahead. Multiple life signs," said Private Valentine.

"Very good, move on."

229

They split up into two groups, one on each side of the passage area. By staying close to the walls, they avoided being spotted along the length of the section. It took time, but after what seemed like an age, they reached the end and another massive doorway that led into a grand plaza. It was surrounded by closed and boarded up trade posts.

"Look's like a giant shopping mall," said Private Cortez.

"Yeah," Private Valentine agreed, "Except this one is closed down and boarded up."

The central plaza might have been filled with scientists, engineers, researchers, and traders in the past, but no longer. The layers of dust and malfunctioning lights suggested it had been abandoned for a number of years.

"I've got a beacon from a lifeboat," Private Valentine said.

Her voice betrayed an odd mixture of dread and excitement. She looked ahead and turned her head left and right before locking down the position.

"Two hundred metres, right beyond that central structure. It's from one of the transports. There are life signs nearby."

The cylindrical building looked much like a control tower, filled with black windows and overlooking every part of the plaza. The marines moved on, but with each step, Sergeant Perkins became more and more suspicious. As they moved away from the tower, he whispered to his squad, "Valentine, Cortez, stay back and secure that tower."

The four slowly walked around the structure and came face-to-face with the distant lifeboat. It looked undamaged, but its multiple doors were open and crates of supplies strewn about the floor. On went the marines, stepping carefully around the discarded clothing, food, and emergency survival packs.

"Don't touch anything," said Sergeant Perkins.

By the time they'd passed the craft, Private Valentine was at the doorway to the tower and busy using her override tools to gain entrance. The door was manually operated, and she pushed it open, while Private Cortez aimed his carbine. It was pitch dark inside, but that made little difference to the two of them. Their visors incorporated a variety of modes, including passive thermal, infrared, and low light sensors. When combined, this provided a detailed picture, even with minimal or no light.

"Sergeant, we're going inside."

"Affirmative, keep your eyes open. We've got a situation down here."

The two marines moved into the blackness and found themselves at the base of a wide staircase. Each step was easily two metres wide and taller than would be expected in a place occupied by humans. Private Cortez stopped and removed a hexagonal device from his leg flap. He pushed it against the wall a metre above the step and pushed it hard. The unit blinked three times, its green light giving a gentle hue to the staircase. Private Valentine smiled, not that he could see her.

"Good idea. Always plan for surprises."

"Exactly."

They began working their way up, ensuring they made as little noise as possible. Step by step the closer they came to the top, the wearier they became. Private Valentine activated her carbine and made sure the rapid-fire mode was active.

\* \* \*

Nate sat in silence as he watched the live video feeds coming in from the marines. He had no tactical control over what was happening, but he did have the direct feed from Sergeant Perkins, and he still couldn't believe what he was seeing.

"Billy, they've got one of the lifeboats. Look."

His friend was still busy checking the scanners and keeping one eye on the progress of Relentless. He spotted something on one of his screens and turned to Nate.

"Sorry, I missed that. Have you seen this? Jack's drone is back aboard, but the LT has flagged it as inoperative."

Nate shook his head and pointed to the mainscreen showing the view of the inside of the station. More important, he enlarged the imagery coming from Sergeant Perkins.

"Is that what I think it is?"

Nate nodded slowly.

"Yeah. And it looks like they've just found survivors."

A single red light activated, and then a dozen warnings went off at once. They looked at each other, but it was Nate who spotted the shape far off into the distance.

"No...you have to be kidding me!"

"What?" Billy asked.

He moved his eyes from the screens and to the virtual window on his right side. From here he had a perfect view of Sector Seven, an area of broken asteroids seventy kilometres from their current position. Red diamonds moved over the window and then hovered over the new shapes. There were six smaller diamonds, and a single massive one.

"No...it's Sword of Mognathus. They found us!"

Nate immediately grabbed the emergency override and hit it. Lights dimmed and systems started to shutdown. He then manually deactivated the navigation computer and guidance system and started an emergency shutdown of the engines and powerplant.

"It's a trap, just as I suspected. Power down anything we don't need, we have to go silent. Just keep visual and comms running."

Something caught his eye, and he looked left. The feed from Sergeant Perkins was shaking, but as it settled, he found a stunning view of the interior of the station. More lights were flicking on, and it looked like the base was coming to life.

"I really don't like this."

"Nate, our electronic warfare system is detecting a Byotai transmission from inside."

He looked to Nate.

"I bet they are calling for help. Or sending a warning."

His expression changed in an instant from intrigue to outright panic.

"Jam it."

Billy continued moving his hands over the computer unit as he ran multiple electronic warfare applications. Unlike Nate, Billy was something of an expert when it came to this kind of work, and when he looked back to his friend, his expression could not have been happier.

"Not a problem. I already had the system in passive monitoring. Unless they get outside, they'll have no chance. As far as any ships are concerned, nothing is happening down here."

Nate grinned.

"Good work, Billy, damned good work."

His attention was drawn from his friend to the feed coming back from Sergeant Perkins. The marines had moved to the other side of the lifeboat. There before him were at least forty people, each cuffed to a long loading platform flanked by a number of caterpillar tracked loading tractors. All wore Alliance uniforms, and many showed signs of violence. One, an older man with a bloodied face was calling out. Nate had no idea who he was, but he recognised the Captain's insignia immediately. Nate looked to Billy.

"I don't like this, not at all. Make sure we are ready to leave. This smells like..."

Flashes of light blocked off part of the feed. For a second Nate thought it was interference, but then he saw one of the marines spin about and fall to the ground. More sparks crackled along the floor as the squad took fire from the same direction as before.

"We're under fire. I repeat; we're under fire."

\* \* \*

Private Valentine reached the top of the steps when she heard the first shot. A heavily encoded ad-hoc network connected the marines, and it provided tactical data to each of them. What one marine saw, they all saw, and she could see that one marine had been hit hard. This was no civilian weapon. It was a piece of equipment designed to blast through flesh and armour with equal ease.

"Incoming!" Sergeant Perkins shouted.

Valentine instinctively wanted to go back down to help her comrades, but based on the ballistic analysis already conducted, the gunfire was actually coming from the tower. A single door blocked their path, and it was slightly ajar. She reached for her flank and pulled a small flash grenade from the flap. There was no need to prime it; she could do all of that from the computer system in her suit.

"Ready?"

Private Cortez nodded. She rolled the device along the floor and through the gap in the door. Both marines pulled back and waited. At the same time, another gunshot rang out, but thankfully this one missed. The doorway flashed white, and then they were inside. The visors dimmed for a brief moment, and when the light returned, they could see the five Byotai. They wore civilian clothing, but augmented with an odd selection of webbing and armour plates. Two waited at the window ledge and took aim with a long-barrelled rifle. Of the three remaining, one was fiddling with a tubular weapon, perhaps a missile launcher. The last two were off to the left and hidden from the tall window overlooking the rest of the great plaza. Both were busy using an armoured communication computer, and clearly annoyed at something. Private Valentine's onboard translator repeated the words in their own guttural language.

"Drop your weapons!"

The Byotai with the tubular weapon dropped it and reached for a sidearm. Private Cortez put two rounds into his body; both centre mass. The accuracy was impressive, and he was dead before he hit the floor. Both of the Byotai at the communications rig leapt up, and one struck the thin wall to their left. They clambered through the wreckage and vanished from view. The pair at the window released the long-rifle and opened fire with small fully automatic carbines that hung about their sides. Private Valentine sidestepped as she returned fire. Three rounds glanced off her right leg as the armour did its job. The triple-barrelled L52 Mark II carbine punched holes into their improvised armour, yet neither fell down.

*Damn it! Okay, then.*

Valentine stepped back and activated the high-power mode. The first triple-shot hit the nearest of the two in the neck. He fell to the ground clutching at the gaping wound. The second turned and ran past the window, and she fired again, but this time the weapon merely hissed. It was the first failure she'd encountered with the carbine, and the timing couldn't have been worse. Instead of reaching for her sidearm, she ran at the Byotai and slammed him into the window frame with all of her mass.

At the same time, Private Cortez crashed through the wrecked wall and then rolled to the side. His timing was perfect, as the two panicking Byotai fired shot after shot. Cortez stayed down for a few more seconds, until the two turned and leapt to the steps that took them back to the ground floor. Cortez rose to his feet and took a step after the two as they ran. There was noise back in the room, and he was torn before his pursuit and helping Valentine.

"Screw this!"

Leaving the two on the stairs, he doubled back and ran into the room. He found Private Valentine delivering a powerful kick that sent the last warrior through the window frame. He ran over to her and leaned out. The broken body of the warrior lay on the hard surface, along with the sniper rifle.

"The others?" Private Valentine asked.

A loud bang shook the structure, and Private Cortez deactivated his visor so that his comrade could see his face. He was beaming, a smile that spread from cheek to cheek.

"What, those two?"

Private Valentine struck him in the shoulder.

"You're too bad, Cortez, much too bad."

They looked out from the window, and below them were the rest of their squad. All were working to free the many prisoners who had been tied up and left to rot as bait. One marine lay on his back while a pair of the recently released crew helped to patch his wounds. Cortez shook his head.

"The Sarge was right. If we'd carried on, we'd have been picked off from up here."

Private Valentine reactivated her own visor and then walked back into the middle of the room.

"Let's get back down there. We've got work to do."

They worked their way down the stairs and past the bodies of the two Byotai killed by the proximity charge. After checking both were dead, they headed back to Sergeant Perkins. He was speaking with the battered looking ship's Captain.

"Sergeant, the tower's secure."

He glanced back at them.

"Excellent. Jackson took a round to the chest. It's serious but he's stable...for now."

"What happened here?" Valentine asked.

The Captain was on his feet and checking a pistol given to him by Sergeant Perkins. He looked at the young marine but then turned his attention to Sergeant Perkins.

"They are just the sentries. The ship left a garrison, perhaps twenty, maybe thirty Byotai. They are experienced and looking for trouble. They went off to look for supplies in the station, and I can guarantee they've heard what's happening here. We should go."

As if to emphasise the point, the sound of shooting echoed out from the other side of the plaza. It was several minutes away even at a run, but it provided a sense of urgency to the situation.

"That's them," said the Captain.

Sergeant Perkins looked to his marines while lifting his carbine to check the ammunition status.

"Contact from Mongoose says that a ship has just arrived. It is definitely time to leave."

The Captain helped lift one of his crew to his feet before realising what Sergeant Perkins had just said.

"A ship. Yes, it must be them. We were ambushed by the Byotai warship five or six hours ago. We had only one escort, and after she was gone, they hit us with boarding parties. I lost most of my crew before I gave

236

the signal to surrender."

He looked back at those around them and then nodded towards Sergeant Perkins and his marines.

"They have been keeping us here as a bargaining chip. I guess they didn't count on you finding us so quickly."

Sergeant Perkins called out orders to his own marines before encouraging all of them to get to their feet.

"We've got a bird waiting on the platform. I'll bring her in close, but we will have to hurry. Cortez and Valentine, you'll provide the rearguard. Everybody else, move it!"

The marines and crew picked up the pace as they rushed towards the doors. The marines were fast, but the group was slowed down to the pace of the weakest member, and it was clear some of the crew were more seriously injured than others. As they moved onward, the Captain tried to explain more about their predicament.

"We lost a lot of crew in the boarding actions. Now all that remains are thirty-seven, and most were wounded in the fighting. Nearly all our officers are dead."

He continued to speak while the group jogged on, and in a few more minutes, they reached the long passage that led towards the magnetically sealed airlock. Sergeant Perkins waited at the entrance and waved them all through just as the first gunshots arrived.

"Keep moving and get to the door."

On they went until the last had passed. He turned to follow them, but not before speaking to his two marines.

"Hold them back until I give you the signal."

He grabbed Valentine's shoulder.

"No heroics. I want all my marines back in one piece. You got that?"

"Yes, Sergeant!"

With that, he was gone, and the two Privates moved to each side of the doorway. They had a perfect view of the open plaza, and there was no obvious way the Byotai would be able to reach them without coming into view.

"Cortez, you ready for this?"

The marine clipped a new pack onto his carbine and lifted it to his shoulder.

"Hell, yeah, I was born ready, lady."

Valentine laughed.

"I'm no lady, Cortez."

"Second that."

A round struck a metre above them, and then the first of the rabble were visible. Private Valentine lifted her carbine and took careful aim. She could see them coming towards her through the sight. Some wore Byotai military uniforms, and others were dressed like those in the tower.

"Drop 'em."

The two fired at the same time, and their high-velocity slugs slammed into the attackers. Three went down before they scattered, and then came the return fire, a great crescendo of rifles and thermal weaponry that hissed and crackled around them. Cortez fired repeatedly and then slammed in another clip.

"Just like old times, hey, Valentine?"

Private Valentine opened up again, this time sending a wild burst over the heads of another group trying to creep around the right. A spike round flashed past, and Private Cortez cried out. She looked over to him to find the spike embedded in his chest. She moved closer to him so he could throw his arm around her neck. Though badly wounded, he still continued to fire at the Byotai.

"Sergeant Perkins," said Private Valentine, "Cortez is wounded. They are pushing us hard."

"Understood. Drop proximity mines and get back here. The Mauler will be here in sixty seconds."

* * *

238

Nate waited patiently with his hand over the engine activation button. His heart was pumping harder and faster than it had ever done before. At one end of the landing arm were the still closed blast doors, and far off in the other direction the enemy ship.

"Nate, we're in trouble here. That Byotai ship is right between us and Relentless," said Billy.

Nate gave a fake laugh in reply.

"You don't say. At least they don't know we're here, not yet."

With most of their systems off-line, they were forced to rely upon their PDS suits. Luckily, the sealed units provided a breathable air system, as well as heating to protect them from freezing inside the confines of the Mauler's cockpit.

"Look," said Billy.

There was no need to clarify. The forward screen currently showed the view back to Relentless. The warship had clearly detached itself from the transports and was moving directly at the Byotai ship. The detailed schematic showed alongside it, and all the data that the injured Captain Dreuc had shown them.

"That thing is a beast."

Data appeared at key points along the ship, pointing out the armour, weaponry, and defensive equipment.

"Captain Dreuc says she is one of the toughest heavy cruisers in the Imperial fleet."

"I know," said Nate, "She's packing six phased plasma cannons in the bow, as well as eight secondary gun mounts on the flanks."

He pointed at the section towards the rear along the underside of the ship. A bulbous compartment further ahead sheltered the opening to fire coming from the front.

"The launch deck. Captain Dreuc says she can carry four fighters on board."

Nate continued shaking his head as he looked at the specification. Sword of Mognathus was a formidable opponent for any single ship, and as

239

both vessels lined up, he knew it was going to be a bloody showdown, and one difficult to escape from. Icons appeared over Relentless, first one and then a second."

"Galanos is launching fighters."

Two Avengers blasted away from the interior of the warship. They must have been inside so they could rearm for any subsequent action. They moved into a defensive position between the two ships, slightly above direct line of sight to keep the flak corridor clear. The communications unit blinked once, and Billy leaned forward and tapped the unit. The internal speaker activated, but there was no accompanying videostream.

"This is Captain Galanos of the Alliance Assault Ship Relentless. We are not looking for a fight, but if you want one, we're ready."

The two cadets looked at each other, their faces numbed at what they could see. A reply came back almost immediately, and to their surprise it was in English, but with a thick Byotai accent.

"This is Byotai territory. Surrender your ship, and we will take your crew as prisoners of war. Refuse, and you will be obliterated. You have thirty seconds to comply."

Billy tagged the lower section of the Byotai heavy cruiser as the computer identified movement.

"Look."

A pair of massive metallic layers parted and revealed a hangar section. Spindles extended outwards, and four fighters were jammed inside, like four bats hanging upside down. One by one they released from their mounts and moved away from the ship. As they did so, their membrane wings fully deployed.

"They look like moths," said Billy.

Nate has seen the shape before, but when he spotted the insignia on the wings, it sent a shudder through his body.

"They are Hawkmoth Light Fighters and that one, that's DuFarl's ship. I'd recognise his markings anywhere, The Death's Head Squadron. Just like it was back in the Star Crusader contest."

The other three moth-shaped fighters left the ship and headed towards the pair of Avengers, now outnumbering the Alliance craft two to one.

"Ten seconds."

The image from Sergeant Perkins returned after what had seemed like an age. To Nate's surprise, he could see a gun battle was still raging.

"I need emergency evac for civilian personnel. Be at the door in thirty seconds, and make sure you come through the shielding."

Nate had no idea what he was talking about, but he was already reaching for the control when Billy said what they were both thinking.

"How can they get inside without suits? And what the hell is the shielding thing?"

Nate had already hit the engine start, and the units spluttered into action. The Mauler was a big ship, and it took a little effort to lift her from the platform even by a few centimetres. Nate spun the ship around so that its right flank pointed at the tall black doors.

"We'll get as close as we can. Hold on!"

Nate's control of the Mauler was as smooth as any experienced combat pilot, and he skimmed along the long platform as though the craft was fitted on wheels. Closer and closer came the outer door, and then to his surprise, the entire thing opened up. This was not the small door the marines had opened, but the entire black slab that must have been more then forty metres wide. Something inside shimmered blue, like a thin energy shield.

"Here we go."

Without checking to look inside, he slid the Mauler through the massive opening and then hit the ground, the low slug skids sliding along the metallic floor. The doorway may have been big, but the Mauler still barely made it inside. The vessel shuddered violently, and some of the internal seal broke as the vibration increased. And then it stopped as quickly as it had begun.

"We're coming in," said Sergeant Perkins.

The view from the right-hand virtual window stunned Nate. The marines were coming out from another much smaller doorway, along with a number of personnel wearing Naval uniforms. He deactivated the side doors to the hold, and they slid open. They filed in, and then there was silence. Sergeant Perkins reappeared at the doorway and took aim with his carbine. The muzzle flashed repeatedly as two more marines staggered through the doorway towards him.

*Valentine!*

Nate watched her stumble trying to help another wounded marine. She dropped to one knee and twisted about to look back. Another marine jumped out of the Mauler to help, and soon there was a vicious firefight that stopped them making it to safety.

"Billy, help them."

Try as he might, due to their current position, there was no way to target the doorway. All four of the gun turrets were positioned on the front of the Mauler, and their limited rotation made shooting this far to the right impossible.

"I...I can't get..."

"Hold on," said Nate.

The doors were still open when he blipped the power from the four massive engines. It was only a subtle shift, but by rotating thirty degrees, he allowed two of the turrets just enough of an angle to target the opening.

"Oh, yeah," said Billy.

Both turrets opened up and hammered the narrow gap with incredible firepower. In space the guns seemed deadly, but on the ground, and this close, they were devastating. Wall, floor, and armour was torn apart with such intensity the entire area vanished in dust. One of the marines moved out of the side, and then another. Finally, Sergeant Perkins said what both of them were praying for.

"All aboard, get us out of here."

Nate needed no encouragement and manpowered them away from the shielded platform while swinging his nose about to face the enemy. He never saw them, and Billy made sure not one of them would get a shot off. Once clear, he spun them around and hit maximum power. They accelerated away from the starbase at high-speed and on a direct path to Relentless.

"Out of the pan and into the fire," Nate said under his breath.

The hatch at the rear of the cockpit opened up and in came the shape of Sergeant Perkins. With no gravity in the Mauler, he was forced to struggle, twist, and drift to get close to the two of them.

"Well done, both of you. What's the plan?"

He looked at the forward screen and the growing shape of the Byotai heavy cruiser. In the excitement of their escape, none of them had noticed that the battle had already begun. Both capital ships were slugging away at each other while the four Byotai fighters were nowhere to be seen. Nate connected to Relentless, and an image appeared of the Captain.

"Cadet, did you get them all out?"

Sergeant Perkins moved closer so that his face was in front of the cockpit camera.

"We're all out, as well as the survivors of the transports."

"Good. I am launching more fighters to cover your withdrawal. Get on board Relentless and fast. We cannot..."

A series of bright explosions along the flanks of the Alliance ship briefly interrupted her. The image vanished, and it took three seconds for the systems to reconnect.

"Uh...Billy. What the hell is that?"

It took a moment for one of the external cameras to lock onto the objects and magnify them. Nate found it difficult to swallow, realising what he could see.

"Lightning Fighters."

Captain Galanos' image finally returned, and she looked shaken by what had happened.

"The cruiser just blasted through the forward plating and to the engines controls. That was one shot in a million. I don't know..."

Another series of flashes flickered along the length off the ship as Relentless returned fire towards the Byotai ship. On the videostream it looked like an ancient battle between wooden ships, as they both fired using every weapon at their disposal.

"Pilot Lewis. The fighters came in and finished the job with missiles. The explosions came back as far as the power management controls. I need time to get the systems back in action."

Captain Galanos' face tightened.

"Lieutenant Higgins is launching now. Just do something, do anything to get the cruiser's guns off Relentless, or we'll be stuck here forever."

Her image disappeared, and Nate found he was back to seeing the shape of the enemy ship, and the constant barrage moving back and forth between them. Sergeant Perkins was silent for perhaps the first time ever, and that worried Nate more than anything.

"Okay, son, what's your play?"

Billy turned to the marine, opened his mouth to speak, and then stopped. He moved his attention back to Nate.

"We can move close and try to harass the cruiser. We might get lucky."

Nate deactivated his visor and glanced at the two of them. His face was serious, but Billy could already see that his friend had an idea. It was a look he'd seen plenty of times before in simulation.

"Remember the Siege of Titan scenario, with the..."

"Assault landing?" Billy said, completing Nate's sentence.

Sergeant Perkins began to look frustrated.

"Okay, boys, what's going on here?"

Nate altered the port thrusters and then tagged the underside of the Byotai ship. The Mauler spun around and headed below the ship.

"Get everybody that can fight into PDS kit. There are full stocks in the rear."

It took a moment for Sergeant Perkins to realise what he was saying.

"Wait, you want to attack the cruiser?"

Nate grinned.

"I'll land you right in her belly. Can you hurt her from the inside?"

Sergeant Perkins struck Nate hard in the chest.

"I wonder about you flyboys sometimes, but then you do this. We'll be ready. Just get us aboard in one piece, and we'll do our job."

244

The marine drifted back into the main compartment and sealed the cockpit behind him. Billy swung his guns around, checking for targets.

"You remember what happened last time we tried to do this in the simulation, right?"

Nate's smile vanished as quickly as it had arrived.

"True, but this time it will be different."

Billy spotted two Hawkmoth Fighters moving into view as they accelerated directly at them. Both released missiles, but Billy was already firing. With the computer controls non-functional, he was completely reliant upon his own experience with the weapons. Most of the shots went wide, but at least a few struck the one to the left, and it spun out of control and vanished from view. The second screamed past dumping countermeasures. Billy adjusted the guns as the Mauler jinked left and right to avoid the missiles.

"How so?"

Nate couldn't look away, as he was desperately trying to avoid being blown up.

"Because this time we can't fail. We've got people depending on us."

The Mauler rolled three times and narrowly avoided colliding with a pair of Lightning Fighters. The Alliance space fighters continued onwards, their guns blazing away at the Hawkmoths.

"We've got your back, Nate," said a familiar voice.

Nate looked to Billy with an amazed look on his face.

"That's Rex."

# CHAPTER FOURTEEN

Rex tugged on the control column and then pulled it hard to the right. The manoeuvre was normally an easy one to pull off, but with full manual controls and his body being pushed about, he was finding it tough. Another of the Hawkmoth fighters swept past to his right and then vanished from view, with an Avenger and a single Hawkmoth right behind it. He saw one of the drones disintegrate, while the Death's Head marked fighter spun about as if it had lost control. The pilot's skill was exceptional, and just as it vanished from view, it changed course and came right at him.

*Roll and evade.*

Rex pulled on the controls once more, and the blood rushed to his head. The integral pressure suit tried to compensate, and then the two fighters screamed past each other. Five projectiles punctured his fighter's nose in the flypast.

"They're all over me. I..."

The forward guns of the third Hawkmoth hammered away at his left wing until flames spread through the fuel lines. Rex instinctively redirected coolant and then vented the engine. The flames died, but so did half of his thrust. He performed another roll and spotted a Lightning coming in from above. Its forward guns blasted away and cut the Hawkmoth fighter to pieces.

"Thanks...that was close."

The fighter moved in on Rex's flank and took up a position slightly ahead of him. At the same time another Lightning moved up to Lieutenant Higgins' other flank.

"Stay together and keep moving. We need to buy some time for the marines."

The formation of three fighters swung around and gave chase to the Hawkmoths. As they turned away, the last Avenger drone moved closer to the defensive flak corridors put up by Relentless. The Death's Head fighter followed right behind and moved so close it looked as though they would collide. The drone exploded in a violent blast that obscured the area of space long enough for the enemy fighter to peel away.

"That's three on three. Stay close, you get only one life in this fight."

The last Alliance fighters changed course and chased after the main enemy fighter, while the other two split off to attack ANS Mongoose. Rex's forehead tightened as he realised what was happening.

"Sir, two of them are heading for Mongoose."

"Affirmative, I see them. Break off the attack and follow me."

The lead Lightning fighter lifted up, rolled, and then turned around to chase the two spacecraft heading for ANS Mongoose. Only the leader, the so-called Death's Head fighter remained, and it was heading right for Relentless. A video message request appeared on Rex's forward display, and he pressed it to find the face of his rival appear. It was the young Byotai cadet from the starbase, one that had been their competitor, and now one of the bloodthirsty rebels.

"Rex, so nice to see you. Are you ready to surrender?"

Rex heard his leader issuing orders, but his attention was taken completely by the fighter as it suddenly rolled to the right and raced around in a wide circle. This was the classic opening gambit that signified the start of a duel.

"Rex, listen to me, dammit! Get back in formation!" Lieutenant Higgins ordered.

Jack began to move away, but for reasons of friendship and loyalty stayed back to help his friend. Nothing was going to drag Rex away from this fight, and if that was the way it was to be, then Jack would be with him. Rex altered his course and made for the Byotai fighter. At the same time, he switched off the audio communication from Lieutenant Higgins.

*DuFarl is mine!*

The three fighters accelerated away from the battle between the two capital ships. And with every second, they became less able to assist either Nate in ANS Mongoose, or the battered, but still fighting AMS Relentless.

\* \* \*

Nate's chest was pounding as he dodged the incoming fire. There were only a few secondary gun mounts on the lower portion of the heavy cruiser, and few of them were aiming at him. While the massive battle continued between the two main ships, there seemed little point in worrying about an unarmoured assault transport, and that was exactly what Nate was hoping for.

"Get ready, we're going in!"

They were moving in fast and directly at the narrow hangar section of the ship. The closer they moved, the larger it looked until they were now just a hundred metres away. Huge doors were already moving to try and seal the ship, but Billy was ready. He took aim and opened fire with all four turrets. The hardened slugs punched through plating, motors, and hydraulics, quickly locking the doors in the open position. Warning sensors announced an increase in gravitational forces as the internal gravity generators pulled the Mauler in.

"Hold on!"

The Mauler was a tough craft, and as they made the final approach, Nate hit the impact mode. Vents closed and motors pivoted back to avoid damage. Three seconds later they crashed into the ship with a violent crunch. The shaking went on for nearly four seconds, and they punched through the broken and twisted metal. Nate glanced over to Billy who was holding onto the gun mounts to keep him steady. Then they stopped and everything became silent.

"We made it."

He was talking mainly to himself, both confirming what had happened as much as trying to reassure him. He then checked the external cameras. The side doors were blocked, but the belly hatch and ramp were clear.

"Sergeant Perkins. The belly ramp is the way in, good luck."

He then deactivated the unit, and the door opened. Any air inside the passenger compartment vanished instantly as it was sucked out into space. Though they were inside the ruins of the ship, they were far from the safety of its innards. The marines, as well as seventeen crew in PDS Naval gear left the Mauler and moved into the ship.

* * *

Sergeant Perkins was first out and dropped down into a broken storage section. Mounts on the walls were filled with metal spars and tooling, and thick cables ran in all directions. Flames licked through the interior, and it took a few seconds to get his bearings.

*Okay, how can we cause the most damage as quickly as possible?*

He knew his squad had a variety of small arms with them, but they were not equipped for a major assault. Relentless contained only a basic level of ammunition, and heavy weapons had been avoided due to travelling into the territory of a supposed trustworthy ally. This part of the ship was designed for fuelling, arming, and launching fighters.

*Ammunition!*

A single change to his scanners quickly identified the location of a motorised loading track that ran off inside the ship. He moved his head a fraction as he checked on the route. At the same time his suit built up an internal layout of the ship via its scanners.

"Ammunition bins are seventy metres this way."

More marines came in behind him as he moved on to the target. Right ahead was a single door, and he spotted something moving towards it. Without thinking, he lifted his carbine and fired. The first round struck the Byotai crewman in the shoulder blade, and he went down.

"Follow me!"

Private Valentine dropped down the ramp with a large pack fitted to her armour. It looked like a radio unit, but it was actually one of the many thermite demolition charges carried by marines. Sergeant Perkins reached the door that was still ajar and swung it open. It was big enough for two marines to travel through at a time. He didn't hesitate and jumped in, with a pair of marines close behind.

"New targets heading this way."

It was one of the Naval crew who carried a Marine Corps carbine in her hands. She pointed off into the distance where the long pipes along the floor and ceiling vanished into dust and steam. Pulses of blue energy ran along what appeared to be thick fibre optic cables. Private Valentine stepped through the doorway just as the Byotai defenders appeared. There were five of them, and they ran along the section of deck right at the marines. Gunfire raged back and forth, and casualties were inflicted on both sides.

"Keep moving."

The marines advanced one step at a time, even as more defenders appeared. For every marine brought down, two Byotai were killed, and still they kept going. By the time Sergeant Perkins reached the end of the corridor, he'd been hit three times, and his PDS armour was struggling to repair the breaches in the outer plating. The passage split off into four directions, but based on his scans, he suspected the one to the right was what he wanted. Without waiting for the others, he leapt inside and found two Byotai waiting in front of a massive motorised conveyer belt system. Huge crates of ammunition and missiles were stacked in mounts on the walls.

*Good timing.*

He ducked down as one fired a pistol and then struck him in the face with the butt of his carbine. Private Valentine was in next and fired a burst from the hip, killing one and injuring the other.

"Is this the place?"

Sergeant Perkins nodded quickly.

"Hell, yes. Place the charge and..."

A hole the size of a man's fist appeared in his chest, and he slumped forward and crashed to the ground. Behind him was a large Byotai soldier, resplendent in thick armour and carrying a thermal rifle. It was the same kind of weapon that had nearly killed her before.

"You animal!"

Private Valentine extended the carbine out to the creature's body and opened fire. Two rounds struck it just as it knocked the weapons aside. That didn't stop her fighting, and she reached down for the pistol, only to remember she'd given it to one of the crewmen. The Byotai soldier started to laugh and then pointed his own weapon at her chest.

"Hey!"

Another marine jumped into the room and nearly fell over at seeing the enemy soldier. He fired a long burst that struck the back of the creature and sent him tumbling forwards. Private Valentine sidestepped just in time to avoid it falling onto her. It staggered three more steps and then tipped over, face first.

"Thanks."

She knelt down to check Sergeant Perkins. Incredibly, he was still breathing.

"Help me with him. We need to leave."

With great effort, the two lifted the wounded marine and made for the doorway. More enemy soldiers were flooding the area from the other corridors, and the smoke of battle mixed with the flashes of light to create a maelstrom of death and confusion. Then she stopped, pushed Sergeant Perkins to the marine, and moved back.

"Hold on."

She ran over to the articulated loading machine and placed her thermite explosive charges. The pack contained an integral magclamp that held it firmly to the walls of the ship. Just a few button presses activated the unit and triggered the locking system. It flashed five times, and then a numbered counter popped up showing ninety seconds. She returned to the marine and activated the communications channel.

"This is Private Valentine. The charge is set. Everybody back to the Mauler, now! We have ninety seconds!"

The Byotai Hawkmoth had changed course once more and was accelerating towards a series of rocky ice formation. They were a perfect way to mask his position, and it made it even harder to shoot at him. Rex was determined to shoot him down, but he'd also noticed the messages arriving of the desperate battle aboard the enemy ship.

*They need my help. DuFarl will have to wait.*

Rex spun his fighter around in a flat spin to pursue and fired a short burst at the enemy fighter. His shooting was well aimed, yet the Byotai pilot managed to evade the shooting with ease. The Hawkmoth spun around, fired a short burst, and continued on its course. The return fire clattered about his right engines, and once more warnings were sounding. His fighter was now so badly damaged there was a chance he might not even make it back in time.

"Rex Hampel, get back into formation, now!" Lieutenant Higgins demanded.

* * *

Nate had removed his straps and was under the control panel fiddling with cables. The main power management system had overloaded, and to his surprise the breaker circuit shredded. Instead of just pulling the lever to reset the system, he had to rewire it from memory, and it wasn't easy.

"Okay, knife."

Billy was above him and handing down the small utility knife.

"How much longer?"

Nate cried out as he caught his finger against two sharp plates. He then peeled back the cables to reveal bare metal. He shook his head in stunned amazement at what this was all coming down to. A state of the art spacecraft, now rendered useless due to damaged wiring.

"This is Valentine. We're coming aboard. We have to leave, now!"

Nate could hear the voice from the communications units in the cockpit, but down on the floor he had more pressing concerns. Billy bent down and pointed the torch at the damaged section, nearly blinding him in the process.

"What, are you kidding me?"

"Nate, we've got fifty seconds till the charge blows. We have to leave."

He looked up to his friend and laughed.

"Then shut up and let me get on with this."

He pushed the last three severed cables together and twisted the bare metal into one tight piece.

"Tape."

Billy handed down the electrical tape, and Nate wound a small piece around the connection.

"Okay. Punch it."

Billy hit the engine start just as Nate was climbing back into his seat. The engines roared, and for a moment little happened. The ship shuddered as he applied more power, but they were still embedded deep inside the enemy ship. Billy pointed at the countdown, but said nothing. Nate threw it a brief glance and almost threw up when he saw they had just twenty-three seconds to go.

*Get the hell out of here!*

Throwing caution to the wind, Nate pushed the engines to full throttle, and though the Mauler slid back a fraction, it remained caught up in wreckage. He checked each of the forward displays one at a time until finding what appeared to be the problem.

"No way, that's not good."

He extended a hand to the unit and pointed at several twisted sections of metal that were caught around the nose and front starboard engine.

"Billy, use your guns and clear a path."

He didn't need to be told twice and swung the four turrets around to the front. Each unleashed a hurricane of firepower that ripped apart the metal with ease. At the same time, Nate blipped the engines three times, and with

253

the third the Mauler tore itself away from the wreckage and out into space.

"Yes!"

Nate swung them around and hit the engines. The ship began accelerating away from the heavy cruiser; every second taking them further from danger. Nate began to relax until he saw the terrible carnage ahead of them. The two ships were just five kilometres apart, and the gunfire between them constant. It was now almost impossible to tell what was gunfire and what an impact. Nate saw the shape of a Hawkmoth circling behind them. It was arming a pair of missiles. At that very moment, the thermite charge detonated inside the Byotai ship.

Nate clenched his fist with excitement as flashes erupted from the underside, one of which completely ensnared the fighters. More explosions continued ripping through as the ammunition stores aboard the heavy cruiser shattered the innards of the ship. From the flames and dust came the Hawkmoth fighters. The damaged spacecraft turned back to protect their crippled capital ship, or perhaps even to eject to safety, wherever that might be.

"All fighters, converge on Mongoose," said a familiar voice.

*Lieutenant Higgins!*

Two of the Lightning fighters altered their course and moved into position at the flanks of the Mauler. One left a trail of flame from its rear section, the other had dozens of holes smashed through its wings. Neither looked capable of combat. Nate spotted their call signs via the IFF system, but one was clearly missing.

"Where is Rex?"

The flight-path indicators showed Rex and Jack had split apart a minute earlier, one moving to join Lieutenant Higgins, but the second had gone dark.

"Nate, look!" Billy said.

From just above ANS Relentless, and nearly nine hundred kilometres away, appeared a series of small dark shapes. They appeared at long-range until Nate had tagged a dozen Byotai Komodo Heavy Bombers. The formation moved from the cover of the asteroid field, and behind them came a massive warship of similar shape and design to the heavy cruiser, but this one was at least twice as big. They were a long distance away, but travelling fast and towards the scene of the battle.

As Nate looked at the distant shapes, he barely even registered the missiles coming from above. He had no idea how they had got there without being detected, and not even his reaction could save them. He tensed his body, but incredibly, Jack swung his fighter up and into the path of the attack. The entire volley of missiles slammed down into the spacecraft and blasted it apart in an instant. The Lightning ripped apart as a Hawkmoth dropped down from above, its guns blazing. Another missile struck Lieutenant Higgins' tail, blasting off a section. It sent him into an uncontrollable spin. Nate instinctively drifted to the right and narrowly avoided being hit as the enemy fighter moved below and then circled around to attack. Billy glanced back at his friend.

"Ammunition is gone. We're defenceless."

Nate did his best to get them back on course, but he'd lost the position of the fighter for just a second. Then he saw it coming for him from behind.

"Nate!" Billy screamed.

He turned back around and spotted a Lightning fighter coming right at him. The fighter was blasting away with all of its guns and rushed past, literally smashing into the wreckage of the Hawkmoth. Incredibly, the crippled Lightning was still operational and turned around to move into formation alongside the other two.

"Good shooting, Rex," said Nate.

"Sorry to keep you waiting."

Nate hadn't noticed, but when he looked back at Relentless, it became clear the fighting had stopped, if only for now. There was no gunfire coming from the Byotai ship, yet a fusillade of projectiles continued to strike her from the direction of ANS Relentless. The enemy ship might be crippled, but the battle-scarred Alliance ship was making certain of her victory.

The area of space between the two capital ships was littered with the debris of the violence. Chunks of ships, discharged ammunition, and the bodies of many crew from both sides. The friendly face of Captain Galanos popped up, and this time she looked even more exhausted than ever before.

"Good work, pilots. Get aboard fast. The Byotai reinforcements will be here in seven minutes. It's time to leave."

* * *

For the first time in hours there was complete and utter silence. The Mauler was down and clamped to the deck. Both inner and outer doors were sealed shut. The only vibration now coming from the last few volleys fired by Relentless.

"I thought the Byotai ship was out of action."

Nate looked to Billy and laughed, or at least as close to a laugh as he could manage.

"I think the Captain is making sure. There's no harm in giving them an extra burst before we leave, is there?"

Billy shrugged and then looked back to the door. The metal bars that clamped the door in place were now to the side, and he kicked at the door, making it swing open and letting in the cool air of Relentless' hangar deck.

"Well, what are you waiting for?"

Nate clambered out of the cockpit. He stumbled and landed face down. One of the rescued transport crew helped him to his feet and reached out with his right hand. Nate hadn't even realised it was one of the Captains. He lifted his hand to salute, and the man responded in kind.

"I don't know what the Alliance is doing with pilots of your age, but somebody made the right choice. That was one hell of a piece of flying."

The man then moved away, leaving Nate waiting next to the Mauler. Billy dropped down alongside him and leant against the hot metal plating of the Mauler. Only now could they see quite how badly damaged the vessel was. A loud howl built up inside the ship as the engines powered up, and both of them grabbed onto the Mauler tightly. It was only for a moment until the dampeners could compensate for the forward momentum. Off to the right were the smashed shapes of the two surviving Lightning fighters. Rex and Lieutenant Higgins climbed down their respected ladders and to the deck. Crew and civilians alike were smiling about, and a good number were clapping and cheering.

Both pilots walked past the odd selection of people until they reached the Mauler. Lieutenant Higgins gave one of his rare smiles and nodded.

"You gave her one hell of a beating. Still, at least you could follow orders."

He looked back at Rex and shook his head.

"I'm sorry about Flight Cadet Ironside. We lost a lot of good people today."

Rex didn't seem to know what to say, but Nate felt obliged to say or do something.

"Jack put himself on the line for the rest of us. None of us will forget that."

Rex nodded in silence, and then stepped forward towards Nate. For a second it looked as though they would come to blows, but instead he reached out with his right arm, and Nate did the same. They shook hands for the first time.

"I couldn't have asked for a better wingman."

As their hands separated, the last of the marines inside the Mauler filed out. More personnel wandered in from the internal elevators, including Matilda and Cassandra heading for their friends at a jog. They reached them just as Lieutenant Higgins turned around and blocked their path. He began speaking with them when as a voice whispered close to Nate's right ear.

"Nathaniel Lewis. Thank you for that. You'll make a combat pilot yet. May I?"

Nate turned around and found him looking at the battered and bruised form of Private Valentine. Her armour was burnt and scratched from the incredible gun battles she'd been engaged with. There were also multiple areas of dried blood on her chest and arms. Her visor was open, and she lifted her arms up to remove the entire helmet with a clicking sound. Beneath the armour was that bronzed face he had seen only a few times before. Her long, slightly curly hair was matted with sweat and hung down limply at her shoulders.

"May you, what?"

She leaned in close and kissed him directly on the lips while holding him firmly against her armoured body. They seemed to be there an age, so much so the others began to feel a little uncomfortable. Private Valentine finally stepped back and winked at him before moving off. When he looked back, he found Rex and Billy with their eyes wide opening and grinning like school children. Cassandra and Matilda were now there, and they moved closer in, hugging or shaking the hands of the others.

"Well, that was, interesting, wasn't it?" Matilda asked.

Cassandra looked a little flustered as she leaned in to Nate and gave him a quick, slightly awkward hug. As they parted, Nate noticed the figure of Lieutenant Higgins next to one of the rescued crew. He'd seen Nate looking at him and pointed over to the battered fighters.

"Get some rest, son. You're going to have to help me get the rest of the birds combat ready. This has just turned into a shooting war, and we're right in the middle of it."

Rex walked towards the officer.

"Where are we going, Sir?"

Lieutenant Higgins rubbed at his chin.

"We are heading to the border and joining up with Admiral Churchill, veteran of the Biomech war and senior commander in this sector."

Rex looked back at the other four to make sure they were listening. The man was something of a legend in the Academy after his exploits in the war.

"That's right, Cadets. Orion Command has pulled back all our assets and is mobilising. We're joining the fleet, and if I know the Admiral, he's going to want payback."

He looked to each of them in turn.

"It's time to graduate. Are you ready to stop being cadets, and become my combat pilots?"

Nate heard the words, but all he could think about was that last escape from the explosions around the Byotai ship. The thrill of the chase, the excitement of the battle, but also the loss of a friend like Jack. It wasn't what he'd expected, but he knew there was no place he'd rather be. The others had already answered, and he had no idea what a single one of them had said. So he looked at Lieutenant Higgins and saluted.

"Yes, Sir, that's exactly what I want to be."

www.ingramcontent.com/pod-product-compliance
Lightning Source LLC
Chambersburg PA
CBHW020316200626
46814CB00006BA/2277